I0534540

Slightly Off

A Nate Thomas Adventure, Vol. I

By
Arthur McGillem

Contact the author at:
art@artmcgillem.com

Slightly Off

Art McGillem

"Slightly Off"
Copyright © 2013 by Art McGillem
All Rights Reserved. No part of this book may be used or reproduced in any manner whatsoever without written permission except in the case of brief quotations embodied in critical articles or reviews. For information contact the publisher at 2509 Burnt Pine Ct., Antioch, TN 37013

Publisher's Note
This is a work of fiction. Names, characters, places and incidents are either the product of the author's imagination or are used fictionally. Any reference to actual persons living or dead, business establishments, events or locales is entirely coincidental.

ISBN: 978-0-9898149-3-5   Printed Book
ISBN: 978-0-9898149-0-4   Electronic Book
ASIN: B00ECH2RH6   Electronic Book
Cover Photo: U.S. Coast Guard
Back Cover Photo: Mexico's office of La Procuraduría General de la República
Book Design by Art McGillem

Some of what follows may have actually happened.

Dedication: To Chu, Janice and Linda for their love and support.

In Memory of: Kiku who left us far too soon.

Contents

Slightly Off

Art McGillem

Slightly Off

Chapter 1

"I am just sitting here sweating and not even moving very much", said Jason. Nathan chuckled and responded that "All newbies have the same problem. Don't worry, you will get used to it. The temperature here is always high this time of year but with the low humidity you dry quickly".

Jason thought about it. As he looked around, there was only sand, a few small bushes and the heavily rutted unpaved road. What a God forsaken place he thought. Then he heard it, the bee like sound of a bullet passing close by. "Sniper!" he shouted and dived behind the Humvee. He had begun counting when the bullet passed, eight seconds later he heard the sound of the shot. He was glad that the shooter had missed, but considering the distance unsurprised at his good luck.

None of the team members had returned fire. They had simply found some terrain or a large enough object to provide cover and began watching in the direction from which the shot had originated. Wilson was looking through his scope and carefully scanning for movement. "There he is, about 800 meters at my two o'clock and getting his hat." Wilson hurried over to the Humvee to get a solid rest.

"He is pretty far out to get a sure hit, oh shit, he just disappeared from sight!"

Jason jumped into the driver's seat and started the Humvee.

Nathan shouted, "Hold on! We are not going anywhere and certainly not fast! That is probably a trap. We need to get over there but watch out for IUDs or mines."

"Ok Captain, you are right."

Captain (CPT) Nathan Thomas knew that these were good men that had just gotten a little excited. For most of them it was their second or third tour in Iraq and they fully well knew the dangers of hot pursuit. Because of the stress, Special Forces team members rotated in and out of combat assignments at about six month intervals. This schedule allowed them to decompress and spend time with family and friends without losing their combat edge.

"Say Corey, you take the point, but keep your eyes open. Abdul, you man the 30 cal on the Hummer and keep an eye open along the horizon as we move forward. Jason, since you are already sitting, you follow us slowly and keep well back; we don't want to walk home. Ok, move out." Nathan commanded.

The team spread out. Nathan took the road bed, the most dangerous. Wilson took the left side of the road, about 20 feet outside the road bed and Corey took the right side of the road also about 20 feet to the side and they all began the slow forward march, eyes constantly on the move.

Lieutenant (LT) Abdul Nabi of the Afghan Special Police moved to man the Humvee mounted M60 machine gun. His job was to act as interpreter and insure that Afghan culture and traditions were not infringed by the team members. He was also a regular member of this particular special operations team. Nabi, a Pashtun had a full beard as did all of the team members, out of respect for Afghan male traditional practice.

Abdul spoke loudly, "We have movement at about 1000 meters at one o'clock. It looks like a head just above the horizon. Jason, stop the truck I may be able to get him. Yes, he is watching us through his scope." They all jumped when Abdul fired a short three round burst. Sand kicked up just in front of the sniper and the head disappeared.

"Those three rounds were a little short, so he is probably still active. The sniper was watching, not shooting, so he may have something that is command detonated. If he pops up in the same place we will know, but it will also be the end of him. Jason keep the ride still, we will wait awhile."

Nathan stopped. The sand farther ahead was slightly darker on the right side of the tire tracks and not as wind-blown. He held his right hand up in a fist, everyone stopped. He pointed at the suspect location and gave hand signals telling the men to spread out and move toward the last place that Abdul had seen the head. Everyone knew to stay well out of Abdul's field of fire. As they neared the crest, the land fell away abruptly into a shallow waddi. When they arrived at the place where the sniper had been, the sniper was gone, but he had lost some blood there. Footprints led south toward a small village and a man could be seen entering through the cotton field.

"Wilson, use your scope, is he still carrying the rifle?" Abdul was shielding his eyes from the sun but could not see a weapon. Wilson said, "He doesn't appear to be carrying anything."

Nathan set the team to looking for the detonator in the sand near the bloody spot. Wilson removed his Kbar from its sheath and began carefully probing the loose sand around where the sniper had lain. He wanted to insure that no booby trap had been planted near the detonator. Wilson gave a whoop when he found it. He pulled on the wire to make sure that it went in the direction of the road.

Wilson asked, "Do we blow it now or look for the weapon first?"

The Captain said. "Luck is with us today. Look for the weapon. We will blow this shit on the way back."

They were about half way to the village when Wilson spotted the weapon. It was well off to the side of the tracks, in among the cotton plants. "Well look at this, very unfriendly" he said with a flat voice. They saw the wire wrapped around the trigger guard of the Dragunov. Wilson carefully began removing the sand from the area below the trigger guard. The weight of the weapon was resting on the spoon of a US manufactured baseball grenade. Wilson carefully held the spoon against the grenade and removed the wire.

"Well Captain, we should probably toss this baby; not really safe to try to re-pin."

"Ok, check that waddi (deep depression in the sand) to the left, if it is clear and deep enough toss it there, we don't want to hurt any friendlies."

"What friendlies," said Wilson; "this is Taliban country."

"The locals in this province are more pro-American than some of the rest of the country, but this village is not particularly friendly." Nathan made his point. "Anyway, we have the sniper rifle and the IUD and we aren't going into the village; there aren't enough of us for that. Get on the horn and tell Jason to back the Hummer about 200 meters, then we can see what this IUD is all about. When you are ready, tell the guys to get low just in case."

Sargent First Class (SFC) James Wilson did the honors. The IUD exploded with a loud bang. Had the sniper caught them in his trap, they would all have been killed. "Well you sure had good luck on your last full day in this god forsaken place," he said. "Tomorrow you will be flying home."

"This isn't actually a god forsaken place, the residents are just misdirected in their faith, and I am not exactly going home. I thought that my tour with SF was over and I would be going back to an MI (Military Intelligence) assignment. They are sending me to something called SFOD Delta. I have heard some scuttlebutt about it, but nothing to sink my teeth into. You guys know anything about it?"

After swapping knowing looks all around, Wilson said with a grin and wink, "You will fit right in Captain. We have all been in SF at least ten years, so the word has gotten around. We can't tell you what it is because then we would have to kill you, but it will be a really exciting and rewarding time. Not everyone gets offered the opportunity to join."

"Geez, my stress level had dropped in the last few minutes, but it is sky high again now!" Nathan joked.

They all chimed in, "You will get to fire your weapon every day, run six miles before breakfast, get into the best physical condition of your life, travel and see the world, and all on Uncle Sam's nickel."

"I am in great shape now; Jump School, Ranger School, SF Training; none of that was a cake walk," said Nathan.

"You think!" said James, "Delta makes all of that look like Sunday school. Don't get me wrong, it is all worth it for a single man. Wives don't last long with the husbands gone so often and without any explanation of where they are going or when they will return. Hell, in SF you are lucky if you can keep a wife for three years. The wives keep complaining that we come home every six months or so with a hard-on and a ruck sack full of dirty clothes, hang out at the team house rather than home and then disappear on short notice without explanation for another six months. Takes a lot of love to overcome all of that."

"Well let's saddle up," said CPT Thomas, "We don't want to be out here after dark."

Back at base camp, CPT Thomas and the team reported in for debriefing. After the debriefing and after action reports had been filed, the Executive Officer came into the room.

"Captain Thomas, was there a reason that you did not pursue the sniper into that village?"

"Well, Sir, there were only four of us, plus LT Nabi, and in the past that village has not been very friendly. We did get the sniper rifle and destroyed the IUD."

The XO (Executive Officer) Major Trump looked at the team and said, "You have gone into other villages with a worse reputation than that one with your team before to get your man. What made you hesitate this time?"

"Well, Sir, I just had an unsettled feeling about that village. I would not say that I had a specific reason. Maybe it was just that the guy walked into the village. He did not run or look back. It just did not look right, that is all that I can say." CPT Thomas replied.

"Well, considering your past record of aggressive pursuit, I was just surprised that you stopped," the XO said with a grin. "Could it have been because you are going back to Bragg tomorrow?"

"No way, I didn't even think of that. Just the way he walked rather than ran to the village must have made me extra cautious. Too bad though, he may live to fight another day."

"Well, let's all go over to the team house. I hear that they have some cold beer over there! I'll spring for the first round, since the Captain will be leaving us tomorrow." The XO said and was glad to see the smiles all around.

It was party time at the team house. The whole unit was already assembled with drinks in hand. Lieutenant Colonel (LTC) Ronald Reginald jumped up and said, "The guest of honor has arrived, all stand and attention to orders." There was a loud scuffling of feet and chairs and soon all were standing at attention.

"Captain Nathan Thomas, front and center!" said LTC Reginald. "Attention to Orders! Captain Nathan Thomas is hereby awarded the Silver Star Medal for conspicuous gallantry in the face of the enemy. On November 4th, 2009, Captain Thomas and his team were surrounded by a large enemy force of about thirty Taliban insurgents. Although all six team members were wounded they continued to defend their position. Captain Thomas distinguished himself by moving out of the night defensive position (NDP) under the cover of darkness to individually eliminate as many of the remaining Taliban members of the attacking force as possible pending the arrival of the rescue team. When the rescue team arrived in the early dawn hours, the remaining Taliban fighters fled and Captain Thomas returned to the NDP and his men. The men reported hearing individual shots during the night and the Taliban stopped actively probing the NDP; since they were under attack from behind their position. The rescue team found seventeen Taliban dead around the NDP. CPT Thomas had accounted for ten of them during the night. CPT Thomas had sustained two flesh wounds before leaving the NDP to take the fight to the enemy. He is hereby awarded the Purple Heart Medal, third award for those wounds. Command Sergeant Major (CSM), would you do the honors and pin the awards?"

"Yes Sir and gladly," replied the CSM. "Congratulations Captain and thank you for a job well done." The Command Sergeant Major took the Silver Star ribbon from the holder and pinned it to the battle dress uniform pocket on the left breast, then shook the hand of CPT Thomas. Next CSM Williams took the Purple Heart ribbon with three oak leaf clusters and pinned it to the right of the Silver Star and again shook hands. "Sorry for your pain sir, but you saved a lot of lives that day."

A loud "AMEN" was heard from near the back of the Teamhouse. SSG Jason Shady was one of the wounded that day. His head wound had knocked him out, but in a few days he had healed from the concussion and was back to full duty. "Sorry that I slept through most of the action sir." Everyone laughed at that comment. SSG Shady had a red face, but everyone there knew the story of what had happened that night. "I would be honored to buy the next round, Sir."

Fort Bragg and Pope Air Force Base

Chapter 2

CPT Wilson stopped at the guard shack at the entrance to Fort Bragg. The Military Policeman (MP) on duty asked to see his ID card and a copy of his orders. He had already noticed that the car did not have a Post Registration Sticker. CPT Wilson was in uniform and was surprised at being stopped. He asked the MP why he had stopped him.

The MP replied, "Well Sir, we have been told to stop all vehicles that do not have on post registration. I just asked for your orders because I thought it likely that you are new to Fort Bragg and might need directions."

"Well thanks for the consideration, but my Green Beret should have tipped you that I have been here before. Although you guessed correctly; I do not know exactly where the building is that I am heading for. Perhaps you can help me with that?"

"JSOC (Joint Special Operations Command) is over on what was Pope Air Force Base. Just keep straight on this road until you get to the airfield, then follow on to the right. You cannot miss the large JSOC sign out front. JSOC is on Gordon Road, Building 3-2847. The Information Desk can help you after that. The info desk is manned 24/7. Be sure to get that on-post registration ASAP, it will save a lot of Stops." The MP handed CPT Wilson the ID card and orders, saluted, and said "Have a good stay Sir."

As Nathan drove toward the JSOC Headquarters building, he noticed that not much had changed since he was here about a year ago. Smoke Bomb Hill, home of the Green Berets, looked about the same. It is probably the only place on earth were you can see a Master Sergeant (MSG) and a SFC sweeping the streets or cleaning up pine straw. The SF (Special Forces) teams are rank heavy due to the extensive training and experience necessary to become a Green Beret.

The JSOC Information Desk was manned by a young woman with a bright smile and a helpful attitude. She pointed me toward the in-processing office sign and said, "Start right there Sir, they will get you to where you are going."

A Staff Sergeant greeted me as I entered the office. "Good afternoon Sir, may I have a copy of your orders." Not really a request, more of a demand. SSG Waters looked at the orders and said, "Oh SFOD-Delta, come with me Sir." She handed my packet to MSG De Jesus and said "Here is another one," and walked away.

MSG De Jesus said. "Have a seat Sir. I need to check with Delta to see where they want me to send you." He picked up the phone and dialed, then gave my information. He listened for a few minutes and then put the phone down.

"Well Sir, you are going straight to Camp McCall. Do you remember how to get there?" He was already getting a map out of his desk drawer. He reached into another drawer and pulled out a folder with my name on it. "We have been expecting you, so all of your paperwork has already been processed. When you get to Camp MacKall, they will make arrangements for billeting and equipment issue."

"Yes I remember how to get there, not much has changed around here in the last year." I took the map and packets from his hand thinking, Camp MacKall, this is no staff assignment. Camp MacKall was all Green Beret territory when I left. I pointed toward Reilly Rd and settled in for the long drive to Manchester Rd then to King Road and finally Hoffman, NC where Camp MacKall is located.

I pulled up to the Guard Shack and a heavily armed MP ambled over and asked for my ID and Orders. I handed them over and he obviously had been expecting me. He said, "Drive straight ahead to the first building on the right. You will be met by Lieutenant Colonel McMasterson, the Executive Officer." He gave me back my paperwork along with a snappy salute.

LTC McMasterson, I had heard of him or rather heard his legend. He had started with Jump School right after coming on active duty, then Ranger School, and Special Forces Officer Course. He and his teams had notable successes in both Iraq and Afghanistan operations. He had been on the fast track for General, but he decided that he would stay with Special Forces and Special Operations regardless of the impact on future promotions. He was very good at planning and executing the operations. He had always fought to be a member of the operational team on the ground. No more, his wings were clipped and he was just viewed as too valuable an asset to risk. He must be fifty-five or sixty years old, but he looked like he could still max the PT (physical training) test and unless you knew something about his history, you would think that he was in his forties. Proof that regular physical activity can help keep you young.

I got out of the car and gave the Colonel a snappy salute; that was returned immediately, with the admonishment that "once a day of that is enough! Let's go over to the team house for a talk. You have some decisions to make before we decide what to do next."

The Team House was one bay in a barracks with a bar and coolers, tables and chairs; nothing fancy. McMasterson said "Want a beer or something else?"

"Beer is fine", I said.

McMasterson brought over two Bud Select and set them down. "You have some choices to make, but you do not have to make them right now. You have been selected for a special operation that we need to get started on soon. You speak Spanish and you were raised around the water with a lot of boating experience. That is what put you in this picture."

"You may not know a lot about SFOD-Delta, but it is all-volunteer and we really are the best of the best. The selection process is viewed as physically strenuous and mentally tough. You are in regardless of how you choose to proceed. You can go through selection or opt-out. The reason that I mention it is the other members of your team. They all went through selection. If you do not go through selection, you will be a question-mark for them. The down-side is selection starts tomorrow. The up-side is that I know how you kept your team conditioned in Afghanistan, so you should not have any problems. Selection for this group will take three days. I know that you are jet-lagged, but a good night of sleep should take care of that. Do you have any questions?"

"I sure do, what all is involved in Selection and what is the mission?"

"Selection is basically a PT Test, marches with a full ruck sack, endurance and land navigation course, some weapons qualification and some psychological testing successfully completed by each individual candidate. Most of the guys here are graduates of Ranger School or Marine Corps Recon, so I doubt that you will have any problems.

Your training and experience are in line with the others. As to the mission, I cannot talk about that until I have your decision about Selection."

"From what you say, I get it that if I want to be fully accepted by my team mates, I need to do the Selection. What happens if I somehow fail Selection?"

"We are careful whom we invite. Mostly Selection is failed because of an injury that happens on one of the exercises. So with a little luck, you will not become badly injured. Selection is a tough three days though. If you fail selection, you are out and we have to find another candidate. I do not want to explain the mission until the Selection issue is resolved."

I thought it over for a few seconds, "I will take Selection. Mutual respect is key to team cohesiveness, the men would not say much to me if I opted out, but they would talk among themselves. I will do the Selection and let the chips fall where they may."

The Colonel was all smiles, "You just passed the first test. Let's find you a bunk so you can get some rest before morning. Reveille is at six o'clock, followed by breakfast at the dining facility. I will show you where everything is along the way to the BOQ (Bachelor Officers Quarters)."

As we walked to the BOQ, the Colonel explained, "We are rank neutral during selection, everyone is a candidate, no special treatment based on rank. Everyone still wears their rank insignia on the uniform, so you do not need to remove them. After everyone draws their equipment in the morning, we will relocate to the training facility. All of the candidates live together in a barracks. The situation is a lot like what you experienced during Ranger School."

"On the left, there is the dining facility. The food is pretty good. We will meet there for breakfast then go over to the supply hooch to draw equipment. Wear your most comfortable boots and bring your shaving gear. You will not be back here for three days."

I was curious. "What about uniform changes?" I asked.

The Colonel grinned, "What uniform changes? Best you can do is stuff an extra pair of sox in your pocket and maybe sock liners if you have any. The course used to be five days. We are trying something new with the three day schedule. You still remember how to sleep standing up? Well, here we are at the BOQ. Just grab an empty bunk, get some shut-eye, and I will see you at breakfast."

Nathan popped a smart salute that was promptly returned. "See you in the morning sir," he said. He walked into the BOQ and found an empty room. The room was really spartan; steel bunk, wafer thin mattress, small table next to the bed, wall locker and a chest of drawers. The walls were a light green and the floor was black and white tiles. At least the window had some lively multicolored curtains. The latrine was about three steps down the hall. Not much different from Ranger School he thought. Nathan went back out to his car and brought in his well-traveled B4 bag and extra boots. Nathan looked at the bed and was about ready to begin putting the sheets and blanket on when he heard a knock on the door. The door was open, so I just turned around and said "Come in."

Standing before me was one of the largest men I had ever seen. He was about six foot five and probably went two hundred seventy-five pounds. None of it was fat. His cover almost touched the top of the door frame. His BDU's showed that he was Lieutenant Gleason. LT

Gleason, said "McMasterson sent me over, the mess hall opens in about five minutes, he suggested that we get a good meal and some sack-time before morning, Sir. I just got here today myself."

"Ok," I said and dropped the pillow on the bed as I grabbed my hat from the table.

The LT was all enthusiasm as we moved toward the Mess Hall. "What have you heard so far? It sounds like the first week of Ranger School, drop dead within three days or make the grade."

"Sounds like that to me too," I said. "By the way, just call me Nathan"

"Oh, I'm Lyman Gleason, just call me Lyman. Sorry, I guess that this casual SF environment is making me forget my manners."

"Well Lyman, it looks like you have been around some; Airborne Wings, Ranger Tab and SF Patch. A pretty quick training schedule for a Second Lieutenant."

"Yeah, I think that it is my size and prior enlisted service. I joined ROTC (Reserve Officer Training Corps) my sophomore year in high school, but only made Major by the time that I graduated. I joined the Army, went through Basic, then Ranger training and Officer Candidate School (OCS), and then SF Officers Course over at Fort Bragg. Not necessarily in that order. I guess that I learn pretty quick and I should make First Lieutenant next month. MMMmm that menu looks good."

It did too, country fried steak, mashed potato with gravy or sweet potato, green beans, corn, garden salad, banana pudding or apple pie and coffee, tea or other beverage. Here, everyone goes through the serving line, but Officers and Senior NCO's had their respective tables separate from the rest of the dining tables.

As they sat down at the table, Lyman asked, "And where have you been lately?"

"I joined ROTC in college and then Airborne and Ranger School right after I came to Active Duty. I went to Iraq as a Ranger from the 75th; then back to Bragg for SF Officers Qualification Course and then on to an SFOB detachment from 7th Group to Afghanistan. I came here from Afghanistan."

Lyman looked at me; then said, "Must be more to it than that from the salad on your blouse!"

"I just did my job like everyone else. It is nice that someone appreciated my efforts."

"Looks like a few took exception. That Purple Heart has a couple of clusters."

"There is always someone that would rather that we were somewhere else rather than in their way. At least, they are no longer around to complain and I doubt that they are with their seventy virgins to celebrate either."

"Well, that was a good dinner. I think that I will get back to the Q and finish making that bed. Take care, see you at breakfast."

I headed back to the Q, then I made the bed; nice and tight with neat corners and a white collar. Then I took a quarter out of my pocket and flipped it onto the bed. Sure enough the quarter bounced high and landed on the floor. Yep, I thought to myself, I can still do it. Then I grabbed a towel and headed to the shower.

SFOD- Delta Selection

Chapter 3

Reveille sounded way too early, but Nathan had managed to get eight hours of solid z's. He jumped up, showered quickly, shaved, dressed and headed for the Mess Hall. The Flag was flying briskly at full staff as he walked by and rendered a snappy salute. It was a good morning to be alive.

Nathan went through the chow line. Nice choices: eggs any way that you wanted them including a vegie stuffed omelet, bacon, sausage, liver pudding, steak potatoes, grits, toast and jam. Army coffee was always good and welcome. Then he saw Lyman already seated and headed over. "Morning Lyman mind if I sit?" Nathan asked.

"Come on ahead Sir and welcome." Lyman responded with good humor.

They ate quietly and then began sipping coffee. "Have you seen the XO yet?"

"Not yet," said Lyman.

Just then, a Master Sergeant walked in and announced "All of the new folks for Selection please form up outside in about five minutes." You could easily tell who we were; we all had shaving kits and bulging pockets this morning.

Anyone who had been through Ranger training knew that you needed more than a change of sox to get through. APC's (All Purpose Capsules aka high power aspirin) and salve for blisters were top items. Extra boot laces could be used for all kinds of things as could a sparking steel and a really good pocket knife. It was only three days, but we expected them to be challenging.

As we assembled, the MSG waited until all ten of us had arrived. Then he said, "Men, the XO will be here in a few minutes. Just line up in front of me, I will call Attention and salute the XO. He will then put you At Ease and give instructions about what will follow. We will then board the duce-and-a-half parked to the right. Everyone load into the back and then we drive to the supply point to draw equipment. I hope to see you all back here in three days, good luck to all of you."

With that said, LCT McMasterson came out of the Headquarters building. The MSG shouted "Attention" and saluted the XO. The XO returned the salute and said "At Ease men."

"Today begins the Selection process. The process stresses you physically and mentally, but I expect that most of you will do well. We always seem to have a few people that get hurt along the way and that is just the way it is. Take care of yourselves. I hope to see all of you back here on Friday. Master Sergeant Dwell take charge of the Selectee Candidates."

MSG Dwell called "Attention", saluted the XO and waited for him to move away. Then said "When I say fall-out, mount the truck; Fall Out."

We all moved to the truck, dropped the tailgate and climbed aboard. It was about five miles to the training camp and supply point. We drew a poncho, a poncho liner, pistol belt, first aid packet, two ammo pouches, canteen with cup, canteen cover, mess kit, entrenching tool, rucksack with shoulder straps and belt, Kevlar helmet, twenty feet of parachute line, a Kbar knife, compass, a map of Camp MacKall, an XM203 submachine gun, five 30 round magazines and three days worth of MRE's. We carefully packed what we could into and onto the rucksack and pouches. The rest went into our pockets. Everything was clean but heavily worn. That was ok with me as it was well broken in and did not poke and pinch like new equipment could.

The Supply Sergeant had us check each item and then sign for the equipment. We had seen a group of men gradually assembling near where we were while we drew our equipment. There were six of them, none was wearing any rank. The Supply Sergeant called to them, "Ok Top, they are all yours."

"Men, welcome to Selection. We do not go by rank here. If you need to speak with one of us, I am TOP. Everyone else is called Cadre. While you are here you will unquestioningly obey any instructions given by myself or any of these other five men, we are your training cadre. We are here to help you succeed, but that does not mean that we will make it easy for you in any way. Anytime that you feel that you have had enough, put your helmet under your arm and come to one of us. If you have an injury, it is up to you to tell us. If the injury is bad enough that you cannot speak, we will decide for you. Enough of the negative stuff."

"Now, here I have some plastic bags and tags. First I want all of the cell phones. Next I suggest that you leave your wallets and personal papers here. Keep only your ID card. You can make the choice for yourself except for the cell phone. If you have a GPS it must be put in the bag."

We all gave up our cells and filled out the tag. No one had a GPS.

Top then said, "Form a line and come up to that table over there where the Cadre are standing. We want to weigh your rucksack. It should weigh about forty-five pounds, any less and we will add rock to make up the difference." We formed a line and weighed in. The weapon and web gear were included in the 45 pounds. As we weighed the equipment each weapon was thoroughly check by a Cadre and the owner. The weapon was then put on safe.

Top called us to "Form up into two columns with all web gear and weapons on. I know that you all had a good breakfast this morning. We are going over to the Lister Bag to fill your canteens with water. It is time to shake it down, so we are going for a short run."

No one bothered to ask how far. It turned out to be six miles and we all made it with no sweat, well, a little maybe. The cadre ran with us, but they were not hindered by any web gear, rucksack or weapons. We suspected that we were near the end of the run when we saw what looked like a mess tent in the distance. Sure enough there was a tent and a pair of trash cans with heaters in them for washing the mess kits.

Top called us to a halt and said to fall out for lunch. Then he said we all had MRE's and that the mess tent had heat tabs so we could heat our lunch. We should clean our mess gear before we left. He said that we had thirty minutes to be ready to leave. We had all been through this before, so we dumped an MRE into the canteen cup added some water, found a heat tab, broke it in half and cooked lunch. There was another Lister bag for us to refill our canteens, none of us missed the opportunity.

An American Army surgeon William Lyster came up with a collapsible rubber lined canvas bag with a tight fitting cover that could be filled with water and a chlorine solution to purify the water and in about 1917 the army adopted it as a standard piece of equipment.

Slightly Off

Art McGillem

We cleaned our canteen cups and were ready to go in three zero minutes. We all saved the other half of our heat tab for later use. Waste not, want not, with a little luck.

We formed up and double-timed for about two miles. We could see a target range coming up on the right and sure enough Top called a halt. "Keep all of your web gear on and your weapon slung, move to the ammo point and draw one magazine of live ammo, move to a firing point and place your weapon on the firing stake. Then step back to the table behind the firing point and wait for instructions."

After everyone was standing behind their firing points, Top said "On this range we will sight-in your weapon. Your magazine has three rounds. When I say assume a good firing position, I want you to move to your firing point, leave your weapon on the firing stake and assume a good prone firing position. A Cadre will hand you your weapon. I will then say load magazine. Remember to keep your weapon pointing up and down range. At this point, I will say load and you can charge your weapon. Then I will say that the range is not safe. Then I will say fire. You will fire three aimed rounds into your target. You will then open the breech, lock the slide to the rear, safe the weapon and remove the magazine. A Cadre will check your weapon and put it on the firing stake. When everyone is finished with the first three rounds, I will announce that the range is safe. We will move down to the targets and see what adjustment should be made to our sights. Then paste over our three round group. Then as a group we will return to our firing positions. We will fire another three round group, check targets. Return to firing position and fire the final three round group. Everyone should be zeroed by this time. Are there any questions?" There were no questions, we had all been there and done that over and over.

"Cadre hand the firers their weapon; Firer, insert magazine, Firer, load. The range is not safe. Establish a good site picture and stock weld, fire at will." It was done quickly. The magazines were removed, weapons put on safe, chambers checked, weapons on firing stake, all verified by the Cadre. Everyone wanted to see their target. Most had tight groupings, but not all in the X ring. Sights were adjusted to move the strike of the bullets into the X ring. Almost everyone was in the X ring on the second round, but everyone wanted to fire the final round and it was done. All weapons were put on safe and examined by Cadre to insure that none contained a live round.

Top commanded "Fall-in, two columns. Right Face, forward march, double-time, follow the road to the right." We double-timed for another mile to another range. Cadre had the ammo point setup. We all took one magazine as instructed, placed our weapons on the firing position stake and waited next to the fox hole.

Top said "This range has pop-up targets. You are to shoot the white dot on the target. There are ten targets and each magazine has ten rounds. Only use one round per target. You will have four seconds to engage your target and fire. Use any unexpended rounds on the last target. The targets will pop-up in random order; the farthest is 450 meters, closest is 20 meters. Firers mount your fox holes. When you have finished firing place your weapon breech open over your right shoulder so a Cadre can verify that the weapon is clear. Cadre give the firers their weapon; firer insert one ten round magazine, load, the range is not safe, firers engage your targets."

It went very quickly, four seconds per target, it was over in forty seconds. Weapons were verified as cleared and placed on the firing position stakes. The Cadre had been on the spotting scopes during the range firing. They tabulated the results and Top announced, "It is a tie between Thomas and Gleason, both got thirty-nine out of 40 in the white. Thomas' out shot was closer to the white than Gleason. All of you had more than seven in the white. Great shooting men!"

It was beginning to get dark, but none of were thinking that the end of our day was nearing.

Top said, "Get your weapons and form up in two rows facing me. Order Arms, Thomas hand your weapon to Cadre and check that all other weapons are clear." I did a Port Arms and an Inspection Arms, then handed my weapon to the nearest cadre. I commanded "Port Arms and then Inspection Arms" that way all breeches were open for my inspection. I took each weapon from the soldier and inspected the chamber, bore and insured that none had a mounted magazine. When I completed the inspection, I reported "Top, all weapons inspected and cleared." Then I retrieved my weapon from Cadre.

Top called everyone to attention, right face and double time. It looked like there was going to be about a quarter moon tonight, but no clouds. If night firing was the plan, we should be able to see well enough. Lyman leaned toward me "I am going to beat you on the night fire. I have eyes like a cat."

"Handy thing to have, I fired back." A little competition just spices the pie.

It was full dark by the time that we got to the night fire range. The range had red lights at strategic points like the ammo point and latrines. Top told us to fall-out into the bleachers and hit the latrine if needed. He called us back to the bleachers a little while later. It was eleven o'clock and we all wished that we were in bed somewhere. The moon provided enough light that we could dimly see the lanes in the range. Picking up targets would be tough.

Top explained that there were going to be twenty targets appearing at random distances and that we would have twenty rounds to get them all. Each target would pop-up for five seconds. The live fire time would be one hundred seconds. The last target would be announced and all remaining rounds should be expended on that target. The icing on the cake is that each target has a white spot that the moon might illuminate for us. The white spot was again the target.

Top said, "Fall-in, a single line facing me. Good luck men. Cadre will give you one twenty round magazine after you have placed your rifle on the firing position stake." Each firing position stake had a notch to help keep the weapon from falling into the dirt.

"Move forward and place your weapon on the firing stake and assume a good prone firing position. Cadre will then give you a magazine. Do not pick up your weapon until told to do so."

"Cadre give each firer one twenty round magazine. Firers pick up your weapon and insert magazine. Load! The range is nolonger safe. Watch your firing lane, Fire."

Picking up the flash of the white spot was a challenge. The firing was over very quickly. It was a difficult series. Several positions fired multiple rounds at the last target. I had fired at all of the targets, but hitting the white spot was tough, the spot was in all different places on the target. Each target had come up twice, so each white spot should have two holes.

Top said, "All weapons on safe, remove the magazine and place the weapon on your right shoulder, breech open. Cadre check them out. Cadre report. All weapons are safe and clear. Place your weapon at sling-arms and return to the bleachers. Cadre score the targets."

"It looks like Thomas wins again," Top announced. "He collected eighteen white hits and the two that were out were just to the right of the white spot. Looks like a trigger control issue. Once again Gleason was second. He hit sixteen white spots. His off hits were in line and low. Looks like anticipation of recoil. Congratulations to you both. Excellent shooting."

The lights came on with their white glare and we were all blinded for a few seconds.

"Cadre has been busy putting cleaning supplies on the tables behind the firing positions. You have fifteen minutes for weapons cleaning. When you are done, take a seat in the bleachers." Top ordered.

We all disassembled our weapon, ran solvent soaked patches, then clean patches down the bore, cleaned the breech, magazine well and bolt; then reassembled our weapon and waited in the bleachers. Lyman slipped up next to me, "Well, looks like I lost again." He looked sad, like he was not accustomed to coming in second.

I said, "You didn't lose, I just didn't tell you that I have cat eyes also so maybe you relaxed a little. I just guessed where two of the white spots were on two targets. I did not see them on the second go round, but guessed the location from the first round."

"Yeah," said Lyman. "I had the same problem. They never pulled this one on us in Ranger school. I will be ready next time."

I laughed, "Probably the next time they will make sure that the moon is well hidden just so we don't get too full of ourselves."

Top and the Cadre stood in front of us, then Top said, "Ok, good job and time for bed. The barracks is eight miles down the road to the left. It is a straight shot, no turns. See you at Reveille formation in the morning."

So we were suddenly confronted with an eight mile run, jog or walk.

Lyman laughed, "I've got you now. Running is something that these long legs know how to do. See ya in the morning."

I jumped up saying, "You have about three inches on me, but you are carrying another thirty pounds. I bet we get there about the same time."

"Yeah, but I will get there first though." The race was on. Eight miles is pretty far. Lyman ran on ahead with a long easy stride. I decided to warm-up first and began a quick-time stride. Soon Lyman was out of sight. Several others passed me as I did the warm-up. Through the next hour I caught and passed all of them except Lyman. When I got to the barracks, Lyman was just dropping his rucksack. I had made it in sixty-four minutes; just over seven minutes per mile.

"Hi Lyman, good run," I congratulated him. "I really thought that I was going to catch you. Our stride is about the same. We have two more days of this so we had better hit the sack."

We put our weapons in the rack, dropped our rucksack and web gear at the end of a bunk, made the bed and were asleep before our heads hit the pillows. It was 0230 hours.

Slightly Off

Art McGillem

They actually let us sleep until 0530 hours. That is when the lights came on and Top said, "Reveille in thirty minutes, uniform of the day is full gear including weapon."

We fell-in at 0600 hours and saluted as the flag went up. "You will notice that you have a different group of Cadre today. Today is land navigation exercises. We will warm-up with a double-time march to the breakfasting area. It is close by, only four miles. Then you will break into two man teams for the land navigation exercises. Break into a column of twos. Cadre take them to breakfast."

With that we were off at a quick pace. It was a quiet time, Cadre did not call cadence to relieve the boredom. We were all left to our own thoughts. As we got to the breakfast site, we halted. We went to the mess tent for heat tabs, cooked our rations, ate and cleaned our mess kits. I noticed several of us had boots off and were taking care of blisters or sore feet. I wondered how they would do in the next forty-eight hours if their feet were already giving them problems.

Cadre called us together after our thirty minute breakfast break. Lyman and I were assigned as one team. We knew that whatever came, we would be the best. Each team was given a set of map coordinates and told to be there in four hours. We were told that if another team or team member asked for help, we were not supposed to give it. The mission was more important than even an injury. If an injury was involved, we were to write down the coordinates and report it when we reached our objective. We were not to arrive early at the objective.

I asked Lyman, "How comfortable are you with compass and map navigation?"

"No problems, piece of cake," he replied.

"Me too," I said. We looked at the map coordinate we had been given, then at the map. "It looks like we are headed to the spillway at Broadacres Lake coordinates are 35'16.45"N by 79'32.49.46"W. We are at 35'00.44.43"N by 79'30.17.13"W. That only looks like 4K. I wonder if they are putting any surprises in our path? What do you think?"

Lyman agreed, "That looks about right and this is supposed to be a tough course. No telling what surprises they have up their sleeve. What say we head northwesterly and stay just inside that tree line? It will take us a lot longer than if we just schlepped down the road, but we should see any surprises well in advance."

I agreed, "We could push the pace just a little in the event that they are timing us and didn't plan any surprises."

My compass said that we were heading WNW (west north west) as we made for the distant tree-line. There were just enough trees to allow us to move without being in direct view. I would call this area heavy scrub with single open canopy. We stayed well back from the dirt roads, they were not even graveled. Just as we made the tree-line, small arms fire erupted to the south of us. Lyman looked at me and nodded. I grinned back. We were going to practice noise discipline just to be safe.

Lyman led off and we had moved about a hundred yards when he held his right hand up in a fist. I stopped immediately. Lyman was looking to the left down at a bend in the road that was just behind us and about three hundred yards away. There stood a Cadre with his weapon at port arms. He had been waiting for us. Then there were a few shot from both north and southwest of us. We could almost hear the wheels grinding, where are my guys he had to be thinking. Then suddenly he turned around and began slowly observing the tree-line that was hiding our evasion route. His visual search passed by us and he turned back to the road.

Lyman signaled to move ahead while the Cadre's back was turned toward us and we started off moving a little more quickly than before. Soon he would come to the trees to see if we had passed that way. We covered the distance to the spillway without seeing another Cadre. We approached the spillway very cautiously and saw a second Cadre hiding behind a large low growing pine tree. Lyman pointed at his eyes and then at the Cadre. I just nodded, then signed for a quiet kill. The Cadre was watching the roadway. I picked up a stick to simulate a knife and signed for Lyman to wait for the other Cadre to arrive. Surely he would be following our trail by now.

I slowly high stepped it down toward my Cadre. I was a half-step away when he heard me. I slipped the branch under his chin and said, "Quiet now, Lyman is waiting for your buddy." The Cadre gave me a sheepish look and nodded. We sat down to wait.

Lyman came down to our position with the other Cadre in tow about ten minutes later. We walked down to the spillway where another Cadre was waiting. He had been talking on the radio as we walked up. He said, "Congratulations, you guys and one other team made it in to their target. The rest got captured. Interesting you and the other team just came back from combat assignments. Your paranoia level must still be high. Good job no matter how you look at it. We are being picked up by truck in a few minutes, so take a break until then."

"How did you catch him" I asked. Lyman chuckled, "Remember that big pine behind us with the limbs all the way down to the ground? Well, I just crawled under it and waited. He was walking along looking at the bent grasses where we had walked. He actually walked right past me before I told him to halt and drop his weapon.

He just said, "Ok, you got me come on out, game over."

"Thomas, that high stepping really works, I saw the whole thing. That Cadre didn't hear a thing until you were right next to him. Watching that was chilling!"

"Yeah, I could have shit my pants when you said drop the weapon and do not move. I hadn't gotten to the point where you turned off and got behind the pine tree, so that voice from nowhere really made my hair stand on end." Both of the Cadre were smiling, who doesn't like to play cowboy and indian.

"Yeah, me too, chimed in the other Cadre, it took a second to realize that you were using a stick rather than your Kbar. Thank you for that."

The duce-and-a-half arrived and we climbed aboard. We picked-up three more teams and then went back to a fenced holding area. Top was there and we had missed another meal. We were not going to have lunch, I would have bet on it.

Top had us fall-in facing him. "You are numbered one to ten from my left, your right. In the building there are ten rooms with the number above the door. Find your room and enter. You can get as physical as you want, but you will probably get it back double later. Remember your SERE (Survival, Evasion, Resistance and Escape) training. Only two teams survived and evaded today. Now it is time to resist, but there is no escape. Go to your rooms and good luck."

We went to our rooms and entered. I had a glimpse of four men before the hood came down over my head and the lights went out. I struggled briefly, but did not try to hurt anyone. These were all hard men and would give more than I gave, with four to one odds. I felt myself being strapped into a chair. The water was cold as it soaked my hood and clothing. My rucksack and web gear had been removed as soon as the hood was in place. A breeze was coming from somewhere and making me very chilled. It was difficult to breathe through the wet hood.

A voice demanded, "Thomas, what is your unit?"

I responded, "Captain Nathan Thomas 370221020." Something hit me on the head and more water was thrown on me.

"I did not ask you about that nonsense. Search him, I want his wallet and any papers. Check all of his pockets." Something hit me on the head again.

Someone said "All he has is an ID card and some heat tabs."

"Captain Thomas what is your unit, quickly before I lose patience?"

"Nathan Thomas, Captain, you already got the SSN (service number)." This time someone knocked the chair over and more water.

The voice said "Ok, want to play tough. Lock him up."

I felt myself being untied and lifted from the chair. My hands were now tied behind my back and I felt myself being pushed into some kind of a box. Then the door slammed and they began banging on the walls. I was in a metal wall locker from the sound of it and the banging was deafening in its intensity. The banging stopped for a few heart beats and water began to pour into the box. Surely these guys aren't going to kill me. In SF school they put snakes in the box with you. That was really creepy, makes your hair stand right up on end. It makes my skin crawl just thinking about it. The water is getting pretty deep. The hood is wicking up the water making it hard to breathe. The water was covering my nose and I began to struggle to keep my nose above water. I was worried that I was going to pass out. No more air to breathe, getting fuzzy.

Suddenly, the locker was lifted upright and the stars began to disappear. I could breathe again. Then it was back into the water and it refilled quickly and I was losing consciousness again.

This time when the locker was upright, the voice asked, "Thomas what is the name of your unit?"

I was panting hard but said "Nathan Thomas, Captain, you know the rest." This time the locker fell on its side and water shot up my nose making me choke and gag.

I heard the voice say, "He isn't going to talk, bury him."

I felt the locker being picked up and moving. It felt like I was being lowered and it was getting quieter.

"Captain Thomas this is your last chance, I cannot waste any more time on you. Either you answer my question or they begin filling in the hole."

"Let me catch my breath for a second,' I said.

"Captain, I am waiting for your answer."

"I am a little disorientated, what is the question?"

"Fill it in; he won't even answer simple questions." Then the first shovel full of dirt began falling on the locker. I began thinking that I was going to be a training accident. The shovels full of dirt were falling regularly and it was getting quieter.

I found out later that they put a foot of dirt on top of me and left me there for two hours. They had oxygen piped into the locker so I could breathe. No one gave any unit information.

They dug us up and we all assembled in front of the prison camp. Top was there to congratulate us for our mental toughness. It was 1800 hours and we were all hungry and thirsty. Our field kitchen had been set up next to the prison camp.

Top said "You have thirty minutes to eat then it is lights out. We will wake you in the morning for Reveille."

I looked at Lyman, "What did you do, put up a fight?"

"Yeah, and I almost won too. I could see that there was only four of them and they were a little slow getting the hood on. I took a shot. I guess that I got what I deserved, they worked on me pretty good as a payback." We finished eating and didn't bother getting undressed, just fell on our racks and went to sleep.

It was about 2130 hours when all hell broke loose. Weapons firing in the barracks woke us up. Cadre said "Everyone outside, uniform is all equipment with weapon."

Top stood there waiting patiently. "You didn't think that we were really going to let you sleep all night did you? This is the last test. You all have map and compass. It is a timed event, so hustle along. There are checkpoints along the way, we call them rendezvous aka RVs. Insure all RVs are found and that you are logged-in. You are not to ask help from anyone. You will not be ambushed or hindered by Cadre on your way. Distance, time and terrain are your only enemies on this exercise. Feel free to use roads, trails, bridges, etc. as necessary to reach your destination. Do not accept rides from locals or other military members that you may see. This exercise is an individual effort. Good luck! Cadre, give each candidate his destination list and send them on their way."

I looked at my list of six RVs and the destination. I got out my map and a grease pencil. I called the checkpoints RV1 as Start through RV6, the last the destination, and marked them on the map. Some of the others had already taken off. It looked like my route was about twenty-four miles as the crow flies. Crows don't have to worry about hills, valleys, streams or rivers. So I set out, it was 2200 hours.

The first RV was about three miles and was near the junction of Thunder and Dwyer roads. There were roads that went most of the way there so I could make good time. It would be only a little shorter going cross-country, but likely would take considerably longer. Brush and weeds really slow the feet and gradually drain energy on long walks. Twice cars stopped to ask me if I wanted a ride. I told them thank you, but I was out for the exercise. They were used to seeing soldiers out jogging with their rucksacks. The drivers had just said ok and left with a friendly wave.

Cadre logged me in eighteen minutes and twenty seconds after the start, 2218.20 hours. I stopped by the Lister Bag to refill my canteen and splash water on my face before setting out for RV 2.

RV2 was about 22 miles away by road, but only about half that by going directly southwest. Between Ellerbe and Richmond, RV2 distance could be cut by about half. I could head down Derby Road to Ledbetter Road as far as Millstone Road. At the Millstone Road junction, I would begin going cross-country. The terrain looked fairly flat, but there were likely to be lots of pine trees which could limit the amount of tangle-foot. Tall pine trees drop lots of pine needles and limit sun reaching the forest floor eliminating most of the low growing shrubs and weeds. Using the roads would add about one mile to the distance, but save considerable time. My rucksack was beginning to bite into my shoulders. Jogging around with the rucksack the last two days had begun to chafe and irritate. I had gotten soft in Afghanistan where we went almost everywhere in a vehicle. No need to hump a rucksack. My team did do PT every day with a two to four mile run included.

My map was showing a lot of roads in the area, so time must be an important factor in deciding how well we did on the course. So I began jogging down Derby road and turned right onto State Road 1442. The roads even had signs. As I jogged along, 1442 became Ledbetter Road. There were forests on each side of the road. At one point, I heard running feet to my right heading toward me. I stopped and squatted down near a tall bush beside the road. In a few seconds three doe deer ran across the road near me. I wondered what had scared them, but heard nothing. As I stood, the buck charged across the road. He had apparently been slipping along behind them.

I reached the intersection with Millstone Road. Now to head west-south-west about five miles to RV 2. The terrain was mostly open forested land with a few farmed areas according to the map. I skirted a pond and freshly plowed field and went along for about half a mile and found a dirt road that went in my direction and followed it for another mile. The dirt road ended at Green Lake Road. I crossed the road and picked up a residential road that looked like it was going in the right direction, but it curved northerly and I started cross-country again. I skirted to the right of a large farm pond, crossed a fire break, and came to what I was sure was Lee Thee Church Road. I stayed to the right of a small pond and kept going. The ground was very uneven with little cover. I could see a tree line ahead and wondered if the ground would be easier to travel. When I reached the trees, the ground was covered with pine needles and little else. Time to make-time. I hitched my ruck higher and stepped-out. The ground was gently rising within the forest and I was glad when I reached the crest and began heading down toward RV2, about a quarter mile away.

The Cadre was sitting in a Jeep waiting for me. This leg had taken two hours and fourteen minutes; thirty-eight minutes, twenty seconds past midnight. I asked if he had any water, but he just looked at me and wrote the time in his log. He handed me a note that said, avoid all civilian and military contact. My canteen was half full, but I suspected that I would not see another Lister Bag until the end of the course. Ok, time to look for a water source along the way to RV 3.

RV 3 was about three and a half miles as the crow flies. Only one major water feature seemed to be in the way. There were a lot of residential areas along the route that I had to travel. I suspected that capture was also part of their plan, so I could not use the roads to cross the lake. It would take a lot of extra time to avoid contact, but the darkness would be a significant help. My night vision was destroyed by the light around the jeep. I put the red filter on my Maglight.

I headed east away from the jeep. Once out of sight of the Cadre, I stopped to let my eyes become adjusted to the night. Good thing that I did, I noticed movement about two hundred yards from where I stood. I moved slowly more northerly toward a band of trees that I had recently passed through. Avoiding contact was going to add time and distance. I made it to the trees and began walking more easterly. I stayed in the tree line and slipped from tree stand to tree stand until just before I re-crossed Lee Thee Church Road. Most of the lights in the homes were out as I passed by. Only one dog barked when I came too close to its property. The dog went quiet as I got farther away. I took my pack off and slung my weapon barrel down in preparation for crossing Lee Thee. I walked quickly across the road between a store and some homes. My ruck was tucked under the arm pressing my weapon to my side. Hopefully, I would look like someone carrying a large package, not someone with a rifle and ruck.

I came across a dirt road and watched it for a few minutes before slowly crossing it. Quick movement catches the eye. I moved a little farther on and crossed some plowed fields. It would have been nice if I could have used Hall Road. Hall would have taken me in the direction that I wanted to go and eventually to the bridge across the lake. I was going to have to swim the lake; that was for certain. No borrowing boats from unsuspecting civilians. I arrived at what was probably Green Lake Road. I was a little south of where I had crossed it earlier. The next stop would be at the edge of Ledbetter Lake.

Ledbetter Lake was quite large according to the map, but was elongated and curved around. I was at a fairly narrow part of the lake, but not at one of the narrowest points. I decided that I would cross here. I sat watching the other side of the lake for about thirty minutes, nothing was stirring over there. Everything inside my ruck was inside a waterproof bag. I stripped of my clothes and added them to the bag. I placed a condom on the barrel of my weapon and slung it across my back, held the ruck in front of me and waded into the water. I frog-kicked across the lake, pushing the ruck in front of me. I made it to the other side with a sigh of relief, nothing was stirring. I figured that it was about two hundred yards through the trees to RV 3. I untied my boots from around my neck and hung them upside down on a bush to let them drain. I put my uniform back on, then the boots. They felt squishy, but did not make any sound as I walked. I high stepped my way to RV 3 and saw the Cadre nodding in the jeep. I kept high stepping until I was standing right next to him. Then in a loud voice, I said "Thomas here."

He came instantly awake, smiled sheepishly and said, "Nice move." That "nice move" had taken me a full hour plus eighteen minutes to go three miles. The time was now 0155.20 hours.

RV 4 was 10.6 miles to the east; on azimuth of 99.2 degrees. The problem is that there are a lot of homes and businesses along that route. I can go about five miles on an azimuth of 82 degrees and then turn right when I see the lake, on azimuth of 114 degrees and hit RV 4. The map showed some favorable terrain, mostly flat, but maybe not much cover.

Well at 2 AM, most people are not out looking for strangers, but I still had to watch for Cadre. They knew about where I would go to reach my check-points. I headed east-north-east and soon saw a schoolhouse ahead. My canteen was empty when I had arrived at RV 4. I slowly approached the schoolhouse to see if I could get water there. I saw the Jeep in the nick-of-time. I slipped a little north to keep the schoolhouse between me and the Jeep. I came to a house set back from the road. No dog barked, so I slipped closer. I could see the hose bib on the side of the house and decided to give it a try. I put the canteen under the spigot and cracked it to just a dribble. The canteen took forever to fill. Then I was on my way again. Someone had dug a deep hole in the yard and I went in and down. They had left a shovel in the hole and it made a deep gash in my shin.

I guess that someone heard me fall, because the lights in the house came on, then the back porch light. I was already out of the hole and had gotten to the stand of trees to the north of the house when the porch light came on. I stopped moving. After a little, the porch light went out. I did not move for another fifteen minutes. A lot of the civilians help the military during exercises and work for the Homeland or Insurgent forces and are used to reporting unusual activities.

I used some of my water to rinse the gash in my shin. I was surprised that it hurt as much as it did. Not as bad as a bullet, that was for sure.

I headed east again. I could see the lake about three hundred yards ahead. I got the compass out again and faced to 114 degrees. I could see the lights of Hoffman to the left and Marston to the right, so I was confident that I was on track. The trick would be crossing Highway 177 without being seen. It had taken me an hour to cover this last five miles. The time was now 0250 hours. I crossed Highway 177 just north of the bend above Marston. Oncoming traffic or someone south of there would not have direct line of sight to see me cross. I used the same package carrying technique that I had used before.

I figured that I was a little north of where I needed to be so adjusted my path to 125 degrees. I saw a tall tree that I could use as a guide and put the compass back in my pocket. I hit Hoffman Road and decided to cross it and come to RV 4 from the back side. The terrain on my side of Hoffman was open farm land without any cover. There were trees on the other side.

I slipped across Hoffman as I had done with the others, entered the trees and began slipping southerly. I could see the road to my right and sure enough there was a Jeep parked partly concealed in the trees on my side. I decided to bypass the Jeep and head for RV 4.

RV 4 was at 34'58.79" N by 79'31.61W and I arrived at 0350 hours. Cadre was waiting. He said "I thought that I saw someone cross Hoffman up a ways. Good technique, it wasn't my job to catch you and I guess that luck was on your side. Tom must have been looking the other way. You didn't waste any time, but you weren't hurrying either. Good luck on your last leg. Speaking of legs, that looks like blood on your trousers, need any help?"

"Nope, just a scratch, I'll be able to hit the showers soon."

With that, I headed toward RV5. The direction was about 22 degrees, just Easterly of North. Most of the way was pine forest, an easy walk, but dark at four in the morning. The direct route was along a road with several cross roads. After getting out of sight of Cadre, I decided to go more northerly along a tributary that fed from Scotland Lake; less chance of meeting Cadre along that route. The sky was beginning to lighten. Avoiding clumps of bushes became easier as the light increased. My canteen was empty again. I decided to wait until I got to the end before looking for a drink. I had water purification tablets in my ruck, but they made the water taste bad and it was a cool night, so I wasn't very thirsty. I stayed about a hundred meters from the stream as I walked along. Pine forests make easy walking, but care must be taken to avoid stepping on limbs that have fallen and are partially covered by pine straw. The sharp crack of a branch breaking can bring unwanted attention. Soon I saw the lake on the left. I kept going and saw a small cluster of homes ahead. A dog began barking from one of the yards. I moved deeper into the trees and the dog went quiet.

Still within the trees, when I reached 35 degrees 49 minutes by 79 degrees 12 minutes I turned right to about 85 degrees and headed for home. I arrived at RV 5 at 6 AM. I was the second one in; Lyman had beaten me by two minutes.

Top was there to greet us. He said, "Go on over to the mess tent for some breakfast. RV 6 does not exist. We will meet after all of the guys are in. Just stay around the mess tent. The latrines are behind the tent."

Lyman was breathing hard. "What happened, someone chase you in?" I quipped.

"Yeah, I heard you back by the lake and just decided to leg it in. I took a chance and crossed the road to get away from you. We were lucky, no one was watching that way. Let's get some breakfast. I ran out of water about an hour ago."

"Coffee sure sounds good to me, food too," I agreed.

Top stopped by the table. "Thomas, stop by the medic tent when you get finished. A farmer called in to say that he found a shovel covered with blood in a hole that he had not bothered to fill-in yet. He said that the shovel was very rusty. He asked if we had been running any night exercises in the area. The checkpoint had called in to say that you nicked yourself pretty good someplace near there. The blood was still pretty fresh on your boot. There will likely be plenty of time before the last men get in."

"Do we have weapons cleaning set up? My sidekick and I went swimming on the way back."

Top chuckled, "Yeah, we will do that after the meeting. Everyone got the chance to go swimming or get caught crossing a bridge."

The last man came in at about one PM. We were told that the meeting would be at 2 PM.

Top called us all together at 2 PM. "We had a good exercise here. There are a few things that I would like to say. Most of you played the game fair and square. Some of you cut corners and got caught. Some of you were pretty cagey and careful. I respect that; because initiative and independent thinking are what we need to survive in this game. Those of you that viewed this as a game lost some points by getting caught doing something you were advised not to do. You cannot trust civilians to be looking to your best interests. They are looking toward their best interests. Two of you were hurt during the exercise, neither of you accepted help. The Cadre would have gotten a medic for you, had you asked; but it would have cost you. Thomas, you can take the rubber off your weapon now, unless you are planning on goosing someone. If you think that I am knocking him, think again. My guess is that he is the only one who protected his weapon while swimming. Good habits are useful when you least expect, even in a training situation. He also is the only one to ask about weapons cleaning. I would be proud to serve with him. He would bring me back alive if he could."

Top looked at the group. "After weapons cleaning, stop by the Team House and pick up your orders. Thank you for your efforts. If you did not pass selection and decide that you want to apply again, please do so. There is no penalty for trying again. The tables and weapons cleaning supplies have been setup outside. Gods-speed and good luck on your next assignment men."

We went outside to clean weapons. Lyman couldn't resist, "Goosed anybody lately?" He laughed. I had completely forgotten the condom on my weapon and ripped it off with a flourish. I tossed it into the trash can.

"I just did not want rust in my bore if they inspected," I quipped.

Lyman finished cleaning his weapon, turned it in to the arms room and headed for the Team House. I finished and followed. I got my envelope and followed him outside. He opened his envelope and then had a big smile. I opened mine and had the same reaction. We moved toward the BOQ to get our gear. Our orders just said report to a building on Fort Bragg for further processing.

Top was waiting for us in the BOQ. He extended his hand saying, "Congratulations and welcome to Special Forces Operational Detachment – Delta. You two and the Recon Marine are the only ones to graduate from selection this round. He is going to a different location than you two are."

"The Colonel is waiting for you back at the Team House. Go through the main room to the office in the back. Good luck to you both."

We shook hands again and grabbed our belongings and headed for the Team House. On the way, we dropped our stuff in our cars.

LTC McMasterson was waiting for us when we knocked on his door. "Enter," he said. We entered, came to attention and saluted.

He said "Once a day is enough, grab a seat. When you get to Delta, you will meet two men; Adam and Scott.

They have been with Delta for four years and are experienced operators. You two and they will become a four man team. You will spend the next month with team tactics. Adam and Scott will be your instructors. Major Thomas, you will lead the team, Lyman will be your XO."

"Thomas your promotion came through yesterday, so congratulations again. In Delta we have a loose formality, it is necessitated by the situations that we find ourselves in. Within the Team each of us has to count fully on the other for our very survival. You will shortly find that you are more like brothers than soldiers. Often our appearance is other than soldierly. That condition is predicated on our need to blend in with the local folks and become inconspicuous. Both of you are fluent in Spanish as are the other two team members. During the next month you are all to work on your Spanish since different dialects are represented. You will also need to let your hair grow longer. Facial hair is at your discretion as well. You are going to a warm climate, so you can consider that in your decision."

LTC McMasterson continued, "When you get to the building on Fort Bragg at 0800 hours tomorrow, Adam and Scott will be waiting for you. This is a cellular operation, very limited access by others; strictly need-to-know only. You four will be the only people at that building. All of the phones in the building are secure and checked regularly. If we need to talk to you in person, we will ask you to visit us. None of us will come there. You will have two hours each day in 'the city' to practice live fire and tactics. You will get to where you can shoot the balls off a gnat without touching the body. In about two weeks, you will receive all of the intelligence that we have about the operation that we want you to undertake."

"What would that operation be," I asked?

"I do not know all of the details, but drugs are coming into the US by submarine. We want that activity to stop. The cartels move a ton or more at a time by submarine. We want to identify their contacts, bases and routes and then make it too expensive for them to continue. It is up to your team to decide how best to do that. Lyman has the computer skills that the team will need to develop target data from the intelligence reports that you will access."

"Your facility is within another limited access facility. You will have badges to access the larger facility. Your badge will also allow access to the cypher lock on your building. Your building is also under twenty-four hour video surveillance from the outside. The rest you can get from Scott and Adam. Here are your badges, wear them at all times while you are at Bragg." LTC McMasterson stood signaling the end of the briefing. He extended his hand to Nathan and Lyman and wished them good hunting.

Lyman said, "I'm new around here are there any good restaurants in Spring Lake or Fayetteville?"

"I suppose it depends on what you like to eat and how fussy you are, I answered. I guess that the O Club on Fort Bragg is as good as most. There are lots of Asian cuisine restaurants in both Spring Lake and Fayetteville. Then there are the usual fast food places. I don't remember any good Hispanic restaurants in either city. I haven't been here for a couple of years though so that may have changed."

"Ok, the O Club it is. How about we stop at the BOQ and get cleaned up first." Lyman suggested. "After dinner I just want to sleep."

"Sounds like a plan to me. Meet me in the lobby at 6:30 and we will head out, civvies?" I questioned.

"Ok by me," Lyman replied.

At 1820 hours, I was sitting in the lobby waiting. Lyman showed about five minutes later. "Change of plan if it is ok with you. Ever been out to McKellar's Lodge?"

"Heard of it, but never been there, what's it like?" Lyman asked.

"The menu is kind of limited, but the food is good and the plate is full. It is setup like an old hunting lodge, big fireplace and all. Lots of SF guys go there. You may even see some guys that you know."

"If you say that it is ok, let's go, I am starving," Lyman said.

We headed out Long Street and took a right onto Gruber Road which became McKellar's Road. "This used to be a really comfortable place. They expanded it a few years ago and it is more like a commercial restaurant now. You only need a Military ID to eat. To use the ranges, they have a forty dollar per year fee. Bring your own ammo and targets or they have some for sale. There are range fees also. From what I have heard, we will get plenty of shooting practice at the Delta ranges, but this used to be a good place to come and unwind. We will see if it still is."

Most of the tables were arranged along a window wall overlooking McKellar's Lake. They had put in a serving line like a cafeteria. We joined the queue and each grabbed a tray, made our selections and paid. All of the tables near the fireplace were taken, so we ambled over to an empty table overlooking the lake.

"Too bad it is getting dark. We will not be able to see the lake much longer." Lyman noted.

"They usually turn on some lights along the dock when it gets a little darker, keeps the visual interest going," I offered. It was not very dark, but the lights came on as I finished speaking.

"The lake looks like more of a pond," Lyman observed.

"Yep," I agreed.

I felt a tap on my shoulder, and looked around to see LTC McMasterson standing there. "Good evening gentlemen, I see you have found the best un-kept secret at Fort Bragg. Mind if I sit?"

"Sure, grab a chair, Sir." Lyman and I looked at each other surprised that we had both said the same greeting.

"I hope that you are comfortable at the Forrestal, it seemed the best choice. We could have put you up at the Sink House, but that might have drawn too much attention," McMasterson said. He continued; "You will be here pretty constantly for the next few weeks, then you will move south. Your quarters here will be kept for you, like a permanent residence, so go ahead and get comfortable."

"That forty-five bucks a day is kind of high, we could rent something larger and less expensive for less," Lyman complained.

"Probably true," observed the Colonel, "But Delta will be picking up the tab, so do not worry about that. You need to setup local bank accounts tomorrow and get your pay on auto-deposit. Most of your expenses will be taken care of by Delta one way or another. Tomorrow you will meet Captain Duke Garcia. He is heading down to Colombia about the same time as your team. He will be your Handler down there and let you know when things change or new information has come to light. Have a good night and don't forget to get some sleep." The Colonel stood and departed.

"What have we gotten ourselves into," observed Lyman. "Looks like a CIA op to me, tomorrow should be an interesting day."

"Yeah or worse, in Colombia it might be DEA, I added." We finished our meal and went to the car.

As we pulled out of the parking lot, Lyman observed, "Colombia, your seamanship skills, submarines, drugs and Spanish looks like it might be a DEA op. They have a bad rep for keeping secrets and losing agents."

"I guess we will know for sure tomorrow."

"Sure enough; meet you in the lobby after breakfast at 0700 hours," I suggested.

The Briefing

Chapter 4

We arrived at the compound just off Armistead Street at 0730 hours, showed our badges to the Security Guard at the gate. He did not salute since we were in civilian clothes, but said, "Haven't seen you men before, from your ID, you are looking for the building just behind me to the left."

We passed through and went into the indicated building. A long haired, bearded Mexican was sitting in a chair tilted against the wall. He was reading from a folder with a Secret cover sheet on the front. The chair dropped to the ground and he stood.

"I am Duke Garcia," he stated. He extended his hand to each of us and we introduced ourselves. He continued, "Just call me Duke. That is my real name. My Dad really had a thing for John Wayne. I am just thankful that he did not choose to name me Marion. I use Alvaro "Duke" Garcia down south. You will each need to pick a Hispanic name to use down south. Adam is Adan Mendez and Scott is Juan Diaz. You should all use the names that you select during the next few weeks. Mistakes down south are often deadly. Adan and Juan have been here two weeks already, getting the Intel in order. They should be here any time now. There are lists of first and surnames on the desk under the window for you to pick from." Lyman and I walked over and began looking through the lists.

After a time, Lyman said, "I am going to be Leon Abadia, should be anonymous enough. Picked a name yet Major?"

"How about Natanael "Nate" Calero," I asked?

Slightly Off

Art McGillem

"Interesting choices, a "lion" and "god given" both good and fairly common." said Duke. "We will start to work on the new passports, driver's licenses and legends; just in case someone gets curious. A lot of the police down there run checks for the cartels, so it is best to establish a good cover. I think that all of you need to come from Mexico City. That will help explain your accents and give credence to the fact that you do not have a long standing gang affiliation. I will be the one sticking my neck out. I am an Embassy Liaison Officer to the Policía Nacional de Colombia or Colombian National Police in Bogota. The National Police come under the Colombian Department of Defense, but are separate from the military."

"You will be in a safe house in Sincelejo near the Caribbean Sea coast. You could quickly move up or down Highway 25 along the coast. North to Tolu or if necessary South to Cali or any other city on the Pacific side. I considered finding a place in Tolu, but you would just have been too conspicuous. Perhaps also a little bit far North since the cartel's subs also seem to be working the Pacific coast."

Just then, the door burst open and in came Adan and Juan. Duke introduced us all around and explained our new names. He asked us to introduce ourselves to each other in which ever dialect of Spanish we felt most comfortable.

When we were finished he said, "Yes, Mexico City it is, that should be believable enough given your strangely accented dialects."

"I just got a report of another possible drug submarine dropping-off a cargo near Galveston, Texas. They think that it carried almost two tons of cocaine based on the word on the streets."

Juan stood, "This could take a while. Anybody make coffee yet?" He was moving toward the door to a hallway with connected offices.

Duke said, "I had just set down to read this Intel Report when Nate and Leon arrived. I guess that it is on you since you asked first. Whoever gets here first usually makes the first pot; then it is on whoever takes the last cup to make the next pot. We are going to be here most of the morning getting the lay of the land. We have the range at 1300 hours."

The Range

Chapter 5

Duke said, "Follow me" and headed down the hallway. He stopped at a metal door and took out some keys to open the lock. "I am going to give you the weapons that you will carry from now on. We will take them into country for you. We want you to become familiar with them. If for some reason we cannot take them into a country for you other arrangements will be made. You will have to decide which of you will become the sniper. All of you will become familiar with his weapon so that you can use it effectively if necessary. You will all select a pistol and something like an HK MP5 or MP10. We limit the choices to insure logistics supplies the correct ammunition. The nine millimeter ammo is available all over South America, so supply is not an issue. The standard issue Baretta M9 is a good choice, but you can use the H&K USP .45 caliber if you wish."

We all opted for the H&K .45 sidearm. The MP10 is an ugly weapon but light and very good. The MP10 uses 10mm ammunition which might not be easily found. We all chose an MP5 and a sight adjustment tool. Night vision goggles and optics came next. We were given the newest light weight body armor.

Duke said, "That is enough for now. We need to clean the weapons and thoroughly check them before going to the range. Today will just be sighting-in and target practice getting used to these weapons. We have a three hundred meter range for today."

We had all fired an MP5 before, but were not very familiar with the one in our hands, so Duke showed us how to break it down and re-assemble. The particular model we had is the MP5SD6 variant; collapsible stock, three round burst trigger group and integrated suppressor. He cautioned us to do it several times and increase the speed each time. We all knew the value of intimately knowing the tools of our trade. The sights are difficult to adjust without the special HK tool; but once set they do not move.

Duke said, "Ok, let's get those weapons back in the arms room and head to lunch. Put a tag on your weapon before you put it in the rack. Tags are here on the right. You may want to change the MP5 for the newer UMP9 if they get here before you leave. We are expecting them any day. They are lighter and have more attachment options than the MP5. I hope that they get here soon. I want to get one for myself."

After lunch, we loaded our weapons and ammunition into a Humvee and headed to the range.

At the range, Duke informed us that we would first zero our weapons on the one thousand inch range. He reminded us that our group needed to be about one and one-quarter inches high at one thousand inches to give us a battle sight zero at three hundred yards. He said that he would be the range officer so that we could all work together. His weapon was already waiting his return to Colombia.

We all placed our MP5s on the sandbag at four firing positions; then went to the ammo point to draw a spotting scope and three magazines with three rounds each. We would do our own spotting for the zero exercise.

Duke said, "Mount your foxhole, load your weapons, the range is hot, commence firing."

I fired my three rounds and checked the spotting scope. All three rounds were touching in exactly the right spot above the bullseye. I looked over at Lyman, Scott and

Adam; each was making sight adjustments. I laughed and said "all of my rounds hit just right."

Duke said, "Everyone continue with the zero. After your nine rounds are expended, if you have not zeroed your weapon, hold up your hand and I will bring you more ammo. I kept firing and had a nice hole about three-quarters of an inch in diameter just above the bullseye.

I moved my spotting scope to check Lyman's target. He had two small groups one slightly low and to the right of the point of aim the other in just the right place above the bullseye. Scott and Adam had both achieved a good zero with good groups.

Duke then said, "Good job men. Safe your weapons and lock the bolt to the rear." He came to each position and checked the chamber and bore then placed the weapon on the sandbag. "I know that we are all professionals, but I am just following the range rules so we can all be safe. Now we will move out and paste the holes in our targets. Then we will move the target out to three hundred yards and return to the ammo point. We will do this as a group and all return to the ammo point at the same time."

We moved the targets and returned to the ammo point.

Duke explained the next exercise, "First we will fire twenty rounds at the black dot, single shots. Then we will paste the targets, return to the ammo point for another magazine and fire three round bursts at the same target. Then paste the targets and return to the ammo point for the final magazine. The last magazine will be sustained fire until empty. The idea here is that you will see why auto fire is not a good practice. The maximum effective range of the MP5 is about two hundred meters, so we are stretching the capabilities here. Have fun but pay attention to what you see. This will be your main weapon and you will need to know how it performs for you."

At three hundred yards we could barely detect the bullseye. Our groups widened to between two and four inches on the slow fire. Good enough groups to likely hit a target. On three round burst, the groups widened to about six inches and were more vertical. For the auto fire, we all kept our MP5 at the shoulder. We had all learned long ago that firing from the hip was for emergencies only and not a very good solution even then. In any case, many of the rounds missed the target completely as the magazine emptied.

Duke laughed, "Good shooting, sort of. Once we get in-country, if we need to go long range, we will have weapons for that available. Now safe your weapons and let me check them." We filed past for a quick weapons check, then over to clean our weapons.

"Tomorrow we will work on the Intel packages. Next day, we work on hostage rescue tactics. We do not know exactly what we will run into on the operation. So we will just get used to working as a team. You all went through Ranger training, so you know where this is all headed. Know your sector and keep out of the other man's sector." You could hear the concern in Duke's voice as he explained.

The next morning, we all assembled in front of the Colombia map in the office. Duke explained, "See the rivers in Colombia, we are only interested in the larger ones that are wide enough and deep enough to submerge a submarine capable of carrying a minimum of one ton of cocaine. The subs run at night. Most of them cannot fully submerge, but must have a viewport above water for navigation. The pilot needs to see where he is going to keep the sub from being observed or hitting something in the water. Here are pictures of two submarines that have been captured entering rivers in Mexico from the Gulf of Mexico."

Nathan looked at the pictures and exclaimed, "Wow, pretty sophisticated. What are they made of, fiberglass?"

"Yes," answered Adam. Adam continued. "You would be surprised to see how ingenious the design. They can surface and submerge with ease. From the reports they like to run on the surface during the night and submerge during the day. When running on the surface, they get fresh air inside the sub. The air within the sub can become hot and fetid during the day when they must remain submerged."

"They are easily observed from the air during daylight, if someone is lucky enough to be looking and flies directly over the sub. With only a small tower above the surface, it becomes very difficult to detect them when they submerge. The latest trend is for fully submersible subs. We are working on techniques that we can use to interdict them when they are fully submerged."

"We have some informants in Colombia who often supply information that a sub is about ready to leave Colombia." volunteered Adam.

"That is true," added Duke. "We often get information in time to stop a sub from sailing, but by the time the Colombian government gets organized, the sub has disappeared. If troops show up where a sub was built or launched, the Cartel will not use that site again. What we propose to do is observe a sub being built and loaded. After the sub sails, we track and then destroy it at sea. The

Cartel knows nothing until the sub fails to arrive at the destination. One of the subs that was captured had communications gear aboard, so the Cartel may begin worrying when a contact schedule is not met, but they cannot know what has happened to the sub and crew. The sad part of this operation is that we do not take prisoners. The interdiction method insures no survivors among the sub crew."

"I am not sure what you mean here," interjected Nathan. "You mean that we murder them?"

"No," said Duke, "At least not exactly. We have developed high explosive rounds that will blow the sub apart with such force that everything in it does not survive. The rounds can be deployed by aircraft, Predator or shoulder fired Grenade Launcher. You have to remember what we are dealing with here. These people are criminals, ruining American lives with their poison. We are just stopping their illegal and insidious activities. I am ok with it myself. I have personally seen the damage that drugs can do to people and families. Either by family members killed in drug wars, addiction, robberies, or home invasions. If any of you have second thoughts, this is the time to say so. You will just be sent back to your units without any negative comment. Remember, this is a war. They will not hesitate to kill you. They will kill you on just a suspicion, they will not wait for proof; these are not good people that we are chasing. I do not see what we will be doing as anything more than cancelling an aircraft, warship or tank. I hope that you can all see it that way."

"Yeah, I see your point," said Nathan. The others nodded agreement.

"Right now, we think that many of the subs exit Colombia into the Caribbean Sea. So we are going to concentrate on the rivers that empty into the Caribbean. After we eliminate a few, we will move south to interdict the rivers that empty into the Pacific Ocean. We do not currently believe that subs launch into both bodies of water at the same time. How we actually proceed will depend on how reliable the Intel is at the time that we get it. The wall map is fairly small scale, so a lot of detail is missing. Pay special attention to the roads and where they go throughout the country. You will have maps and GPS when you get down there, but the more familiar you are with the territory the better chance you will have to get where you need to be if you are denied those aids for some reason. There are maps and stacks of Intel reports on the table over there. I am going into the office to catch up on some paperwork. Read through the reports and locate the activities on the maps. It will help you focus on Colombia as an operations area." Duke let his chair legs drop to the floor and walked to the office and shut the door.

We all sat quietly for a minute. Then Adam said, "I read in the New York Times an article about these subs. It said that if the sub and crew were about to get caught, they would scuttle the sub. It would sink in just a couple of minutes and all of the evidence would disappear. Then they would be rescued and sent back to their home country. I guess that we are about to take a more aggressive approach to eliminating this problem. I suppose this is another black op to take out the bad guys. My cousin got involved with cocaine and he finally became a distributor to support his addiction. A rival gang killed him in order to take over his territory. These drug traffickers are at the beginning of the distribution chain and I have no problem with eliminating them. They will not hesitate to kill us if we make a mistake and are discovered."

I spoke up, "Yes, that is probably the best context for what we are about to do. The weapons that we will carry are used through-out the world by a lot of different military and civilian organizations. So a rival gang might be suspected. Duke probably already has a legend prepared for each of us. So we will be on our own over there. We had better get familiar with the cities, roads and rivers in case we need to move quickly."

"Wow, listen to this." shouted a surprised Scott. "These narco subs cost one to two million to build and can carry up to about nine tons of cocaine. There were between twenty and forty of these babies sent to the US of A back in 2007. I have been thinking way too small about this whole deal."

"Listen to this," Lyman added. "Something called the Black Market Peso Exchange has laundered about 5 billion dollars of drug money for the cartels in the past year. There is a US law that deposits of over $10,000 must be reported. Many of our banks have ignored this law in the past, but the FED is applying more enforcement to make it work. The cartels are adapting with multiple bank accounts and a system of runners to deposit the funds. Foreign banks still seem to ignore the law and even setup special rooms where the drug money is brought in by the box to be counted and deposited. The various accounts are then used to move the money around to pay debts for cartel purchases. It seems that in Colombia the drug industry contributes more to the local economy than the legitimate businesses. No wonder the Colombian government is slow to stop these activities."

I added, "I guess that is why our services are needed. The Colombian government has a bitter-sweet quandary to overcome and is therefore hesitant to act. Our problem is that it is killing our people and causing a significant cash flow out of the country. Makes me want to leave today and sink some subs."

"Amen to that," confirmed Scott.

We spent the rest of the day studying reports and maps.

Hostage Rescue

Chapter 6

Duke started the presentation, "Our rules of engagement will be somewhat different from SWAT tactics. In what we are directed to do, there are no friendlies to be concerned about. That said, there could be circumstances where we would not want to hurt civilians. You all went through the hostage rescue and city incursion training during Ranger training, so the only difference here is a new team. We will practice as if innocent individuals could be present; hopefully, that will not occur."

"You will all wear comm gear during training and on the operations. With comm gear, you can keep your voice low or just use clicks to indicate an answer or status. Nathan will assign our numbers, one thru five, rather than using names. From today forward I want you to use your in-country names. You will enter a structure in numerical order, you need to keep each other informed about what you see or are doing that was not in the pre-entry discussions. If you run out of ammo for your weapon and are going to reload or change weapons, drop to one knee and announce reload. The next in line will cover your position and both surveillance areas while the reload or change occurs. After the reload is complete, let the team know by standing and announcing ready. The operation can then continue. You can communicate by voice or touch as is appropriate, just make sure that you all agree on what method will be used during the pre-op briefing. Nate, this is a good time to setup your team."

I thought for a few seconds, "Juan is 1, Leon is 2, I am 3, Adan is 4 and Alvaro is 5. I will change these placements as we practice for two reasons. Some of us will be a better or quicker point man than others; it will take some practice to get that down. We will finalize that before we leave for Colombia. The other reason is that we all need to feel comfortable with changing our sector coverage and the things to look for in that position. Trip wire, loose or damp sand, dead vegetation and such all mean something and noticing can save our asses. I want us to practice without Alvaro quite a bit. He may not be able to go with us on all operations, that just remains to be seen. We all need to keep sharp about being the rear guard. As we all know that is an important position and often the first to sense an ambush."

Alvaro got us moving, "Ok, here are your comm sets. I put them on the charger before we left yesterday, but do a comm check before we leave for the range. After you get the comms check done, come to the arms room for your weapons. We will be using blank ammo today. Remember, blanks can severely wound up to fifteen feet, so stay in your sector."

We practiced clearing a house, changing positions throughout the morning. We had bad guy and friendlies setup in the house and Alvaro changed their position for each run-through. The original team assignments proved to be the one that worked the best. I was the only one to get a powder scorch on my uniform when I stepped to the side to engage a target and Adan tagged my right sleeve.

Alvaro gave us a critique. "You guys make a great team. Only one scorched team member. Any one of us could have had that happen. The bad guy target was partially hidden as Nate entered the room. His peripheral vision picked up the target and he turned just as Adan fired at his target. Both of you managed to still take-out your targets. These things happen and they are just a result of the dangerous work that we do. I can find no fault to correct here. Tomorrow we will be at the range with the H&K M320 Grenade Launcher. The M320 can be fired from the shoulder and has special optics for night work. We will have the H&K416 carbine where we can mount the M320. The HK416 improves reliability over the M4A1 both are semi-auto or full auto fire. You will need to practice trigger control to get two or three round bursts. We will not be using the M320 special ammunition designed for the subs for practice, rather the standard high explosive and illumination rounds. The special round is designed to penetrate several feet of water and explode against the hull of the sub. The 320 can fire all of the rounds that the old M203 fires and is ready for new stuff as well. Have a good night and meet me back at the team house in the morning."

"This M320 is an ugly little sucker," said Nate as he pulled out the butt plate. "Look at this, the barrel swings to the side for a reload."

"Yes," replied Alvaro. "You can carry it on a sling or mount it to the M416 rail system that allows the 320 to mount under the barrel. You can slide the tube open and reload without taking your weapon off of the shoulder. The 416 also has a hundred round box magazine available for when things might get a little hairy. The 320 can also mount on an M16, a nice set of weapons with good systems integration."

With that we went out to the range to familiarize with the M320.

I aimed the M320 at the tank and fired. The tank was at the maximum effective range of 250 meters and I got a direct hit on the turret, almost exactly where I had aimed. "Wow, it takes a horse to pull that trigger," I observed.

"They say that it is pretty accurate out to about 350 meters, then things get iffy," Alvaro added. "I like that it takes longer rounds than the M203, so you get more powerful rounds out to a greater distance. The M79 is more powerful, but less handy to carry around. For mounting on a rifle or carbine, I would like to see a model with the hand grips removed. As you can see, it works well as a stand-alone weapon; good accuracy, and more powerful HE (high explosive) rounds than the 203. It also takes the new sub-killer round that will not work with the 203. I hear that the M320 works with the new HK417. I will stick with the 416 for a while. I like that you can dunk it in the lake and it will come out firing without blowing your head off. The only problem is that they are 5.56mm, not 9mm. It will be the main weapon when we attack a submarine. I am waiting to see if a box-magazine and an M320 can be mounted on one M416; should be interesting."

We all took turns firing the M320 and agreed that it was a fine weapon with useful updates. The improved trigger that allowed multiple firing strikes in the event of a misfire was very much appreciated. The chamber of the M203 had to be opened with the live round still chambered to re-cock and fire; a scary situation. If we got within 250 meters of a sub, it would be killed.

For the next three weeks, we spent three hours each day practicing takedowns with live ammo. The remainder of the time was spent reading Intel Reports and map study.

On Thursday afternoon, Alvaro called us all together. "Well guys, the cake walk is over. You all have a three day pass to have some fun. Monday we all fly out.

Nate and Leon will fly through Miami to the Simon Bolivar International Airport in Santa Marta. Juan, Adan and myself will leave from San Diego. I go by boat to the small port of Buenaventura on the Pacific coast not too far from Bogota. I want to check with my contacts to see what is cooking. Juan and Adan get to fly into Bogota. Rental cars have been reserved for you at the airports. They are four wheel drive Land Rovers that are popular there. Do not be discouraged by their appearance, they are very well maintained and reliable. There will be maps showing your new residence and additional local currency for expenses. Just ask for the package that goes with the vehicle."

"There is one change to our plans. Originally we wanted to put all of you in one residence. We decided not to do that. Four men living together that do not belong to one of the cartels would likely raise questions among the locals. So as you fly, so are you paired for a residence. You can probably find a local woman to do your laundry. Since you will want to keep weapons close by it is probably best that you do your own house cleaning. Both residences are in the countryside, but neighbors are fairly close. The crime rate is high there, you will likely be thought of as foreigners and as such fair game for the thieves. Be very careful about what you leave laying around. Someone might do a B&E just to see who you are."

"Before you leave here today, you will find your new wardrobe, suitcase and accessories in the next room. Go on in and see how the clothing fits. There is a box for each of you to put all of your current clothing, wallets, personal stuff and such into. The box will be waiting for you when the mission is over. Be sure to also change your underwear. We do not want you raising questions about why you have so much American made stuff. Mistakes like that can get you killed." With that, we all walked out to check our new wardrobes.

Leon was standing there with some very high-water pants legs. "Hey, I must have someone else's box. Who has pants that are too long, and this shirt is tight also."

Adan looked at the tent that he had on for a shirt and that his feet did not come out at the pant cuff. He said, "Well, this must be your box and it looks like you have mine. Keep the underwear, but pass the rest of the stuff over."

"Amen to that," said Leon taking off the shirt and pants and tossing them onto the suitcase.

"I hope that they did not make the same mistake in Sincelejo. Be sure to check and exchange whatever is not right the first day. Anyone checking you out will need to discover the same things each time that they enter your residence. They will probably send young women, so be prepared," advised Alvaro.

Bogota and Sincelejo

Chapter 7

Lyman and I got off the plane at Simon Bolivar
International Airport near Santa Marta, Magdalena,
Colombia at three in the afternoon. We could see that the
landing strip ran along the coastline parallel to the
Caribbean Sea. Santa Marta is quite a small airport, I
thought to myself. It looks like it can only handle two or
three C46 sized aircraft at one time. The rain was pouring
down and although the temperature seemed to be in the
nineties, the humidity was not oppressive. We got off the
plane and hurried across the tarmac to the baggage pickup
and customs stations.

The customs agent smiled and quipped "Welcome
to Colombia! Our liquid sunshine helps our crops grow and
our rivers flow. If our airport was a little larger, the planes
could discharge passengers directly into the terminal. Mr.
Calero, what is the purpose of your visit to Colombia?"

"Mr. Abadia and I are here to help your government
survey the rivers and locate places where hydroelectric
power generating stations can be built."

"Ah, we have many rivers near Santa Marta. I can
recommend a very good accommodation if you wish,"
volunteered the customs agent.

"Well, thank you for your offer, but we already
have accommodations arranged in Sincelejo. I know that
the distance is about two hundred miles south of here, but it
will allow us to see a large part of the area that we will be
studying. I think that Hertz should have a van reserved for
us. I hope that they can provide maps."

"Oh yes, Hertz has good maps. They are just down
the hallway to the left. We tend to think in kilometers

(Km) here. The distance to Sincelejo is about 330Km." He stamped our passports and handed them to us. "Have a pleasant stay in our beautiful country caballeros."

As we headed down the hallway Leon chuckled, "Hydroelectric power source survey, when did you think that one up?"

"I had been thinking about a good cover story on the flight over and hadn't come up with a good one until the agent asked and it just popped-out. I don't know why we did not plan for a cover story while we were at Bragg. This one gives us a reason to be on the rivers and all over the countryside. I hope that it does not conflict with anything that Alvaro had planned."

The Hertz van looked like it had just barely survived world war one. The rental agent Juan Sanchez apologized, "I know that it looks a little rough, but mechanically everything is really in top condition. You will not be disappointed."

He handed me his business card and said, "If you have any difficulty, the number on this card is my personal cell phone, please do not hesitate to call." He handed me the keys and watched as we drove off.

Sanchez walked back to the office and took out his cell phone. "Alvaro, your guys have arrived. They have the old green van. You should have seen their faces; I think they were expecting a BMW or something. They told customs that they were here to survey for hydroelectric power stations along the rivers. I didn't know that you were into that kind of thing."

Alvaro, ever ready responded, "Well, the Embassy is into a lot of different things and I get caught-up in all kinds of stuff. I guess that I am just supposed to see that they do not get into too much trouble while they are here.

Thanks for the info amigo, see you next time I am up that way." Good plan thought Alvaro, I should have thought of that myself. I had better pass this new info on to the other team before they talk too much.

Leon took the wheel, started the van and headed out of the airport parking lot. Nate took out his cell phone and began waving it around the van. "What are you doing?" asked Leon. Nate made motions to keep talking and driving as he moved into the back of the van.

When he finished, he said "Bug check. Alvaro gave me an app for the cell that exposes bugs. I gave a copy to Adan before we headed south, but haven't had a chance to give you a copy yet."

Alvaro took out his cell phone and called Adan. "Nate came up with a really good cover. You guys are here to survey the rivers for hydroelectric power generating sites. I hope that will work with whatever you guys said to customs."

"Not a problem," said Adan, "We said we were here to do research for the US Embassy and they did not ask what kind."

Alvaro thought for a minute then said, "You guys are all single, so it is natural that you will find some women to share your house while you are here. Be careful to select the more educated women. They will likely have ties to the cartels and will report on you if asked, so be very careful around them. Everyone will expect you to have handguns and rifles, because everyone else does. No auto weapons at the houses though. I have found a marina to keep the Zodiacs and a boathouse to store your equipment. The location is on a military installation, but nothing is totally secure here. There is lockable storage there and alarm systems to protect your sensitive equipment. Unless something comes up, I will let you settle-in until next week. Enjoy your time by getting to know the locale, bye for now."

Adan called Nate, "I hear you guys are on the ground. Give me a call when you get to Sincelejo and we will arrange to have a meet. Alvaro called and filled me in on the cover. Man, that is brilliant."

"Thanks," Nate responded. "We should be able to find the house ok. The van has a GPS. I am planning on at least six hours to get to Sincelejo, so we will call you in the morning. Our van looks really bad, but the engine purrs like a kitten and it is four-wheel drive. What did they give you to drive."

"They gave us a relatively new BMW 740, it seems popular with the cartel upper echelon around here." Adan winked at Juan. Adan laughed as he heard the choking sound from the other side. "Ok I lied, we have a beat-out looking suburban that has been really well maintained mechanically. I think that it will take us anywhere we want to go in this country. Did Alvaro mention about the women?"

"What women," asked Nate?

"We are encouraged to act like normal healthy single males and find comfort in the local flowers, replied Adan. The only caveat is to be careful of conversations in their presence, since they will likely be reporting to the cartel folks. Alvaro said to seek the better educated variety. I guess that will make our houses unsafe since bugs can easily be hidden. Maybe Sincelejo is a college town, observed Adan."

"What else did he say?"

"Let's see, we have a boathouse that is somewhat secure on a military base and that we are free to acclimatize until sometime next week; get the lay of the land so to speak. That was about it."

"Since you are already in Sincelejo, have fun. We will call you in the morning," said Nate.

"I am not inclined to worry, but give us a buzz when you get to Sincelejo," requested Adan.

"Ok", Nate replied.

"What was all of that about," asked Leon. "We have been instructed to consort with the local ladies as part of our cover. Alvaro explained our cover to Adan and Juan. We have the rest of the week to acclimatize."

"We need to find some ladies that look great in bathing suits. What better cover than checking water depth and flow rates in the company of suitably attired curvy ladies," observed Leon with a sly grin. "An assignment like this almost makes going through selection worth the pain."

"We haven't survived it yet," noted Nate.

"A sobering thought," admitted Leon.

We drove along Highway 90 heading along the coast to Barranquilla where we turned south picking up Highway 25. The river and lush mountains once in the distance began appearing on our left as we drove. At about Barranca Nueva we veered away from the river and began climbing into the mountains at about the town of La Biche. Finally we arrived on the outskirts of Sincelejo at about nine pm. We arrived at the house on Diagonal 4A at about 9:30 in the evening. I opened the envelope that Juan Sanchez had given me when we picked-up the van. Happily the keys to the villa were inside.

We picked our bedrooms and set to unpacking the few items that we had brought. We planned to get additional clothing and such locally. Leon had his door open so I knocked and stepped in. "Feel like checking the local sites," I asked.

"Sure he said with excitement in his eyes, I am not tired either." We headed out on the town.

We found the Restaurante Bar El Corral on Troncal de Occidente Calle and parked. We went in and were seated by a very attractive senorita. Our server, Sarita, was pretty and friendly, so after a drink and dinner we asked her where a couple of guys could go to have a good time.

Sarita said "If you guys let me practice English, I will show you myself. I have a friend that might want to come along, but we will not finish work for another hour. Leave your car here and go across the street and have a beer in the bar. The women there are not good so do not plan anything with them. We will have a good time."

Sarita walked in the door an hour and a half later accompanied by her stunningly beautiful friend. Sarita and I were already getting along well, so the beauty was Leon's prize. Sarita was happy when I greeted her and stood by her. She said, "I would like you gentlemen to meet my friend Carmilla. Carmilla this is Nate and Leon. What would you guys like to do?"

I spoke up, "We are new to Colombia and Sincelejo. We are here to study your rivers and will probably be here for at least a year. We would like to learn about your culture and customs. Perhaps a night club where there is music and dancing would be a good start so we can make some plans. We are pretty much free for the next four days. We would be very happy if you two can find the time to help us learn about Sincelejo."

"To be honest there is not a lot to do in Sincelejo. There are a few restaurants with a bar and music. Sometimes it is fun to go to the coast and spend time on the beach. It is nice to get high up in the mountains and look down into the valleys, but it is often cold up there. Cartagena or Santa Marta have more entertainments." Carmilla offered.

"The Hotel Santana has a band, we could go there and listen to the music and have conversation to get to know us better," said Sarita.

"If you want to go, we can take my car, your van doesn't look too comfortable, Carmilla offered."

"Is the van safe to leave here?" Nate worried.

"Yes, this is a good place that is why I work here. Carlos does not let any of the bad people hang around," Sarita said.

Sarita's car turned out to be a Toyota Prius, small but comfortable. Leon folded into the back seat with Carmilla and I got in beside Sarita. Sarita looked at me and asked "Would you like to drive, I think that I can trust you?"

"If I knew the city better, I would say yes, but I think that you should drive this time. Yes, I am trustworthy," I replied. I looked up into the rear view mirror and saw Carmilla and Leon huddled close together looking at her cell phone screen and laughing.

Sarita saw what I was looking at and smiled. "Carmilla has this funny app on her phone. If she takes your picture she can do weird things to it that are very funny and clever, beware."

Hotel Santana looked like a modern office building with parking on the lower level. We could hear the music from the band floating down to the street. We went up to the top floor and as the elevator door opened we could see the skyline of the city. The window walls were open to let in the cool night air.

"We will take a table and listen to the music," said Sarita as the Hostess approached.

"Good evening." she said, "Where would you like to sit?"

"A table not too close to the band and near the windows por favor," I replied using my best North American Spanish accent.

The ladies excused themselves for a few minutes. Leon exclaimed, "Wow how did we ever get lucky enough to meet those two! Carmilla is really beautiful and what a sense of humor, not to mention what a figure! We should take them to the beach tomorrow," he managed in a hushed tone."

"Sad to say, but they probably have to work tomorrow," I mused. We had ordered before the girls went to the powder room and the drinks arrived. I sipped my beer and wondered what tomorrow would bring.

Sarita and Carmilla came back all smiles. "We called our bosses and got tomorrow off. We can go to the beach at Tolu and enjoy the sun," said Sarita. "That is assuming that you have the time and interest."

"That would be great," I said. "We did not bring any swim suits, so we will need to go shopping first, can we do that?"

"Yes, said Carmilla I need a new suit also. I gained some weight this past year and last year's suit may not fit."

"If you did offered Leon, it all went into the right places."

Carmilla looked him dead in the eye and said, "You don't know me well enough to flirt like that, you are making my face red." You could tell that she was not really upset by the quip, just telling Leon to slow down.

"I uh," Leon stammered, "Didn't mean to make you uncomfortable. I was truthful though in what I said." His eyes told her that it was a compliment not a flirt and her expression softened even more. We all had a second drink and then the girls said that it was time to go.

We all got back into the Prius and headed back to the restaurant. I wrote down the address for our house and Sarita and Carmilla agreed to pick us up at eight o'clock. They dropped us off at the van and said good night even though it was two am.

I had just finished shaving and brushing my teeth when I heard a car pull into the yard. I knew that Leon had gotten up at about the same time, so we were probably ready except that we had not had time for breakfast. I looked out and there were Sarita and Carmilla coming to knock on the door. Their arms were full. I opened the door to see two smiling faces and hear that breakfast has arrived.

"We just got here last night and haven't had time to check and see if we have dishes and flatware," I warned.

"Not to worry, we have come prepared. Where is the table," asked Carmilla. I led her over to the table and she began setting out breakfast. Sarita was eyeing me and I turned to look at her.

She said, "Are you guys US military?"

I gave her a surprised look and said, "No, but we both got out of the military about a year ago. We both went to engineering college on ROTC scholarships and had to spend four years in the military after graduation. Why do you ask?"

"What is this ROTC, asked Carmilla?"

"Reserve Officer Training Corps is a way to get an education paid for by the US Government. The catch is that for each year of school you are obligated to spend one year in the active military. Leon and I met when we took this job. We have similar backgrounds, so we usually get along ok. Besides, surveying rivers for hydroelectric power facilities is a fun way to make a living. I mean it is a little boring measuring the depth of rivers and the flow rate of the water, but being outside in the sunshine beats being in a cubicle in an office building any day."

Breakfast turned out to be cornbread, scrambled eggs with beans and rice mixed in and fruit. A very good way to start the day. Both girls were bright eyed and filled with excitement. I guess that we were new toys to brighten their day.

Sarita said that Tolu was about an hour away and the shops would be open by the time that we got there. Sarita turned out to be a skilled driver on the twisty mountain roads and got us to Tolu in just under an hour. Along the way, Carmilla suggested that we go to Isla Mucura where we could rent a cabana for about 15,000 pesos (about $8 US) a day and enjoy the beach and food there or at Club 100.

"After we get our swim suits, we can take a short boat ride to the island. This time of year we will not need a reservation. Tolu gets busy around a holiday with mostly Colombian folks. We get few foreign tourists in Tolu," Carmilla explained.

Sarita parked on the main street in Tolu and we entered a foot path between the buildings. The path quickly opened into an open air market where almost anything sold locally could be purchased. There were pigs, chickens, goats and other animals in cages or tied with a rope displayed for sale. Televisions and other electrics were displayed under tin roofs.

Sarita and Carmilla gave a happy "Oh, look," as we approached a stall with mounds of bathing suits. The store had blankets stretched between poles for a changing room.

Carmilla grabbed a couple of two piece swimsuits that caught her eye and disappeared for a quick change. Next to the changing room was a full length mirror. Carmilla popped out from the changing room and looked at herself in the mirror.

Leon said, "You sure do nice things for that swimsuit Carmilla!"

Carmilla looked at him with a shy smile, "Yes, it does fit well, but the color is not quite right."

Sarita appeared in front of the mirror in a blue and white one piece that really displayed her full bust, narrow waist and flaring hips to the best advantage. I looked at her admiringly. She caught my eye in the mirror and asked, "Does this suit look good?"

I smiled, "Yes, I think that it is perfect. Please let me purchase it as a gift for you."

Sarita looked at me thoughtfully for a moment. "Thank you, but I think not. It would be a very personal gift and we have only just met. To be fair though, you guys can pay for the boat and cabana. We might not have come here again this year and we might not have needed new swimsuits."

Leon and I both said, "Deal" at the same time. I continued, "We understand that you are helping us get to know the area and we do not want to burden you. Please let us take care of all of our expenses. We are pleased to do so."

Carmilla asked, "This deal, is that like umm we are in agreement?"

"Yes," Leon said, "We want to take care of all of the expenses since you are really helping us and we enjoy your company." The girls nodded agreement.

Leon and I each picked a pair of swim trunks. The girls paid for them and the beach towels also.

Sarita explained, "You guys are good not to insist on paying for our swimsuits, so your reward is that we will buy your suits. Remember, here in Colombia most asking prices are negotiable. The asking price will usually be about twenty percent more than they expect to get. If you pay too much or too little, that is not a good thing."

"At a gas station, you pay the price at the pump. If prices are posted for things inside, that also is the price. Places like the open air market, you can negotiate even if a price is posted."

The girls changed back into street clothes and we headed down to the beach to find a boat.

Carmilla advised, "The boat ride should cost about six thousand pesos for the four of us, do not pay more than that. You guys do the negotiations."

Leon and I approached the closest boat owner. I asked, "We want to go to Isla Mucura, how much to take the four of us?"

The boat owner looked at the four of us, as three other boat owners drifted closer, and said, "Seven thousand five hundred pesos." There was a murmur from the other boat owners and they leaned closer.

"Oh, I was thinking that four thousand seven hundred pesos would be about right for such a short trip." The other boat owners smiled and were quiet. After about fifteen minutes of negotiation I had gotten the price down to five thousand nine hundred pesos and agreed to the price.

The waters of the Gulf of Morrosquillo were quite clear and the bottom remained visible even at thirty foot depth. The boat captain surprised us with his excellent English. He sounded like a New Englander when he asked, "Ayah, what brings you to Tolu. Your Spanish is quite good, but forgive me as I do not get to speak English very often."

I answered, "We are here to study the rivers and locate sites for hydroelectric power generation stations. I am surprised at your New England accent. How long have you been down here?"

"I am Jason Escobar and I was raised around the Chesapeake Bay area from the time that I was five until age fifteen. My family was originally from Tolu and we moved back about fifteen years ago. That was a good job of negotiating the price, how long have you been down here?"

"To be honest, Sarita told me what the price should be and that I should negotiate. How well did I do?"

"A fair price would be six thousand pesos next week, but the price you settled for was also reasonable. Why did you stop there?"

I replied, "Sarita said six thousand was fair and I was already below that, fair is fair. When you offered five thousand nine hundred pesos, to press lower would have been unreasonable and bad faith."

"I am pleased to meet you sir, please call me Jason."

"I am Nate Calero and this is Leon Abadia." We all shook hands and Jason asked how long we planned to stay on the island.

I said, "I think just for today, but it is so peaceful and beautiful here that I will likely want to stay longer." Sarita and Carmilla had been quietly talking.

Sarita looked up and said, "Perhaps we could get two cabanas and stay until tomorrow afternoon." Carmilla nodded her approval.

"Here is my cell number, call me when you want to come back. I will pick you up right here at the dock." The boat captain said.

We were pulling into the dock. The girls had brought beach bags and Leon and I grabbed them and jumped onto the dock. We then helped the ladies up to the dock.

We walked a little way down the beach and found some small cabanas. Carmilla said, "I will go and get the cabanas for tonight. We will get two cabanas and it will cost sixteen thousand pesos.

I gave her two ten thousand peso notes and she disappeared up the beach.

"We will take these two right here next to each other," said Sarita. "Girls here, guys over there. Go on in and change clothes." When we came out Sarita had already spread towels out for us to lay on.

"I am going in for a quick dip," I said.

Sarita dropped her tanning lotion on her towel and said, "race ya." I let her stay about three steps ahead of me all of the way.

We swam around for a while and Carmilla and Leon joined us. Sarita swam toward the beach and I followed her. When she got to her towel, she dried off and handed me the tanning lotion.

"Please do my back," she said as she stretched out on the towel and rolled over. "Ooh that feel good" she said as I began rubbing the lotion on her back. Her suit was very low cut in the back and as I neared the bottom, she looked over her shoulder at me and said "It is ok to go lower." She watched the bulge grow in my swimsuit, but said nothing as I rubbed the lotion lower and lower. We swam and sunbathed the rest of the afternoon. A hostess would occasionally appear to see if we wanted anything to drink or eat. It was a perfect day.

We went to the restaurant for dinner and enjoyed the music and a few drinks. Then we walked back to the cabanas and said good night to the girls. A little while later there was a knock on the door. I opened it. Sarita was standing there, "Leon, Carmilla is looking for you in the other cabana better hurry; she is very impatient."

Leon lost no time asking questions.

As she entered the cabana Sarita said, "It has been such a perfect day, we could just not let it end yet." As her body melted to mine she put her arms around my neck and gave me a warm soft kiss. "Be gentle, it has been a long time for me."

"For me also," I said. We kissed for a while and then lay on the mat.

She moved her hand down and felt my erection. She pushed herself up and then removed my shorts. "Oh, I knew you would be large when I saw your excitement earlier today." She was wet with excitement as she slowly took me in.

Carmilla tapped on the door. "You guys awake yet? Let's go get some breakfast."

Sarita said, "Give us fifteen, we will meet you at the restaurant."

As we approached, Carmilla looked from Sarita to me and back. "Good morning, looks like all is well with you two. Leon is a real heavy sleeper, so we got plenty of rest. After we eat, let's get some bicycles and explore the island."

"Yeah, I do not think that I remember seeing a car or bus here," I said.

Sarita explained, "There are not cars here, bicycles and foot are most popular. The bicycles come in different sizes, besides the standard one, there are several that carry the driver and up to three passengers. Everyone works the pedals; it is very good exercise. I have heard that there is one bicycle that holds sixteen people, but I have never seen it."

"Should we take some drinks with us, I asked."

"No need," replied Carmilla; "There are fruit stands all over the island and we can get a fresh drink at any one of them. Please excuse us while we powder our noses."

Carmilla waited until they got to the ladies room, "You always get the best ones. Leon was good for one time and went to sleep. I could tell, I bet you guys didn't sleep at all."

"There is no way to tell, but you are right I was very lucky, Nate is a great lover. I think that I am going to try and keep him," said Sarita.

Carmilla complained, "Darn, I was hoping that you would agree to switch and we would stay another night. Leon did not bring any protection, good thing I am on the pill."

Sarita responded, "Nate didn't bring protection either and I am not on the pill. We managed quite well though. His tongue is like a pillar of fire."

"Oh you rat" complained Carmilla, "Now I really want to swap, you know that is my favorite thing."

"Nothing doing, you picked Leon first, besides I don't want to have Nate slip into that beautiful body of yours. You really look great in that swimsuit. Besides, you wouldn't want Nate anyway, he is so big that I almost couldn't get all of him in."

"Oh, you are so bad Sarita!"

As Sarita and Carmilla approached the table, "It is almost ten o'clock, soon it will be too warm to enjoy the bike ride. Let's just go back to the cabanas and relax, maybe lay out on the beach," said Carmilla.

Nate and Leon had been looking out past the veranda at the Carribean not talking. They turned and "Ok, sounds good to me," agreed Nate; Leon nodded ok.

Later they were alone and Sarita said, "Carmilla wanted to swap dates with me, do you want to go with her?"

Nate looked at Sarita for a second and then smiled, "No, I like you and want to be with you. Carmilla is very attractive, but there is something about you that makes us special. I hope you agree with my choice."

Sarita did not answer in words. She put her arms around Nate's neck and the whole thing started over again. Two days later they called Jason to pick them up.

The girls dropped them at the house in Sincelejo and they exchanged cell numbers. "I do not know what my schedule will be for the next few days. So can we call you?" Nate asked.

Sarita explained "Carmilla and I both work Monday thru Thursday afternoons and evenings usually one til ten pm. We are free after work on Thursday. If you want to have breakfast together, call the night before."

Nate and Leon said their separate goodbye's and the girls drove off.

"Nate, Carmilla doesn't seem too excited about me. I wonder what I am doing wrong."

Nate responded, "It is too soon to tell. I know that I was surprised at how this date worked out. I was totally unprepared to spend the night with Sarita, but I sure am glad that I did. I didn't have any rubbers and I hope that does not turn out to be a problem. I guess that I will know in about three days. Sarita was not on the pill either."

"Well, Carmilla was on the pill, but I didn't have any protection either. You are probably safe since no pill probably no sex. I think that perhaps I was too casual since I fell asleep right after the first round. I fixed that on the next opportunity. This morning it was really great, so maybe everything will be ok."

Nate's cell rang, it was Alvaro. "You guys really work fast. You got the two best looking chiquitas in Sincelejo to take you out for the weekend."

Nate interrupted, "How did you hear about that so fast, we barely had time to get our thoughts together on it ourselves."

"There are eyes everywhere. Use Jason Escobar if you need a boat. Do not put him in danger though he is a good guy with a local family. Your GPS has an entry for Boat Dock 1. I decided not to use the military port. I will meet you there in about two hours. Depending on how many checkpoints you encounter, you may be a little late. Be sure to carry your passports. They will check for weapons, you are new in country and did not realize that you should carry any. When we meet I will take care of that. There are actually some in your safe house, but I will have to explain how to find them. They are for emergency only. See you soon." There was a click and Alvaro was gone.

"Got your passport?" I asked.

"Yep" said Leon, "Let's roll."

We headed out Diagonal 4A to Carrera 17, Carrera 3, US 90, to Calle 29, left onto Carrera 20 then right onto a dirt road arriving at the Boat House 1. Alvaro was already there and we were only thirty minutes late. The checkpoints were no big deal. They just looked over the van and checked our passports. When we said studying rivers for the Embassy, they all seemed to lose interest.

Alvaro asked, "How many checkpoints?"

"Six I replied, not heavily armed and not very suspicious of us."

"Good," he responded. "Sorry that you didn't get the Land Rovers. Come on inside. Obviously this is not a boat dock. We own this house and the one over there on the point. We will keep a zodiac at each one. We have a gatekeeper at each one when they are not in use. He is really an undercover member of the National Police. We are pretty sure that they can be trusted."

Adan and Juan arrived and came to the door. Alvaro let them in. "How was your drive up?"

Juan said, "What a pain we must have had to stop every twenty kilometers for a checkpoint. They did not really take much interest in us though. Basically, they just looked in the vehicle and checked our passports. One did ask us if we had any weapons, when we said no he just shook his head and waves us on through. I would feel better with a good old .45 in my pocket though."

"Let's take care of that now," Alvaro said. He went to a cabinet and unlocked it. When he opened it there were a couple of old shotguns in it and a rifle. He looked back over his shoulder to see our expression. We looked very disappointed. He pushed in on a gun support and the back of the cabinet rotated and the base swung outward to reveal a small arms cache. He handed us each a relatively new

HK.45 and four full magazines. We also got two boxes of ammo each. "You probably will never use this much ammo, but it is better to have more than you need. At the boat docks we have our main weapons. I am going to give you each an old M1 carbine that is chambered for the .45 ACP cartridge. Probably no one will try to confiscate this oddball relic from you. Here are three full magazines each for the relics."

Leon looked and said, "Sure wish that I could carry one of those HK416s instead." "Yeah, but you would not get through the first checkpoint with it, probably get dead instead," warned Alvaro. "You will carry them on missions though. Anybody tries to stop you make them dead. When you are on the water, you will not have any friendly support available. Duck and run if you can or eliminate the threat if necessary. The other boat docks have the same cabinet arrangement."

"I have decided to have Adan and Juan station at Safe House 3. Rincon Sucre is a very small town and you may need to go to Cartagena to find companions. It will be more difficult there since so many rich folks inflate the cost of women. Stay away from the hardened prostitutes. Find some more educated ladies to keep you company."

"The boat dock and safe house are both setup the same. We keep the Zodiacs under the house, hidden from casual sight. They are fueled and ready to go. The gate keeper will resupply any fuel that you use, so do not worry about that. Soon you will begin using Nate's cover to patrol the rivers looking for likely submarine building activity. Let's go down and take a look at the Zodiac that you will be using for the next few weeks." Alvaro lifted a ring set into the floor and a staircase could be seen descending downward. He went down about seven steps and hit the light switch. We all followed him down.

The Zodiac that we saw was the standard 15 foot long by six foot wide Combat Rubber Raiding Craft (CRRC), it looked like a standard F470 model. The motor was the standard 55 horsepower outboard. Alvaro continued, "This is a standard military surplus Zodiac configuration. The one over under the safe house has twin engines, a silencer package and ArmorFlate. A sub can still hear you coming though if it is submerged. You will probably want to use it for your kill operations. The one here can be folded up and carried in the van if necessary. There is also a trailer for it that the van or suburban can pull easily."

"I want you to scout the Sinu River from the Dam to the coast first. We think that they are building at least one sub somewhere along that river. We have only rumors, nothing definite yet. Later we will look over the Cauca river below the San Jorge confluence. On the rivers during the daylight hours take the girls along if they want to go. Be casual, but check water depth and flow rates from bank to bank as you go. The river police may leave you alone after they have followed you and become convinced that you are really doing a survey."

"The Zodiac is kind of small, so I would suggest one team work the shoreline looking for potential building sites. The other team will take the boat and do the hydro survey, maybe switch roles day-on day-off. The girls will be a useful distraction. Got any questions?"

"What about weapons," I asked. Alvaro advised, "Carry your .45s everywhere you go in this country. That means both rifle and pistol. Be casual with them, close but not intimidating or nervously. Remember, there are bandits in this country. If they think that you are interested in gold or emeralds, you will also be in danger. If you play it cool, the FARC will even leave you alone. Either the bandits or the FARC will kill you if they feel threatened in any way. Anything else?"

Leon asked, "We may need to purchase gas along the river, are there funds for that?"

Alvaro chuckled, "Yep, but do not go around flashing a big wad of cash. These are mostly poor folks along the river. Complain about the cost and often you should negotiate because the gas will be hand pumped from a 55 gallon sized barrel. My suggestion would be that each Zodiac has two five gallon cans, when you empty one, refill it at the next opportunity. People will get used to seeing you and the boat that way. Stop at each village or town to let the people get familiar with you. You will be amazed at how fast news travels around here. Anything else? If not, then come back tomorrow morning and explore the Sinu River."

Adan said, "Nate, I think that Juan and I will head up to Cartagena. Rincon only has two cantinas and the women all looked like hard working farm girls. We are hoping for something more interesting in Cartagena."

"Sure," I said "and happy hunting. Send us a text each night and we will answer back within about half an hour so we can know that all is secure. Short comm both ways, ok?"

"Sure enough," Adan responded. We climbed into our vehicles and headed home.

We stopped at Sarita's restaurant for dinner. Later she came by the table to say hello. "Hi Nate, I was hoping that you would stop. I would like to talk with you after I finish work tonight. Leon, is it ok if Carmilla comes along with me."

"Sure, I will always be glad to see Carmilla," Leon had a big smile.

We drove back to the house and set to checking and cleaning the weapons. We had just put them down and taken showers when the girls arrived.

Sarita took my hand saying, "Excuse us. I want to talk to Nate for a few minutes." As we entered the bedroom, Sarita closed the door and said; "Sit on the bed for a minute. I want to explain something to you. My first lover was also my fiancé. He was killed the week before we were to marry; that was almost three years ago. I do not know what happened to me when we met, but somehow I really wanted to be with you. You are my first lover since Juan was killed. I think that it is important that you know this, please do not think badly of me."

I stood up and gently pulled her to me. "I do not think badly of you and I am glad that you told me about Juan and you. It must have been very difficult for you when he was killed. I have been warned that this can be a very dangerous country. What happened to Juan?"

"He was driving in the mountains when his truck went off of the road. When the police went to the scene, they found that he had been shot as he drove along the road. The Police blamed the FARC. We may never know the reason he was shot. It took me a long time to get over it. I think that I am over it now or I would not have had that strong attraction to you." Sarita smiled and stretched up to kiss me fully and warmly.

We started to go out into the main room, but Leon and Carmilla were not in sight. Sarita pulled me back into the bedroom. "Is it ok if we stay tonight?" she asked.

"Carmilla already said that if Leon was interested she was going to give him another chance. I started the pill this morning. Did you get any condoms today?"

"No, I said; we went to Rincon today to meet the other team members and just got back in time for dinner. Besides I do not think that either of us knows where to buy those kinds of things."

Sarita laughed, "There are many places to get condoms here in Sincelejo, but they might be difficult to find in Rincon. Most of the markets and medicine shops along 4A will have them. If you promise to be only with me, we can stop using condoms this weekend. The pill will have taken effect by then. Is it a deal?"

"Yes, I cannot imagine anyone more attractive or desirable than you. I should tell you that I have not been with anyone for a long time also."

"You first then me," she said as she removed my pants and pulled me to her. Her full moistened lips parted to welcome me in.

In the morning, I said, "You first then me and proceeded to make her writhe in ecstasy." Carmilla knocked on the door. Sarita answered, "Fifteen more minutes and I will go with you to get breakfast." Her beautifully manicured hand was wrapped around me and moving rhythmically.

Rincon

CHAPTER 8

We arrived at the Rincon boat dock just before noon. Adan and Juan were down checking the Zodiac. They looked up as Leon and I descended the stairs. Adan asked, "Do you think that we can hump this to the water? The CRRC is about six hundred pounds without anything extra inside if I remember correctly."

"Don't know til we try," I responded. "Usually there are six to carry the boat. Leon and I might be a little weak this morning. We got our horns trimmed."

"You aren't the only ones," said Juan. "We got lucky yesterday. Cartagena is the place to go hunting for beautiful women. I don't think we have found anything permanent yet, but they gave us their cell numbers." Adan was just smiling.

"Everyone grab a hand full and let's find out if we can move this beast, I said." We got the CRRC to the water edge and then loaded in the extra fuel cans. I went to the van and brought our weapons over and put them into the Zodiac. "Leon and I will take the first ride. See if you can find roads to keep us in sight. Put Berrugas in the GPS and see if you can keep us in sight. We will pull in at a dock there and meet you for lunch. They are sure to have a cantina or somewhere to get a meal." We got into the Zodiac and headed southwest along the Caribbean coast.

The coastline looked more like a barrier island strand. We rounded the point and motored into the Gulf or Morrosquillo and headed along the shoreline. We found several docks with associated buildings as we motored along. These settlements were isolated, but did not look like they were large enough to build and load a submarine without attracting attention from the locals. A stream was found near Berrugas with buildings near and large enough to house a sub. There was also a road large enough to land good sized cargo aircraft. We tied up the Zodiac on the jetty at Berrugas and found a nearby restaurant. We went back to the Zodiac and called Juan to let him know where we were. While I was on the phone, a pair of fishermen walked up and began a conversation with Leon.

The fishermen wanted to know if we were fishing or just riding around. Leon explained our search for rivers with good flow rates. They said that there were several small rivers flowing into the gulf, but no really large ones between Berrugas and Tolu. They said that handline and net fishing was good in the Gulf if you knew where to go. I resolved to bring a cooler and fishing gear from now on.

I asked the fishermen, "Is that restaurant good?" The fishermen nodded. I asked if they would like to join us for lunch and they both nodded with good humor. We each had a beer with our meal and then another.

I asked, "Is there a good place to buy some fishing gear?"

"Yes" said Jota, "We will show you after you finish your beer." We finished our beer and paid for the lunches and drinks. Jota took us to a house on a side street and knocked on the door. An old gentleman answered and Jota explained our needs. The man took us to a building behind his house and unlocked the door. Inside was quite an assortment of fishing poles, reels and line; plus nets in many different sizes. He asked us where we would be fishing and I said mostly close in along the coast or in the rivers. He showed us several poles and reels that he thought would be the correct size. He said that all of the reels were imported from the USA or Japan and that he made all of the poles himself. We bought what we needed and paid the man. We were careful not to show a lot of cash and negotiated acceptably.

Leon took out the small cast net and caught us some bait. I went over to a small store and bought a foam cooler and some ice. We fished on the way back and kept five large grunt for dinner that night. We got back to the boat dock about dusk and Adan and Juan arrived to help store the Zodiac. We gave them two of the grunt and kept the others in the cooler.

"Say Adan," I began, "Since you and Juan haven't hooked-up yet, how about running a quiet recon on the buildings that Leon and I saw off of the small river just east of the pointe?"

Adan agreed, "Sure thing, but I thought that you said it didn't look deep enough to float a sub."

"What I am thinking is that they quietly build the sub in the buildings. The most likely building of the four is right next to the river. That would just take a few people. Then they float it out to the dock at night and load the cocaine or whatever and sail away before dawn. The Gulf is easily deep enough to run submerged. The locals would only occasionally notice more than usual truck traffic, like a resupply for some the farm. I bet the crew arrives with and loads the drugs into the sub."

"Ok, we will slip in at about oh-three-hundred hours. Want to meet back here about noon? That would give us some down time before we report what we found." Adan asked.

"Sure," I said, "Then Leon and I can take the Zodiac and scout the other side of the Gulf." We headed back to Sincelejo.

Slightly Off

Art McGillem

The girls did not come that night, so Leon and I awoke refreshed and decided to take a more leisurely recon of the coastal area between Tolu and Rincon. We drove to Tolu and took Carrera 2 heading north. After a few miles, the road took a sharp turn toward the coast. We followed it for about forty miles until it ended at the edge of a river. We named that junction River N of Tolu-2 and turned back looking for a road heading East. The roads were all hard packed dirt and would likely be a mess when the rains came. There were police checkpoints on each side of town. The police looked at our weapons with little interest.

We found an improved road heading generally north toward Rincon and followed it to Pita Abaja and continued northerly, turning left toward Pita Arriba. We intersected with Calle 29, the main road toward Rincon. This area was mostly flat farmland. We turned left onto Carrera 20 and were in the home stretch. We did not cross anything that could be called a river although there were many small streams spread across the area.

It looked like the northern coastline of the Gulf of Morrosquillo only had two rivers deep enough to possibly interest the cartels. On the eastern and southern coastline only one river looked promising, but there is a large mangrove type area on the eastern coastline that could harbor building activities in the densely vegetated area. The Gulf or Morrosquillo provided relatively secluded access to the Caribbean Sea, so exploration is definitely in order. We would have to scout the area from the Zodiac and check any large buildings or heavily forested areas found nearby.

When we arrived at boat dock 1, Adan and Juan stumbled from their rooms looking for coffee. Adan reheated a pot of coffee and reported "You sure guessed right on this one. The sub is almost finished, but we did not find any drugs. We were worried that we were going to be found out. They have four dogs at that farm. They started barking and wagging their tails as soon as they heard us. They run free and came right up to us, so we gave them some meat laced with a sedative and they became quiet very quickly."

"How large is the sub?" I asked. Juan answered, "Looks about thirty-five feet or so and the tube looks to be about nine feet in diameter. I bet it will carry about eight tons of cocaine."

Adan added, "You can go in tonight if you want, we have plenty of sedative laced meatballs for the pups. Alvaro left some GPS transponders here for us to use if we can find a good place to attach them to the sub. If you install it tonight, they still have all of the fiberglass and resins laying around for us to use. I found a place inside just in front of the sail where the GPS will plain disappear from sight once it is covered with that blue fiberglass and resin."

"What about the antenna?" I asked.

"According to Alvaro none is needed," responded Adan. "Alvaro says that this is mostly battery." He was holding up a rectangular object about two inches square by six inches long. Adan continued, "If you enter through the sail, face the fore point, take two steps forward turn around and look toward the stern and look directly up. There is an open space that looks like a wooden stiffener was used to support the hull as two sections were seamed together. Once that cavity is covered with fiberglass and resin, it will look just like the rest of the hull. With a little luck no one will notice."

"I think that it is worth the risk. Worst case, we destroy the sub; best case we destroy the sub and the drugs," Nate suggested thoughtfully. "Any of you guys worked with this fiberglass and resin before?"

"I did a small fiberglass boat for my little brother once," offered Leon. "It should not be very difficult. I think that I remember the proportions of resin and hardener; that is the only critical part."

Nate looked at Leon, "Ok, you and I go in tonight. We measure the sub, set the GPS transponder and then get out quickly. What is the best way in?"

Adan was ready for that one, "You can drive easily to within a mile. We haven't seen much traffic on the roads in that area and there are several places where you can pull-off and hide the van. We will draw you a map and give you the GPS coordinates. As soon as those dogs start showing up, give each one a meatball and then wait a few minutes. After they are calmed down, get to know each one of them. They will be less likely to bark the next time that we visit. Let's put the equipment in the van and then you guys may want to get some rest. We are heading to Cartagena. One of the girls that we met has a friend that wants to meet Juan."

"Ok you guys head out and I will call Alvaro and let him know our plan." Alvaro picked-up on the second ring. I explained that we had found a sub building location and planned to install a GPS Transponder in the sub. Then I explained how we planned to observe the sub until it is launched.

Alvaro came back, "That GPS transponder means that you can track it even if it goes under the water. Most of the drug subs cannot go below thirty feet. When you check the sub tonight, be sure to check the hull thickness;

that will tell us how deep they can go without drowning. Good hunting tonight, call me in the morning."

"I am going out on the veranda and try out one of those hammocks. There is another one if you want to give it a try." Leon looked uncertain, "I have never sat in a hammock before, let alone tried to sleep in one."

"Piece of cake, just do not try to roll over," joked Nate as he sat then lay back in his hammock. A cool breeze was gently blowing across the veranda. "The weather is just right for a good siesta," advised Nate.

Nate woke up to darkness and loud snoring. He rolled out of the hammock and walked over to Leon and began to gently shake the hammock.

Leon awoke instantly asking, "What's up?"

"It is eight o'clock, time to fix some dinner and get ready to check that sub. I guess that Adan and Juan found something of interest in Cartagena. They have not returned yet."

US Embassy Colombia

Chapter 9

Alvaro walked into the conference room of the U.S. Embassy in Bogota, Colombia. Four people were seated around the conference table. Three of them were Senators that sat on the Senate Intelligence Committee. Alvaro had met the Deputy Chairman from Georgia and the Senator from West Virginia, but he could not place the third Senator. The fourth man was the senior CIA spook Ryan Dottmann.

Ryan stood up as Alvaro entered and said, "Welcome Alvaro, I think that you know Senator Tom Wilson from Georgia and Senator Lucy Barnes from West Virginia, but you may not know Senator Jason Tweedle from Maryland. Senator please meet Alvaro Garcia our liaison officer with the Delta detachment for the project named Slightly Off." We shook hands all around and took seats.

Senator Tweedle jumped right in, "Are you really going to kill these subs without giving them a chance to surrender?" He was red faced and out of breath by the time that he finished.

Alvaro held up his hand and replied, "No Senator, that was the initial suggestion, but cooler head prevailed. We will try to make them surface and then take the prisoners to a secure island prison. The sub will be sunk in deep water."

"What happens if a crew refuses to surface and be captured," asked Senator Barnes?

"We can easily disable the sub and cause it to surface. In the unlikely event that the sub does not surface, it may sink. In any case, we do not plan to kill the crew unnecessarily. The plan is to make the crew, cargo and sub totally disappear; without a trace."

"Have you found any of these subs being built, Dottmann," asked Senator Wilson?

"Not yet, we just began looking two days ago," Ryan said.

"I haven't had a chance to brief you yet Sir, added Alvaro. We found one last night and are going back in to get full details tonight. The sub is almost complete. Seems they need to add their electronics for navigation and communications and the sub will be complete except for fuel and cargo. I just got the call before I arrived here."

"How did they find it?" asked Ryan.

"Seems Nate had a hunch about a building near a river and when Adan and Juan went in that night to check, there was a nearly complete sub sitting there," Alvaro said.

"What is their next step after checking it out again tonight? Why not blow it now?" Ryan asked.

"For the benefit of everyone present, our plan is also to remove the cocaine from the market, along with the sub and crew. We do not plan to do anything more until the sub is loaded and moves out to sea. We are going to monitor it each night until it sails with a crew and cargo. Only then will we take it down," Alvaro explained.

"Where is this sub located," asked Senator Tweedle?

Alvaro looked at Ryan for a long second, then responded, "I do not know exactly, I just got the initial report a few minutes ago. We will also want to keep that information compartmentalized and on a need to know basis. The cartel has ears everywhere and we do not want people speculating."

Senator Tweedle looked miffed, "We are all professionals here."

Alvaro responded, "This is our first case, so ground rules haven't been established. I was just thinking out loud, no criticism was intended."

"Who is Nate?" Senator Tweedle persisted.

"Nate is the leader of the Delta team. Information beyond that is need to know only," Ryan responded.

"I should have more information to share tomorrow. If you have questions about other aspects of operation Slightly Off, now would be a good time," Ryan said.

"How do you plan to disable the sub when it is under water," asked Senator Tweedle.

"That would be up to the Delta team. They have several options. They will try to get the crew out alive if possible. Remember, these cartel members know the danger of what they are doing. In the past, when the drug sub was scuttled because they were about to be captured, the cartel did not punish the crew. Any other questions?" said Ryan.

Ryan asked Alvaro to stay as the others wandered out the door. "Ok, what's bugging you, Alvaro?"

"Tweedle seems to be asking the wrong kind of questions. On an operation like this, the less outsiders know the better for everyone."

"Yeah, I agree on principle, but these guys insure our funding, so we need to give them a little extra, so they can puff their chests like they know something."

"I don't like it. I want my guys to survive this operation. I think that I will do some disinformation at the meeting tomorrow, don't press me too much if you hear something unusual like an exact location for something," Alvaro confided.

"Ok, see you tomorrow after lunch," Ryan suggested.

"Sure thing," agreed Alvaro.

Nate pulled the van inside the tree line and pulled the fuses for the brake and tail lights. "If we have to get out of here in a hurry, no point in showing others the way. Set those fishing poles out against the bumper. If someone happens along, it may explain why we are sitting here. The stream should be about a hundred meters in front of us." We locked the van and proceeded on foot toward the farm.

Two of the dogs rushed at us barking and wagging. Leon fed them each a meatball. Two fat old dogs wandered up and also got their reward. Leon went to the other buildings while I checked the sub. Adan had been correct. The sub was thirty-nine feet long and nine feet in diameter. The hull was a full three inches thick with wooden vertical ribbing meshed into the fiberglass. The sub looked very solid. I went inside and found the cavity that Adan had reported. The GPS transponder fit easily. I put the GPS in operation and wrapped some fiberglass cloth around it to make a tight fit into the recess. I found more cloth, resin and hardner and mixed up a batch to seal the transponder in. Unless someone expected to see a recess there, the transponder was invisible to the eye. It was now almost four o'clock in the morning.

Leon came back from the other buildings and said that he had found almost enough materials to make a second submarine. He also saw lights come on in one of the houses. The fiberglass patch over the transponder had dried so we decided to leave. As we were leaving we heard a truck approaching along the road. We hurried over to a large bush and hid behind it.

The truck stopped by the other shed and four men jumped out. They took tools and materials from the truck and carried them down to a boat tied to the dock. After a little time, a man came from the house to the boat and they started the engine and headed west toward the Caribbean.

I looked at Leon and whispered, "I wonder if they are already building a second sub? You said that it looked like there are enough materials for another. Tomorrow we will all need to be ready for a night op. We need to watch this place and also check out that other river that we saw just south of Punta Norte del Golfo de Morrosquillo. There is an air strip not too far from there also. Not much that we can do about it tonight."

We headed back to the van, stowed the fishing poles and headed back to the boat dock. It was already light as we approached and we could see that Adan and Juan were still out on the town. "Cartagena must have a lot to offer," Leon observed.

"We should check it out some time soon," I countered. We dug out some more MRE's added water and warmed them in the microwave.

"After we finish breakfast, let's put the fishing gear and rifles down by the Zodiac so we won't have to look them up in the dark," I said.

"Ok by me," agreed Leon.

Adan and Juan arrived just after we finished moving the equipment. "What did you find last night," asked Adan?

"About the same as you reported yesterday, I said. Something new came up also. I suspect that they are already building another sub out by the Punta Norte del Golfo de Morroaquillo, in the mangrove swamp. Leon and I will check it out tonight."

Leon suggested, "Let's boot that laptop and see what Google Earth can tell us about this area. The info might be old, but it should still be very useful. These paper maps do not show that same types of information. Oh, look at this, a router with a sat phone hookup. Alvaro even setup a Google account for us."

Google Earth let us see the North Point of the Gulf of Morrosquillo and the mangrove swamps along the northern shorelines. Nate used the plus and minus keys to zoom in and out to get the detail that we were looking for.

Night Op Berrugas

Chapter 10

Adan and Juan eased along the dirt road until they were about a mile from the farm. "It is really flat here. We had better kill the lights and hope for the best on this cow path," said Juan.

"Yeah, I am going to stop and let my eyes get used to the darkness," said Adan. He stopped the van and looked out over the hood. "I still cannot see the farm buildings or any lights. I guess that we should park and walk the rest of the way. Have you got the meatballs?"

"Sure thing," Juan said. "I want those dogs to be friendly."

"We should find out soon," said Adan. Juan set the fishing poles out against the bumper of the suburban and turned to check that they were hidden from the road.

Adan had the farm house in sight when he felt a wet nose nudge his hand. He looked down and the dogs had arrived, tails wagging. "Hey Juan, give these pups their burgers. This looks like a good place to keep an eye on what goes on tonight."

"I wonder if Nate and Leon are in position yet," mused Juan.

Nate and Leon had just rounded the point and entered the Gulf. They were moving slowly and the motor was just a quiet purr that was completely hidden by the noise of the surf. They slipped by the structures on the point without anyone coming to look. They went on down the coast until well out of site of the buildings.

"I think that we should just appear to be doing some night fishing just about here. We can pull the Zodiac up on

the beach and put some lines out then sit back until things
get real quiet," said Nate.

Nate had just put his baited hook in the water when
he whooped, "fish on!"

"Why don't you play it for a while and I will mosey
down the beach toward the river and see what I can find,"
said Leon.

"Ok, go ahead, but be careful of caiman's and the
Fer-de-lance. These mangrove areas are usually full of
them," warned Nate.

"Not to worry, you know that I am the careful sort,"
said Leon as he held up his .45 that now sported a silencer.

"Where did you find that," asked Nate?

"When I was cleaning my .45 I noticed that the end
of the barrel was threaded, so I started looking around.
Alvaro had them in a drawer, so I got one for each of us. I
don't think that it would be good if the locals caught us
with them, but it is probably safe for us tonight. You can
decide if you want to let Adan and Juan in on our secret."
Having said that he tossed a silencer to Nate and headed
down the beach toward the river.

During Ranger training in Panama, Leon had
learned that the Bushmasters and Fer-de-lance might move
toward a sound but that the caiman would usually move
away from a human sound. He also found that often the
mangrove completely covered the beach and he had to walk
along the slippery roots until the beach reappeared. Leon
moved along the mangroves and occasionally heard a
splash that could have been a caiman leaving the area.
Leon kept a sharp eye out for the Fer-de-Lance and the
Eyelash pit viper in the vegetation above. The Fer-del-
lance is often aggressive if disturbed, silent and deadly.

One bite and he would be past help before he could get back to the Zodiac.

Leon kept his feet in the water as much as possible. He did not want to leave footprints that someone might question. He came to the break in the beach where the river flowed into the Gulf without finding evidence of the sub. The beach turned back inland and followed the river so Leon kept on. He could barely see the opposite shoreline, but he saw several more or less parallel groves in the beach sand. He decided to wade across to investigate, but the river proved to be much deeper than thought. He swam to the other side a little away from the grooves. He walked a short distance into the mangrove and came upon a work area with a partially built submarine hull sitting on logs. He heard voices and realized that a boat was approaching from the Gulf. Leon moved back further into the mangrove and quietly waited.

The men worked on the submarine throughout the night.

First light saw the men getting back on their boat and leaving. Leon went to see what work had been done to the sub. The motor, drive shaft and propeller had been installed during the night. Leon headed back to where Nate was waiting with a heavy string of fish.

Nate greeted Leon, "I was worried, I thought that I heard a boat early this morning, but it did not come all of the way up here."

"Yeah I know. They stopped to work on the second sub. I had to wait until they went back before I could leave. They installed the motor and drive gear. I guess that they work on it about four or five hours each night. It is on the other side of the river, but I do not think that they can easily drive to it. If motorcycles were quieter, we could probably get there easily."

Nate interjected, "Time to take some riding lessons. Horseback is the answer to this problem. As the crow flies, the second sub is slightly less than two miles from the boat house. When we get back I will call Alvaro and see if he has a source for some really tame horseflesh."

We loaded the Zodiac and headed back to the boat dock. When we rounded the pointe, we could see a man standing in the gazebo. I waved my hand to him as did Leon. He waved back as I held up our string of freshly caught fish.

Nate guided the Zodiac back to the boat dock while Leon cleaned the fish. "You know that you caught 'em, so you should be cleaning 'em," grumbled Leon.

"Next time you guide the boat and fish and I will do the observing and cleaning," offered Nate.

Adan and Juan hurried down to greet us as we neared the boat house. Adan said, "We were getting worried, it has been light for almost two hours. What took so long?"

Leon answered, "We found the second sub, but while I was there a work crew showed-up and I had to stay until they left. Either of you guys know how to ride a horse?"

"Yeah," said Adan, "I grew up on a ranch. I could ride almost before I could walk, why?"

"The best way to approach the second sub is from the land, but roads do not look very promising," said Nate. "I will see if Alvaro can come up with horses and tack. Lots of folks seem to ride around here, so we should blend right in. What did you guys see last night?"

"The dogs didn't even bark last night. They must like their snooze medicine," said Juan. "We saw the work crew come in, get supplies from one of the buildings and then leave in the boat. They did not do any work on the sub at the farm. When they returned just before daylight, they just got on the truck and departed. We followed about twenty minutes later and did not see them."

"Ok, I will call Alvaro and report the second sub and see if he knows where we can borrow two horses. I hope that you do not mind teaching the rest of us how to ride," I said. "Oh no, I do not mind, it should be a lot of fun," laughed Adan.

I called Alvaro, reported the second sub and asked about the horses. "I think that two horses will be enough Alvaro."

Alvaro asked, "I hope that you can ride, some of these Colombian horses are pretty rough."

"Adan has offered to teach us, but I fear that he thinks like you do. We will have sore butts and bent pride before this is over," I responded. "Take pity on us and find some gentle mounts." Alvaro gave a suspicious sounding chuckle.

Alvaro continued, "On another topic, I want you guys to go to Safe House two in Sincelejo. Take your weapons, stay dark and quiet. Use the suburban and park in the front. I want you to watch what happens out the back at the house on the north corner of Garrera C and Calle 22A. Stay for the next three days, very quiet, but do not bring the girls, sorry. If something happens at that house take no action and wait until everyone is gone before you leave the area.

"What has you worried?" I asked.

Alvaro said, "I was asked one too many of the wrong kind of questions yesterday. You are not in any specific danger from these people at this point. They do not have enough information to be dangerous yet. I am going to bait a trap later today and I want eyes on what goes down, if anything does. Go tonight and try to remain unseen. The safe house has dry foods and canned goods, so you can be comfortable. Just do not go in and out often. Anything else to discuss?"

"I think that we will take two of the silencers along unless you advise against it."

Alvaro was quiet for a minute, then "Ok, but hide them in the compartment that I showed you in the suburban. Only engage the cartel hit men if your lives are in immediate danger." Alvaro hung up the connection.

"Saddle up, we are all heading to Sincelejo, but to a new location. We will be there three or four days. If you have dates scheduled, cancel them now. We will all ride in the Suburban and will leave in thirty minutes." Adan and Juan looked saddened as they pulled out their phones to cancel their arrangements.

I drove to the safe house and parked the suburban in the garage. We took all of our equipment out and I rolled the steel door down. The street was empty and it was likely that we were not seen entering the house.

"Get some blankets to cover the windows. No light is to show to the outside. We are on a twenty-four watch out the back to that house over there, I pointed. The cartel may hit the place, but we are not to do anything about it. If we are attacked, we can defend, but only then. We will take turns observing in four hour shifts. If you need to take a leak call one of to take your place, same for meals."

"What is going on," asked Juan? "Alvaro thinks that someone in Bogota may be a leak. He is going to plant some information and see what happens. I think that he has a specific person in his sights," I said. "We just watch until pulled-off. There should be food in the kitchen, so let's see what we can have for dinner."

We ate, prepped the weapons, set the watch order and began the wait.

Safe House 2 ~ The Trap

Chapter 11

Alvaro was waiting when the other four came into the briefing room. He stood to greet them. They took their seats and looked at him expectantly.

"I spoke with both teams this morning. They returned to the Sincelejo safe house on Carrera 12C this afternoon. The cartel did not work on the submarine last night. So the men will check on progress every three days. They will stay away from the area where the sub is being built as much as practical. If activity picks-up, they will observe more closely. Do you have any questions?"

"Yes," said Senator Tweedle. "Why are they returning to Sincelejo, aren't there places to stay closer to the sub base?"

"The safe house on Calle 22A is located near a major road and they can be in the target area within about two hours. Building a sub takes time. We can move them closer if there is a reason," Alvaro explained.

Senator Tweedle chimed in, "I thought that you said the safe house was on Carrera 12C."

"Oh, did I? Well it is a corner house, North side actually." Ryan had a puzzled look on his face, but did not say anything. "There is nothing else to report right now. If you are still here in three days, perhaps I can give you new information after the team returns to check the sub. Any other questions," asked Alvaro.

"You can all go ahead. I have something to talk over with Alvaro. I will meet you at the restaurant for dinner," said Ryan.

"Ok, what is going on? You gave up that safe house on purpose," Ryan asked.

"Tweedle asks too many of the wrong questions," replied Alvaro. "He was very quick to pinpoint the exact location of the safe house. In his position, he shouldn't care at all where the safe house is located. Actually, I did not give up the safe house location. The house at that location is currently empty, but it is under observation at this very moment by the team. If Tweedle is a sleeper, I also gave him a time-line to do something."

Ryan mused, "The three days."

Alvaro continued, "The team has instruction to just observe. They are only allowed to defend themselves if attacked. The team should be safe. Their house is not on a corner."

"I don't like it," said Ryan, "but I can see the logic of playing it safe. See you in about three days."

Cartel Strikes First

Chapter 12

Senator Tweedle picked-up his encrypted Sat phone and dialed a number in Washington DC. Geof Vinson, the senior staffer on the Senate Select Committee on Intelligence answered. "Hello Jason, how are things in Bogota?"

"Not too good from our standpoint, Geof. Is your side secure?"

"Of course it is Jason. You must have something hot if you ask that."

"Yes that scum from Delta have found a sub near completion and are sitting on it. If they wait until the sub is loaded and then destroy it we will lose a million each."

"Well Jason, how do you propose that we stop them?"

Jason had anticipated the question, "They are all in a safe house in Sincelejo. Do you have something to write on?"

"Go ahead," said Geof.

"The safe house is on the north corner of Garrera 12C and Calle 22A. The team will be going back to check on the sub in three days. Perhaps you can put something together before then."

"I think that is doable," Geof responded. "Good work, wish us luck. Anything else that you need Jason?"

"No Sir, just trying to hang onto our cash." Geof hung up the phone. He picked it up again and dialed a number in Cartagena.

A gruff voice answered, "jhola Geof, what is new my friend." Carlos Morena had few friends and Geof was not one of them. Geof was simply a highly paid but useful lackey interested only in the money.

Geof began, "We have a problem. A Delta team is in Sincelejo and they have found one of your submarines. They are going back in three days to kill it and the people associated with it." Geof knew that it was a lie, but he had to protect his time and investment. "Do you want to write this down?"

"I have a pen right here, go ahead."

"The house is on the north corner of Garrera 12C and Calle 22A. I have heard that this is a four man team, but information about this operation is very closely held. What will you do?"

"Do not worry about a thing my friend. Carlos will find these men and take care of them. Have they reported the location of the sub? Obviously we do not have any submarines in Sincelejo."

"No, if the sub's location had been reported, I would know," replied Geof.

"Let us hope that only the Delta team knows, then the secret will die with them. Rest tonight knowing that they will be gone in the morning," Carlos predicted.

Morena put his cell phone down and sat for some time thinking. He could hear his men in the kitchen pestering the cook that was preparing the noon meal.

He called-out, "TJ leave Maria alone and come in here. I have a job for you." His son TJ was tall and slender. His slight build and young look caused many people to underestimate how tough and vicious his son could be.

TJ walked into the room. "Maria seems to like my attention." He said casually.

"She is a married woman and her husband is not someone to take lightly," said Carlos.

"What is it that you wanted to tell me?" TJ asked, dismissing the light reprimand.

"That sub we have under construction just north of Tolu may have been found by some DEA agents. We know where they are staying. Take some men and kill them all. I will call Captain Garcia in Sincelejo to insure that there are no National Police in the area tonight."

TJ looked at his father, "How do we know the address?"

"A US Senator provided it to us. It seems like he does not want to lose his cut of the profits." Carlos could not keep the sneer from his voice and countenance.

TJ said, "Where did this Senator get his information?"

"He and some other Senators attended a briefing at the Embassy in Bogota and I guess that he heard it there." Carlos replied.

TJ looked at his father with a doubtful expression. "I wish that I knew more about this meeting. It seems a little convenient that he has the exact address where this DEA team is staying."

"In any case, the Senator is a reliable source. We can trust his information."

Carlos continued, "Take some men down there and burn the house to the ground. Everyone in that house is to die."

TJ smiled happily, "Yes Father, consider it done." With that, he turned and walked out of the house.

TJ pulled out his cell phone and called Diego Gomez, his right-hand man. "Diego, get the crew together. Bring at least ten men and pick me up inmediatamente (right away)."

Diego arrived with three Land Rovers full of men. TJ got into the lead Land Rover with Diego and three of his men. "Diego, go to a shop where we can get five gallon petrol storage containers and buy six of them. We will then go to the petrol station and fill them."

"Where are we going TJ?" Diego inquired.

"Sincelejo," responded TJ.

"Why don't we get the canisters and gas in Sincelejo?" Diego inquired. "We do not want to smell the petrol all the way to Sincelejo."

"We do not want anyone to remember our purchase on this trip," came the reply.

It was two o'clock in the morning when the assassination crew arrived near the address given by the Senator. TJ told Diego to pull over at an abandoned building with a large parking lot.

"Get everyone over here for instructions." TJ ordered. When the crew gathered around, TJ looked at the men. "There is a building near here that hides four DEA Agents. I want to kill them all without firing a shot. They are here to destroy one of our projects. The National Police have already been told to stay away from this area. The building is old and wooden, it should burn quickly. Place a can of gas at each entrance. Spread gasoline along the walls of the building and we will ignite everything at one time. They should all be sleeping. I do not expect any resistance. If anyone comes out of the burning building shoot them."

The building burned nearly to the ground before TJ gave the signal to mount the vehicles and depart for home.

Senator Tweedle is Suspect

Chapter 13

Juan was watching the target house at four in the morning when three cars pulled up and four men got out of each. Juan put the night vision camera into action to film the upcoming events. The men did not attempt to enter the house. They placed boxes along the four walls and walked back to their cars. The cars moved a little way down Cale 22A and stopped. There was a large explosion as the incendiary explosives in the boxes ignited and exploded engulfing the house. The house burned to the ground in minutes and the cars simply drove away. A Hertz rental vehicle turned onto Calle 22A and slowly drove down the street. Senator Jason Tweedle was caught on camera as he passed the still burning structure.

After the explosion, the whole team gathered at the window. They too saw the Hertz Toyota vehicle drive slowly by. They did not recognize the driver. Nate pulled his phone out of his pocket and called Alvaro.

"¡Hola, quien es este," Alvo queried?

"Nate here, they just hit the fake safe house, burned it to the ground without any warning. No one could have survived that explosion and fire. Interesting thing, a Hertz rental car rolled by just as the fire was getting smaller. We have the whole thing on tape. That was about thirty minutes ago and no rescue vehicles have arrived yet. What do you want to do?"

"Let me think for a minute," Alvaro said. "I didn't expect anything this drastic or sudden. You must have seriously scared some people. In a couple of hours when everything has died down go back to the other safe house in

Sincelejo and wait for my call. I need to talk with my Embassy counterpart to get his ideas."

I interrupted, "Embassy counterpart my ass, I told you who drove by."

Alvaro said, "Calm down it would not be him. He was never a suspect, but I will want that tape. Have you noticed the SuperPharma on Diagonal 4A near your place? Call me when you leave and I will meet you there. Park away from there and walk to the store." Alvaro disconnected and went in for a shower.

When Alvaro finished his shower, he called Ryan. "Meet me in the conference room. I will be there in fifteen minutes. Ryan, it is very important and do not mention this meeting to anyone."

Ryan responded, "What has happened?" Alvaro thought for a minute, "Not over an open line and do a sweep of the conference room before the meeting please." Alvaro clicked off and walked to his SUV.

Alvaro entered the conference room just as the tech was leaving. Ryan was sitting at the table and looked up. "The room is clean. What has happened that is so urgent?"

Alvaro thought for a few seconds. "The fake safe house was completely destroyed early this morning. It will probably be on the news today. Apparently the house was burned to the ground with incendiary explosives. No attempt was made to enter the building. A Hertz rental car drove by the house minutes after the explosion. I think that Tweedle took the bait and called someone. I would appreciate it if you could check the phone records of the visitors. Since this room is clean, it would have to be one of them."

"I was afraid that you were going to say something like this," added Ryan. "I am already checking the phone records, but it will probably be noon before the checks are complete. Do you have anything else?"

"I will be meeting Nate late this morning or early afternoon. I told the team to stay in the safe house until everyone has left the burned out building. Nate has the whole thing on tape, including the driver of the rental SUV. He said all of the images are good quality. Nate did not want to trust you, but I told him that you were never the suspect." Alvaro paused to give Ryan a chance to say something.

"I appreciate your confidence. We have been through a lot together over the years. With NSA help, we can probably tie all of the calls together. Once I have a few solid numbers, I can have our security guys start the queries at NSA. With luck we will also get the voice traffic."

Alvaro thought this over. "Senators, I wonder how high-up this goes?"

"When you are talking serious dollars, the sky is the limit," Ryan said.

Alvaro continued, "Can you keep this just between us until we have all of the calls tracked?"

"Sure thing," Ryan replied, "We will not have anything solid until we see the video and get the phone data. I may want to bring the Ambassador in at that time. I think that he is solid, but he is a political appointee."

"Ok, it will be your call on that, you know him better than I do," Alvaro agreed.

Alvaro rose saying, "I will call you after I have the tape and then we should meet. It is a fifteen hour drive each way to Sincelejo, so I had better get moving." Alvaro walked toward the door. In parting Ryan said, "I may have some good information on the calls by then. Be careful, the bad guys may be wondering how much we know. They just attempted to kill four men and whoever was in that building in cold blood." Alvaro, smiled and nodded as he continued out the door.

Alvaro got into his SUV and drove away from the Embassy compound. He drove a circuitous route to the Plaza de Bolivar, checking constantly to see if he was being followed and parked. He walked to a small beat-up Toyota pickup truck, got in and drove off checking once again to see if he was being followed. He headed toward Sincelejo and the SuperPharma store.

Alvaro mused that driving was less conspicuous than flying or taking an Embassy chopper to Sincelejo. Still, fifteen hours was a long drive in Colombia. Route I-25 was an hour faster than I-45 and more secure although it had fewer government check-points. Should it be necessary, he had Embassy credentials and was heavily armed. He did not really like the mini-Uzi that he carried, but it was less noticeable than most other available weapons.

The drive to Sincelejo proved to be tiring, but without incident. Alvaro arrived at eleven-thirty in the evening and called Nate. "I am going to stay at the other safe house tonight. What say we meet at the SuperPharma at about nine in the morning?"

"Sure thing, said a sleepy Nate. You must have driven. I expected you to fly and call earlier."

Alvaro said, "I did not want to attract attention. Colombia can be a deadly serious place. See you in the morning." Nate went right back to sleep. The team had gotten back from the boat dock and had gone to bed early.

Alvaro awoke to the sound of heavy equipment. He looked out the window that the team had used to monitor the fake safe house and saw the rubble from the fire being scooped up by a front loader and loaded into a dump truck. He picked up his cell and called Ryan. "Morning Ryan," Alvaro greeted, "they are already cleaning up the burned-out building and loading it into dump trucks. I do not see any police or other city agency at the site. Have you heard anything about it yet?"

"Nope nothing at all about a bombing or fire in Sincelejo. You were correct to suspect Tweedle. He called his contact in Washington D.C., who almost immediately called Carlos Morena a known Cartel controller. Then the dumbass flew to Sincelejo and rented a Toyota SUV. I am going to brief the Ambassador privately this morning. He will likely want to include our top Intel guy. Then I am going to suggest that we let it slip that the team was killed and we need to ask Delta for another. I will add that we did not get the location of the sub. Notice that was not a plural sub. That should get your guys and us some free time."

Alvaro thought it over for a few minutes. "Can we keep full electronic surveillance on these guys for a while? There should be some interesting communications going on when we do kill those subs. Maybe we will get to wrap-up a bunch of the bad guys all at once." You could almost see the smile in Alvaro's voice.

Ryan continued, "I will ask the Ambassador about that and let you know. It sounds like a good plan to me. Trapping Senators is a dangerous game with potential serious political consequences. The Ambassador may try to hedge his bets. I will let you know." Ryan clicked the phone off and headed for his meeting with the Ambassador.

Nate met Alvaro at the SmartPharma and they went outside and across the street for some fresh juice. The juice stand was a large one with a lot of open tables. Alvaro picked a table away from others and said, "I see that you brought the camera. Can you show me the tape now?"

"Sure," replied Nate. "Just let me make sure that the sound is off." Nate started the tape and turned the screen toward Alvaro, then set the camera on the table.

"Damn, I sure am glad that I gave them the wrong address. That sequence with the Hertz Toyota SUV is a clincher. The driver is a US Senator named Jason Tweedle. I wonder how long he has been turned?"

"Did you make a copy of the video tape?" Alvaro asked. "Yes, but it is a digital copy saved on one of our laptops. These USB ports on the camera sure can be handy," observed Nate. "You can have the video tape."

Alvaro picked up the camera, ejected the tape and put the tape in his pocket.

"You and your team have some breathing room. We are going to let it slip that you all died in the explosion and fire. We are also saying that you did not give us the location of the sub. We never mentioned subs, in the plural, to anyone. Ryan knows and may brief the Ambassador and select others, but it will be a small group of trusted folks; need-to-know only. We hope to keep the trap open and net all of these bad guys at one time."

Nate sipped his chilled fresh squeezed lime and Lulo juice; then said. "Yeah that should take some pressure off of us. They will still be relaxed at the farm. They can send that first sub within a couple of days if they want. It will probably be another month before the second sub is ready to sail. We can check the eastern and southern coastlines of the Gulf while we are waiting. No telling what we might find." Alvaro sipped his jugo de lulo thoughtfully.

"Nate, take it slow. We do not want any mistakes that will get our people killed. We have our sights on two subs. We should be able to take both out when they sail. That could take as much as two billion dollars' worth of smack off of the streets in the good old US of A. Do not stretch your small team too thin. You will have enough to do covering those two building sites. Oh, almost forgot. After we finish our drinks, I want you to meet a friend. He does not know what I really do here, but he has a large stable of horses. We should be able to find two that will meet your needs. I think that the farmer will provide you with feed for the horses, but you will have to negotiate the price. He will respect you more that way."

Nate thought for a minute. "We should go and get Adan, he knows about horses. He said he rode almost before he could walk. Your friend will be more comfortable working with Adan."

"I see your Suburban over there, we should take it rather than my Toyota pickup, not much room for three grown men in it," said Alvaro. They finished their drinks and got into the Suburban.

Adan looked at the rancho land. "Your friend takes good care of his rancho, Alvaro."

"Yes his ranch and farming go very well," replied Alvaro. "He grows a lot of coca also. You should know that the Colombian government only tries to control coca growth when the US pressures them. To the Colombians, it is a natural crop right up there with coffee beans and fruits. It is just best to leave the coca topic alone with the locals."

"Ok by me, as long as he is not on that sub when we take it down," said Adan.

"Not to worry," advised Alvaro, "He is too well off to get his hands dirty with work. You will see; he does care for his horses though." We arrived at the castle like ranch house and could see the owner coming out to greet us.

"Senior Domingo Alvarez, I would like to introduce Nate Calero and Adan Mendez. They are here to study the rivers of Colombia and help us locate sites for hydroelectric power generating plants."

"Gentlemen, please call me Dom. Alvaro, forgive my saying so, but these men look like soldiers."

Alvaro chuckled, but Adan said, "We both got out of the US Army about a year ago and joined the civilian branch of the US Army Corps of Engineers as hydrologists. I think the old saying goes, "you can take the boy out of the Army, but you cannot take the Army out of the boy." We all chuckled.

Alvaro said, "Dom we are looking to borrow two good horses. We will pay for their use and if you could supply their feed we will pay for that also."

"Dom looked puzzled, why would they need horses to study the rivers?"

Nate was quick to answer. "We also need to check for building sites along the river and learn what roads access those areas where we might want to recommend building a power plant. Adan is an experienced horseman, so he will be helping the rest of us learn horsemanship."

"Who is the rest of us, queried Dom?"

"There are four of us engineers. Nate replied. We usually work in two man teams and take turns on the water. We arrived in Colombia about two weeks ago and are just learning our way around Sincelejo and the nearby coastal areas. Our current plan is to work up-river from the coast checking water flow rates, depth and building sites. Well Dom, we do not want to bore you with our dream job, but we get excited talking about it."

"Ah, Dom said wistfully, the joyful spirit of youth!" Dom continued, "Hydroelectric power is good clean power, very green. I would like to see more of it in this country. Any way that I can help, please ask. Now to the horses." We walked over to a large barn.

Dom said, "We only have a few horses here at the rancho, most are out in large paddocks. What kind of horse are you looking for?"

Adan said, "I do not know what you would call them, but gentled work horses for mounted riding would be my description. They will not be asked to pull a wagon or anything like that. Horses raised in the fields have senses for danger that a farm raised horse never develops. Three of us have never ridden before, but I will see that your horses are well cared for." We walked through the barn and several tall horses eyeballed us. We came out into a corral that had one horse in it.

Dom looked at Adan and said, "We will saddle this one and you can ride him and see what you think." Dom called for Pedro and sent him to fetch more horses from a nearby paddock. Dom picked-up a blanket from the fence rail and Adan grabbed the saddle. The gelding flared his nostrils as Dom approached with the blanket. Adan noticed that the gelding spread and stiffened its legs. Dom put the blanket on the geldings back. Adan placed the saddle on top of the blanket and pulled the cinch strap tight and then stood there. Eventually the horse let the air out of its lungs and Adan tightened the cinch a full two notches more.

Dom nodded approvingly. "Walk him around the corral, get to know him." Adan walked the horse around the corral twice and quickly jumped into the saddle. The horse immediately stiffened its legs and jumped straight into the air, twisting to the left. Adan was ready for it and held on tightly, one hand grabbing a hand full of the mane and the other holding the reins. The gelding continued to buck and whirl until it became tired and stood shaking from its efforts to dislodge the rider. Adan dismounted and Dom sidled up to him and gave him an apple. Adan stood in front of the gelding and held the apple out in his palm. The horse accepted the apple and chewed happily. Adan removed the saddle and blanket, picked up two brushes and began to curry the horse.

Dom looked at Adan, "Would you like to ride that horse, he is not well trained and actually you are the first to remain on his back?"

"I would like the privilege, but the horses must be shared with others and I do not think that the others could handle this ciclon." Dom laughed and thought for a second. "If you take him and train him, there will be no cost for the other two horses. Do you have a place large enough for three horses?"

"Yes replied Adan, but we will have to build some walls to keep them from kicking each other."

"Shouldn't be a problem, the other two horses will be mares," replied Dom.

"Would you be so kind as to deliver them and their feed? I can give you the directions," said Alvaro.

"Most assuredly, when would you like to have them delivered" said Dom.

"Tomorrow would be great," said Alvaro. Dom invited us to the veranda for some fruit drinks.

Delta Is Now Suspect

Chapter 14

Carlos looked at TJ and simply said, "Tell me about it."

TJ explained about burning the building to the ground. "What bothers me is that no one tried to escape the building. No cries for help, no one came to a window, nothing."

"Take Diego and go to the farm where the sub is being built and check on the progress. Let everyone know to keep alert. There may be more of these DEA Agents around. I wonder why Geof called them Delta though." It was not meant to be a question, but TJ got to thinking.

"The United States Army has a Special Forces unit that everyone calls Delta Force. They do very special operations and get almost no publicity. Most people would not even know of their existence if Chuck Norris had not made those two popular movies. The Delta specialty has been primarily hostage rescue, but that could easily change. After the movies, even more information came out on the internet. Delta is as serious as a heart attack. These men are very special and highly trained. There is no way that we killed a Delta Team without any response. They may not have been in that building."

Carlos looked at TJ and began thinking out loud. "There are two subs being built at the farm near Berugas. You already know Camilo Lopez, it is his farm. Go see him and let him know that there could be intruders. He is to keep his eyes open.

Submarine Watch 1

Chapter 15

The stalls had been built in the barn and the horses and their feed arrived. Adan inspected the gelding and the two oldish mares. All were healthy and fit. Their tack was proper for riding and each had a scabbard for carrying a rifle. The two mares were very gentle, like they had been ridden regularly. The first mare stood quietly as Adan saddled her and complained only a little when Adan pulled the final slack out of the cinch strap. Nate, Leon and Juan had been watching the saddling process with interest. Juan finally asked, "Why do you wait to take the last little bit of slack out of the cinch strap?"

"A picture is worth a thousand words Juan," said Adan. "You saddle the second mare Juan and we will watch." Juan put the blanket on the second mare, then the saddle and tightened the cinch strap. He then put the bridle and bit on the mares head.

Adan smiled, "If we were younger, I would let you mount the mare; but I am going to take pity on you this time." Adan walked up to the side of the mare and grabbed the front of the saddle and gave it a strong pull. The saddle swung under the mare's belly. Then he walked up to the mare that he had saddled earlier and swung up into the saddle. "Notice any difference?" Adan asked with a sly grin.

Juan had a sheepish look as he responded, "I guess that last tightening of that strap is important. What is going on? It didn't look like you did anything different, except for the wait."

"That wait is very important." Adan advised. "All horses that have been ridden have a trick up their hoof.

When they feel the cinch strap begin to tighten, they take in a deep breath and hold it. If you don't want the saddle to fall off, you need to wait until they exhale, then you can finish tightening the cinch strap."

Juan thought for a second, "Any other useful tips for us neophytes?"

"I can think of two right away," Adan offered. "Do not stand behind the horse, they do not like it and many will kick at something behind them. Treat the horse well. If you stand too close, they may accidently step on your foot. Do not get mad and hit or kick them. They did not do it intentionally. If a horse is abused it may take revenge by bucking, biting or kicking at an unexpected opportunity. Nate, why don't you and Juan re-saddle that mare and we will practice riding."

Adan worked with Cyclone each day; they were becoming a team. We decided to watch only the submarine that was mostly complete. The other team would continue to scout the coastline. During the next two weeks the first submarine was completed and we waited for the cargo to arrive.

We did not find any other submarine construction along the Gulf coast and began taking turns at night monitoring the completed sub. We all stayed at the boat dock, except on the weekends. The construction crew never came to the farm on the weekends, so we took that as free time also. Adan and Juan appreciated that we would go back to Sincelejo on the weekends so their girls from Cartagena could visit them.

We arrived back at the boat dock on Monday morning. Adan had been out for a ride on Cyclone. He came hurriedly into the boat house. "Tonight may be the night," Adan said. "I saw trucks approaching the farm this morning. If they are smart they already floated the sub and may have already begun loading. We should be ready to move tonight."

"I agree," said Nate. "We should ready both Zodiacs for tonight. Once it is full dark, we will carry them to just above the surf line and activate the GPS Transponder. If the sub moves, we intercept it. If the sub doesn't move then we put everything back before daylight and wait again."

"Leon, tonight you do the honors with the Grenade Launcher. Adan and I will support with those new HK416 with the Beta C-mags. Juan gets the silenced MP5. Leon and I will be in the lead Zodiac from the safe house. We will only use weapons and body armor from the safe house. The armored Zodiac will always be the lead boat. Next attack, Adan and Juan will lead in the armored Zodiac."

Leon looked surprised, "We going to war or something that C-mag adds almost five pound to the weight of the 416."

"I am just being cautious; those hundred rounds might make a difference if the sub crew puts up a fight." Nate said and continued; "Don't forget, we are riding, not walking. Get some rest. We will move the equipment to the boats after dinner."

"Nate, I am going over to check the M320 and ammo. Want me to check-out your 416 and mags?"

"No thanks, I will be right behind you and check it myself. You should carry a 416 or MP5 also. We really are going to war, but maybe we will not meet much resistance."

Adan had already opened the weapons cache in the boat dock and handed an MP5 and silencer to Juan.

Cleaning supplies were laid out and the tedious tasks of checking equipment had begun.

"The 320 sure is an ugly little sucker," observed Leon.

"You could mount it on the rail of the 416 if you wanted to," suggested Nate.

"I think that I will keep them separate for now. I think that I will have more control of the 320 if I am just holding it. I guess that I should carry both the special HE and irritant gas rounds."

"I wonder if the irritant gas round can penetrate the sail area of the sub," mused Nate.

Leon was thinking, "The sail looks a little too tapered, I think that it is likely to ricochet rather than penetrate."

"Yes, I had that thought also. If we use HE on the first round, the sub driver probably dies though."

"I think with that swing-out tube I could easily get in a second shot before they could submerge. I would have the HE round in the chamber to fire if needed."

"Yes we should try that," agreed Nate. "We can hit with the special HE round even as they submerge. My guess is that they will run on the surface during darkness, so we should get the shots that we want."

"Agreed," said Leon. "I think that I want to use this 416 as my backup weapon. There are plenty of thirty round magazines here. We can take them closer to shore if we mount silencers."

Submarine Captured

Chapter 16

Alvaro had returned to the Embassy in Bogota and called Ryan. "We need to meet. I am here, do you have some time?"

"Sure thing, meet me in the Conference Room that we used last time," Ryan responded.

Alvaro was seated in the conference room when Ryan entered. Alvaro pointed the controller at the VCR and the tape rolled. Ryan said, "Oh shit! That is Senator Tweedle without a doubt. What a dim-bulb! We have him and his contacts confirmed; we are just waiting on NSA to deliver the text of the conversations. We have added their phone numbers to the active watch list. I guess that we just have to wait for now."

"The first sub take-down may take place tonight." Alvaro reported. "Nate said that trucks were arriving at the farm and that the sub had been ready for a week already. The team is ready if the sub moves away from the farm tonight. Do you have a sub on standby to take the prisoners to the island if it goes down?"

"There is a submarine in the area, but I will need to check the location. Do you have coordinates of where the team can meet our submarine?"

"I can give you approximate coordinates. We will need to setup a contact schedule so that the team can communicate directly to our submarine. Our submarine should be in the vicinity of 9 degrees 52 minutes 44 seconds North by 75 degrees 43 minutes 10 seconds West during the hours of darkness tonight."

"Come with me," said Ryan and led the way down to the Embassy Communications Center.

"Chief, I need to contact the Ventura immediately, can you do that?" asked Ryan.

"Sure thing Mr. Dottmann." The Chief sat down at the console and asked, "What do you want to say?"

Ryan composed for a minute. Need rendezvous with Delta Team to transfer prisoners in the vicinity of 9 degrees 52 minutes 44 seconds North by 75 degrees 43 minutes 10 seconds West during the hours of darkness tonight, can you comply? Contact Team Pied Pipers on prearranged frequency after darkness tonight. STOP Waiting Out.

"Mr. Dottmann, it will take them a few minutes to answer. I will call you when they respond." said the Chief.

"If you do not mind, we will wait right here Chief," answered Ryan. The Chief nodded and sat at the console waiting for the response.

A message was coming off the terminal. Ventura sends: Will comply with rendezvous. Will contact Pied Pipers at 2000 hours local. OUT.

"Thanks Chief," Ryan took the message and said "Let's go."

Ryan asked, "What kind of comm equipment does the Delta team have?"

Alvaro responded. "They have an encrypted Sat phone with an index that connects to their team communication equipment. They have the Ventura's number so to speak. I just need to call them and say that the Ventura is on station. Of course I will not use the subs real name. The code is "lockbox is open". The Ventura can also monitor the GPS transponder once it is activated by the team."

"Nothing to do now but notify the team and wait. I think that I will go and find some dinner." Alvaro said. Alvaro took out his Sat Phone dialed a number and said,

"The lockbox is open." He ended the call and went out to his SUV to find dinner.

At eight in the evening the shadows were just beginning to cover the landscape. The Sat Phone buzzed. Nate answered, "Major Thomas here, transponder activated but not moving. Over"

A voice came back, "Commander Ryker here, understood. We are on standby. Call when needed. OUT" The line went dead.

Full darkness came in another hour and a half. The Zociacs and equipment were moved to the beach just above the surf line. Just before midnight, the GPS transponder began to show movement. The team launched the armored Zodiac and attached a rope to the second Zodiac to pull it into the water. The exhaust from the motors vented below the water surface so the Zodiacs were like wraiths as they moved toward their prey.

Nate activated the Sat Phone link, "Target on the move. Will follow them until out of sight of land. Over"

The voice came back, "Roger that. Out"

The drug sub was cruising along with only a small portion of the sail above water. The sail rose about four feet above the deck. Nate and the second Zodiac took position behind the drug submarine and followed. The only viewing port in the sub faced the bow, so the Delta Team had no fear of being spotted. Their only vulnerability to detection was the sound of their engines transmitted through the water. The coastline disappeared from sight. Leon loaded the teargas round into the 320 as Nate signaled to overtake the drug sub. Nate increased speed and quickly came up on the sub.

Leon fired the teargas round and it bounced off of the sail. Leon quickly reloaded with an HE round. The sub was slowly sinking from site as Leon fired at the base of the sail. The round penetrated the hull and went out the other side without exploding.

"Experimental ammo," cursed Leon as he loaded another HE round. He put the 320 to his shoulder, but did not fire. The sub was returning to the surface. The hatch popped open and a man holding an AK74 appeared. Nate shot him dead and he fell back into the sub.

The remainder of the crew came out with their hands held high over their heads. There were only three. Adan pulled his Zodiac along-side the sub and motioned the men to get in. Juan had his weapon trained on them just in case they were stupid enough to resist.

The sub was not sinking. Nate needed to see what was going on. He covered the prisoners as Adan put restraints on their wrists. When they were seated at the rear of the Zodiac, Nate told Adan, "I am going to board the sub and find out what happened. You stand off and keep watch."

Nate took out his .45 mounted the silencer and climbed onto the subs deck. He carefully approached the sail and mounted the ladder. Carefully peering over the lip, he looked down the hatchway. The Pilot had been hit in the head by the HE round and killed. The round had continued out the upper part of the hull leaving about a two inch hole for water to enter the sub. Apparently everyone had panicked and began to abandon ship. The man with the AK was dead on the bottom of the sub. The AK lay on the deck next to him. Nate climbed down the ladder into the sub.

"Guess I need to get some pictures of this," he mused half aloud; and began snapping pictures of the dead men's faces, layout of the sub controls, communications gear and cargo. The rear of the cargo hold was full of cocaine and bundles of money. Nate called Adan on his comm and told him to move his Zodiac about five hundred meters West of the sub. Nate began shoving the bales of money out of the hatch. When all of the money was out, he placed a six ounce stick of Semtex explosive next to the cocaine, inserted a fifteen minute time delay pencil into the Semtex, activated it and climbed out of the sub. He then threw the bales of money to Leon and climbed into the Zodiac.

"We need to get out of here fast. Head west full speed about five hundred meters. I think that I see Juan flashing over there." I pointed. Our night vision goggles were set to identify the infrared signals worn on our helmets. I covered the bundles of cash with the tarp and we went to meet Adan and the Ventura.

I called Commander Ryker on the Sat Phone.

The Ventura answered. "Commander Ryker here. We are about one hundred meters West of your boats. We will surface and transfer the prisoners. Over"

"OK, when your deck is awash we will send the Zodiac with prisoners over. There is going to be a loud explosion is about ten minutes. Can we be done by then?"

"Sure thing," said Commander Ryker. I could already see much of the sail emerging from the Sea.

I called Adan. "Motor onto the deck and transfer the prisoners. When the Ventura submerges, meet us at the safe house." We had practiced this maneuver many times in Ranger training.

Leon and I headed back toward the safe house and turned when we heard the dull thump and then huge bang from the exploding drug submarine. A large orange flame shot skyward, but was quickly extinguished. "I wonder if anyone on land heard or saw anything?" Leon wondered aloud. I was wondering the same thing.

We got back to the safe house and began removing the money, weapons and such from the Zodiac. Leon asked, "What are we going to do with the money?"

"I think the whole team needs to help decide that. We will have a meeting on the beach when they get back." About ten minutes later they beached the Zodiac next to us.

"The explosion and fire were not a big or loud as I had expected," said Adan. "I wonder if anyone on land even noticed," Adan continued. "We might have gotten a free pass on this one. You guys were probably a mile or two away when the explosion happened. How did it sound to you?"

"Initially I thought that it was pretty loud," said Leon. "I was expecting it though, so I may have thought that it was louder than it really was."

"I agree you are probably right;" mused Nate. "The explosion just seemed loud because we were expecting it to be loud. The fireball was actually small and short lived."

"How about helping Leon and I move this beast into the safe house and then we will help move yours into the boat dock." We finished moving the Zodiacs and equipment.

"Meet Leon and I outside," I said. Adan and Juan followed us out.

"What's up, did we mess something up?" asked Adan. We were outside by then and away from the beach and house.

I looked at the Team and shook my head. "Nope, listen-up."

"I think that we will be wanted men after tonight. You all saw what happened at the fake safe house. There were four bundles of cash on that sub. I propose that we keep two and turn-in two to Alvaro."

"That is not honest," said Juan hotly and got nods from Adan and Leon.

"I agree, but we should think this through. Do you believe that our government will protect us from the cartels for the rest of our lives? We are single now, but what if we have families later. I think that we need to be able to cut and run if necessary and it takes serious money to do that. There is at least one US Senator hooked into the cartels on this caper and someone else high up. I think that they will eventually get our real names and information and feed it to the cartels. We need to be prepared for that. I do not think that we should discuss this with Alvaro or anyone else. It is our decision as a team. We need to think it over."

Leon looked nearly convinced, "Why not bring Alvaro in?" "He is a good guy."

"I agree. He is career CIA. My guess is that he already has another ID and cache of cash somewhere. If we give him half of the recovered cash we can wait to see what he says. We take what he offers and keep quiet about the rest. He can make his own deal with Ryan. If he suggests reporting one bundle money that is what we will agree to do."

"You guys never heard this from me, but I know several Delta guys and they do keep slush funds for when the government leaves them out in the cold." Leon spoke quietly. "They told me that some of the SF guys that work the real dangerous ops do the same thing. It is really self-preservation. If we get away clean we can always donate the money to a worthwhile charity."

"How would we ever know if we got away clean? The cartels never give up on finding folks that cause them harm. I hate to say it, but I think that Nate is correct." Adan confirmed.

"I will meet Alvaro somewhere and give him the two bundles of money and see what he says. I will call him in the morning if he does not call me tonight." I said. "I suggest that we put our cash in the back of the boat dock storage area. We have some time before the other sub will be ready to sail. I will find a way to get new ID's so we can put the money in Costa Rica. I think that is the best solution since we are all fluent in Spanish. It has been a full day, what say we hit the sack?" We went into the boat dock and hit the sack.

We were all up early the next morning. I said, "You guys make breakfast and I will go get two bundles of money. We can count it to get some idea about where we stand." I brought the bundles back, tore the plastic wrapping off and began counting the bundles of bills. "I count twenty million in these two bundles," I declared. "The other two bundles seem to be about the same size so probably are worth the same amount." "Since Alvaro is at the other safe house, he could show up here at any time. We need to get this cash out of sight." Adan said, "I know just the place we can put it in trash bags and bury it in the horse stall."

"Ok," I said. "You guys do that while I call Alvaro and give him the good news."

Alvaro picked-up on the second ring. "¡buenos dias, Nate. What is up?"

"We were busy yesterday. Come on over to our place, we have something to show you." "Can do, be there in about an hour and a half." Alvaro clicked-off. He arrived at the boat dock a short time later.

Alvaro looked apprehensive. "What is up?"

"We took down the first sub last night. We got three of the five sub crew into custody. One was killed by the HE round and the other tried to gun us down. The three prisoners are on the Ventura. I used about eight ounces of Semtex to destroy the sub and bodies. It will look like an accident if anything is discovered. Just before I blew the sub, I found two bundles of cash. They are down in the boat storage area. What do you want to do with them?"

"Two bundles, did you search for more?" Alvaro asked.

"No it was dark in there and I had already activated the time pencil when I saw them. I just threw them out the hatch and followed them out."

Alvaro said, "Let's get the cash and see what we have.

Alvaro finished counting the cash. "Twenty-five million dollars, that is a respectable haul. They must have been sending it back to be laundered. How much powder did she carry?"

"Just guessing, looked like about six tons based on the volume of the hold," I said.

"Whew," said Alvaro. "The street value of that much smack would be close to one billion dollars US! Good job guys."

"Alvaro looked at each of us for a minute. "I hope that this does not sound strange, but you guys are now marked men. The cartel will eventually find out who you are based on what we know about who in the States is involved in this smuggling operation. You will need to protect yourselves. Uncle Sam will try to protect you by moving you around. The cartel will probably find some or all of you if you do not personally take precautions."

"I will take this cash back to Ryan and see if he will agree to divide it and get you untraceable ID's. We have done this in the past. You will want to setup an account in your new ID in Costa Rica or the Cayman Islands. Think it over and have Nate call me later. I am headed back to Bogota." Alvaro took the captured drug money and headed out the door.

"That sure went smoothly," Adan observed. Juan and Nate nodded agreement.

Leon said, "It will be interesting to hear what Ryan says."

Alvaro will not get back to Bogota until late tonight. We probably will not hear anything until sometime tomorrow." I said. "We should take the night off. Leon and I will go back to Sincelejo. You guys can do whatever is on your mind."

"Our girls are just a phone call away. We will be in Cartagena tonight if you need us." We cleaned our weapons and stowed our gear. Leon and I began the drive back to Sincelejo.

We got in at about two in the morning and decided to sleep until about eight in the evening. We got up and got ready for dinner. We went to the Desde Restaurante where Carmilla worked. After we were seated at a table Carmilla drifted over.

"Where have you guys been?" she asked. "Sarita is really disappointed that you have not called her in so long, Nate. You are in big trouble. You are too Leon." Carmilla had a good pout showing on her lovely countenance.

Leon smiled and said, "We have missed you ladies also. We have been looking for rivers, but have found mostly small streams with insufficient flow to generate any power. Maybe we can get you girls to come along with us next week." Leon looked into Carmilla's eyes as he spoke.

"Your timing is good; Sarita and I are off for the next three days. I do not know what plans she may have though. I last spoke to her on Monday and it is Thursday already. Nate, why don't you call Sarita and ask her? We finish work in about an hour."

I dutifully called Sarita. "Well hello stranger, nearly two weeks without a call. I am so unhappy." Pouted Sarita.

"I am sorry," I said. "We have been cruising the streams and roads up north of here without finding any suitable hydroelectric sites. We have missed you and Carmilla, but we had work to do."

"Where are you now?" asked Sarita.

"We are at the Desde. Carmilla is standing right here," I answered.

"Put her on the phone," Sarita requested.

Carmilla listened for a minute, rang off and then said, "Sarita says that she will meet you at your house when she finishes work. Leon, would you like to accompany me after you finish dinner?"

"Sure thing," replied Leon. "Where are we going?"

Carmilla smiled thoughtfully. "I want you to see my new apartment." Carmilla was really thinking that she wanted to see how much Leon really did miss her. She continued, "Leon, after you finish dinner, there is a dark blue Jeep CJ in the parking lot. Wait for me there. Nate, you can go on back to your house. I promise to take good care of Leon."

"Works for me," I said.

Carmilla said, "Ok guys, see you later." She went back to her customers.

We finished dinner and exited the restaurant. "Want me to wait with you?"

"No thanks, you had better not keep Sarita waiting. Carmilla has a new apartment, maybe she has decided to like me after all." Nate could hear the excitement in Leon's voice.

"Ok call me tomorrow and maybe we can find something interesting to do with the girls." I climbed into the van and headed to the safe house.

Sarita was waiting. "You must have left work early. You got here before I did." I observed.

"Yes, it was a slow night and after you called, I asked the manager if I could leave. Are you disappointed that I am here early?" There was a sharpness to the response that put Nate on alert.

"No after two weeks in the wild, it is wonderful to see you." Nate took her hand and led her toward the door. They went in and Nate spun Sarita into his arms and gave her a long hug. "Umm, you smell good. Steak I think." Sarita punched him on the chest with her fist and turned her face up for a kiss. Nate gently pulled her closer and complied. Sarita pressed her body to his and he could feel the heat from her breasts as they seemed to burrow into his chest. He released her slowly and took her face into his hands. "I really did miss you," Nate said.

"I missed you too, why did you not call during all that time?"

"I thought that it would make me feel even more lonely. I think that Leon felt the same way about Carmilla. I do not think that he called her either."

Sarita walked toward the bathroom, "I am going to take a shower, then we can talk some more." She said as she closed the bathroom door. Nate sat down on the sofa and picked up the newspaper. He was about half way through the first section when the bathroom door opened and Sarita came out wearing only a towel.

"Wow, you do great things for that towel!" Nate exclaimed enthusiastically.

Sarita smiled, "Why aren't you waiting in bed?"

"You said talk and I did not want to presume too much."

Sarita pulled the towel off and gently threw it at Nate. "Presume all you want," she said and ran into the bedroom. Nate quickly followed her.

Nate had full erection by the time he came through the door. Sarita saw this and immediately forgave him for not calling. She smiled and said, "I can tell that you have missed me, come here and let me help you lose those clothes."

In the morning, Sarita came back from the market with a basket full of food and asked, "Have you and Leon done anything bad?"

Nate immediately had a surprised look on his face, "No, I don't think so," he replied. "Why?"

Sarita looked concerned. "I was approached at the market by three men. One of them asked me what you were doing in Colombia. I was afraid; these are bad men, known to be associated with the Escobar Cartel. They are very dangerous."

"What did you tell them?" asked Nate.

"I said that you were American engineers working for the US Embassy and Colombian government to find places to develop hydroelectric power. The man just said, "We shall see" and walked away with his friends. I hope that you did not do anything to anger them. They will kill us all if you did."

"Do not worry Sarita. We have done nothing to anger them," I lied. The likelihood of them tracing anything to us was remote.

While we were having breakfast, Alvaro called. He said, "Are you alone?"

I answered, "Not at the moment."

Alvaro continued, "Ok call me when you are free. Nothing urgent, it is about what we discussed the last time that we talked and about a new development." Alvaro ended the conversation.

Sarita asked, "What was that about?"

"Our contact at the Embassy wanted to know if this was a good time to get a report on what we had found. I haven't called him in the past two weeks either. I will call him back later."

There was a knock on the door and then Leon and Carmilla entered. "Hi everybody, they chimed in unison."

Carmilla said excitedly, "Let's go to the Restaurante Don Parrilla out Highway 25 toward Corozal. Parrilla is a nice open-air restaurant in the old Colombian style and the food is good and at reasonable price. The countryside there is also beautiful."

"That is a good idea. The restaurant is not far and the road is good," contributed Sarita. "The farmers and their families may be bringing things to market. Today is a good time to visit. Tomorrow everything will be very how do you say, busy; no more than busy?"

Leon suggested, "Do you mean more than busy as in hectic?"

"Yes, I think hectic means very busy in a confused way?" Sarita concluded, her voice unsure.

Nate looked at Leon and shrugged. "Sounds like fun, maybe we will get to see some of the famous Colombian cowboys."

"Here we call them vaquero or gaucho," Carmilla corrected. "In some ways it is like your old west. The gaucho's like to show-off their horses and riding skills. We can also get some fresh fruits for tomorrow."

The road to Corozal was well paved and had light traffic. The breeds of cattle grazing in the fields along the route were often different from those that I had seen in the States. Many of the cattle were whitish with a large hump on the back. Carmilla said that they were Brahman and particularly suited for the warm Colombian climate. We made good time getting to the restaurant.

"The Las Brujas Airport is just up the road," said Sarita. "A person can fly from there to Tolu or Cartagena very quickly, but there are not a lot of flights."

Carmilla, parked the Jeep and we entered the restaurant. As we entered the restaurant, I noticed that the building had a large thatched roof. I was about to comment on it when a hostess came forward and seated us at a table with a pastoral vista.

"I have seen several of these thatched roofs as we moved along the rivers and roads here in Colombia," I observed. "Do they work well?"

"Oh, yes they work very well but attract snakes and insects. So we have to keep a sharp eye that nothing poisonous tries to live there. The new tile roofs do not keep the heat out nearly as well, but last longer and are less trouble. I think that the thatched roof is much more beautiful than the tile." Carmilla stated.

We all ate more than we should have. The service was great and the food was even better. We had to stuff ourselves to clean our plates. We stuffed ourselves into the Jeep.

Carmilla said, "If you want to get good handmade hammock, we can turn left up there and go to Morroa. The weavers there make the best hammocks in Colombia. Morroa is also a nice country town. They even have a Cathedral and a statue of Simon Bolivar."

"Sure, I would like to visit Morroa; how about you Leon?"

"Sounds like a nice little town. Can we also go by the airport? I would like to see that."

Sarita thought for a minute. "Yes, the main road kind of circles around the town of Morra and the airport is on the East side from here."

I noticed a statue as we turned toward Morroa. "That statue does not look like Simon Bolivar. Who would it be?"

Carmilla said, "La devanadora."

"What is she famous for?" I asked.

"She is a symbol of the Colombian women and their history of weaving and hammock making. La devanadora means the spinner." Carmilla responded proudly.

We drove on a short distance to Morroa and slowly drove through the town. The town was busy preparing for the Saturday meetings of farmers and buyers. Many men rode along the streets on horseback.

We continued along Route 25 Morroa gradually looping back toward Corozal. The Las Brujas airport appeared to our right. An Embraer ERJ 170 small jet passenger plane was just landing as we approached. The airport could handle good sized aircraft on the long paved runway. I made a mental note. A quick connection to Tolu and Cartagena could be made.

"I notice that most of the buildings and a lot of the houses have grillwork over their windows and doors." Leon thought out loud.

"Yes," Sarita responded. "There are many thieves in this country. Most of the people are poor but honest. In the towns is where most of the bad people are found. Many of our police and military also take advantage when they can. There is also the FARC, they often also kill the people that they rob. Our government considers FARC to be a terrorist organization. They are a communist aligned, Marxist-Leninist revolutionary military force. FARC is very dangerous. They often kidnap for ransom and kill if the ransom is not quickly paid. I hope that you do not fall prey to them."

We continued along Highway 25 as it looped through Corozal and then back toward Sincelejo. We stopped at Los Pasteles to sample the wonderful fresh made fruit drinks and continued on. On the right we saw another monument. Sarita saw me looking at the statue of a mounted horseman. She explained, "That is a monument to the great horsemen of this country. Travel by horse is still a very much needed skill in this country. Roads do not go everywhere, but a horse can go most places, just more slowly."

"Oh, would you like to go riding?" Carmilla asked.

"Horseback is not my favorite form of riding." Leon responded quickly, giving Carmilla a quick wink. Carmilla looked away quickly, but she was smiling.

We stopped again at the Restaurante Don Parrilla and decided to have an early dinner. We would get something for a snack later. We then headed back to the safe house in Sincelejo. Darkness had already descended on our compound when Carmilla drove through the gate.

Sarita exclaimed, "There is someone in the house. I just saw a light flash through the window." Carmilla bumped the horn as Leon jumped out of the passenger seat.

Leon gave Carmilla a sharp look and asked, "What did you do that for?" I was quickly getting out of the back seat. Leon and I both had our forty-fives out.

Carmilla looked at us, "You guys have nothing in that house worth dying for or killing for. Give them a chance to run away." Leon gave her a look over his shoulder as he ran around the back of the house. I continued to watch the front.

The lights inside the house came on and Leon came out the front door. "It looks like they didn't have time to take anything. Did anyone come out past you?"

"Nope," I said. We went inside to see if all was well.

"You guys need to be careful. I told you that others had been asking questions about you. If you pass their test, they will probably leave us alone." Sarita said as she brushed past me and into the house.

We checked the house and nothing seemed to be missing. They did not even take our spare magazines for the forty-fives.

Sarita said, "I am going to get a shower before I fix a snack for us."

Carmilla said, "I am next, you guys can shower while we get the food ready." I got down a bottle of Jack Daniels old number seven and poured myself a stiff shot and diluted it with ginger ale.

Leon said, "Make me one to. I didn't think that I would like that mix, but it kinda gets its hooks into you."

The girls were in the bathroom. So I said in a hushed tone, "We probably should have expected to be checked-out especially after the sub disappeared. We are so far away from Rincon that I had not really given it much thought. Good thing that we did not have to shoot anyone."

Leon looked at me. "I wonder why Carmilla tooted the horn. Kind of suspicious. We might have caught the guy inside."

"Good thing that we do not have anything except some extra ammo here." I said. "We don't have anything much to report to the police either. I guess that I will let Alvaro know about Sarita's warning and the break-in."

"This B and E was kind of sophisticated. Either they had a key or picked the lock. Nothing was broken to get in." Leon observed with a wry grin. "Suppose it was Alvaro."

I looked up kind of surprised. "It would fit after what has happened this week. I hadn't thought of that. I had better give him a call to report the break-in." I walked outside and dialed Alvaro.

"¡Hola!" Alvaro spoke as he put the phone to his ear.

"Good evening to you as well." I said. "We had someone enter the house while we were away today. He ran away just as we entered the courtyard. We haven't found that anything was taken."

Alvaro thought for a minute. "Did you get a good look at him? If so, we can ask the police for some help."

"No such luck, I am afraid. He was out of there before Leon made it to the back of the house."

After a pause, "Maybe someone was just checking you out," Alvaro suggested.

"That is what Carmilla and Sarita thought." I said. "They said it was better to let a thief run away, than someone get shot, since we did not have much worth stealing in the house."

"I spoke to Ryan today and gave him the money. The news will go about the way that we talked about. I want you and Leon to fly to Costa Rica on Tuesday. You can take the girls if they want to go. You will fly out of Las Brujas Airport. Next week Adan and Juan can go. They will fly out of Cartagena. I will make the arrangements for all airline tickets. Let me know if your girls can go. I will ask Adan if they want to take any along. When I give you the tickets, we will talk. Have a good night," Alvaro said as he hung up the phone. He smiled to himself, a few million each and fourteen million for Uncle Sam to keep the war alive, he thought.

We sat around the room with our plates in our laps and drinks in our hands. The girls had made fajitas de polo for our evening snack. I asked casually, "Would you ladies like to go to Costa Rica with us on Monday?"

"We are going to Costa Rica on Monday," Leon asked?

"I just spoke with Alvaro at the Embassy and he thought that it might be a good time to slip away for a few days. We have been working too much the last two weeks anyway he said."

"Never been to Costa Rica, what is there to do there?" The girls were ready for this one. "Shopping, good food, nice beaches, gambling and generally just a good time can be had by all. I think that I can get the time off." chirped Sarita.

"Oh, yes!" exclaimed Carmilla, "They have beautiful beaches there. I am going also."

I called Alvaro back and reported that we needed four seats. Alvaro said that it will be an Embassy flight. We could carry whatever we needed, no need to go through a customs check in either direction. He would have a package waiting at the airport check-in desk for us before we boarded the plane. We would be on a return Embassy flight as well. The flight is just over an hour and we would return on Wednesday.

Sarita grabbed my hand and pulled me up, saying; "Come with me and collect your reward."

We headed toward the bedroom; leaving Leon and Carmilla to their own devices.

We arrived at the airport thirty minutes early. Alvaro was waiting. We introduced the girls and Alvaro led us out a side door to the aircraft. He said, "I will be flying with you to Bogota." He let Leon and the girls go on ahead, slowing me down.

"There are two suitcases already on the plane. The luggage tags are in your and Leon's names. They contain the cash, passports and international driving licenses in your new names. The Banco De Costa Rica at this address is expecting you today." Alvaro handed me a business card with a bankers name printed on it. "Just present this card when you go in. Be prepared to wait to see Eduardo. The account is your personal business and you will receive a credit card to help you access your funds. Call me if you have any difficulties. The return flight leaves at thirteen hundred hours on Wednesday. Stop in Bogota on your way back for the night. Here are your Costa Rican hotel reservations. Leave the girls there while you go to the bank. See you in Bogota." Alvaro boarded the plane with Nate and claimed his window seat over the wing.

Alvaro deplaned at Bogota. The flight resumed fifteen minutes later. Several new passengers had boarded in Bogota and the plane was a little over half full when it landed at San Jose International. The time was about three-thirty in the afternoon. Nate said to Sarita, "Go to this hotel and check us in. Leon and I have something to take care of, but we will catch up with you before dinner time. Here is some cash and my credit card. We have reservations and everything should be taken care of. We will call you for the room number when we get finished."

We took the suitcases with us to the bank. Eduardo made us wait until almost closing time before he called us. "I apologize for the long wait, it is usual in this business. Please step into my office. Do you want to come in together or separately?"

I looked at Nate, "Together," I asked?

"Might as well, that way Eduardo will only have to explain everything once."

" Acordó, de esta manera, por favor," Eduardo purred. "Passport and driver's license please." We each opened our luggage and took out the documents. Eduardo looked at the cash and asked, "How much is your deposit Mister Calero?" "One million US dollars," I said.

"Mine will be the same, "said Leon. "Please place your cash in these trays. I have a machine here that will make the counting easier."

The machine counted up to one million one hundred thousand US dollars for each of us. We each gave Eduardo one hundred thousand dollars as his commission. He created our accounts, setup the credit and debit cards. A machine next to his desk spit out the credit and debit cards.

"Please check the spelling of your names," Eduardo instructed. "We do not want any mistakes." The cards looked fine.

"When can we use these cards," I asked?

"Actually you could use them right now if you wish. Perhaps you need some local currency, we do have a good exchange rate today," Eduardo offered. Leon and I each got five hundred dollars in Colones. We netted about 251,000 Colones. Eduardo assured us that we would have difficulty spending that amount unless we decided to gamble at one of the Casinos.

"If you need more, the credit or debit card will work at the Casinos. Is there anything else that I can help you with, gentlemen?" We said goodbye and thank you, then headed the hotel.

Our reservations were at the Grano de Oro and a taxi was waiting just outside the bank.

I called Sarita on the way she said, "We have a beautiful room on the second floor, room 204. Leon and Carmilla are in Room 206. I knocked on Room 204, and Sarita opened the door.

"You are going to love this room, look at that bed." I looked over and saw a king size bed that looked very comfortable compared to what we had been sleeping on.

"That looks comfortable, have you tried it out yet?"

Sarita grabbed me and pulled me toward the bed. "I was waiting for you, we can try it together." Leon will be here any minute," I protested.

"Carmilla and I have already discussed this. Leon will not knock for at least another hour."

We ate in the hotel restaurant. The service and food were very good. We then headed toward the Hotel Presidente and its casino. We all played the slot machines and lost, except Sarita. She actually won about twenty-five thousand Colones. Carmilla suggested, "Tomorrow lets go to Limoncito Beach near Jaco; it is one of the closest and is supposed to be better than Jaco Beach."

Sarita was thoughtful. "Too bad we ended up in San Jose. The beaches on the Caribbean side are much more attractive, but they are far away."

"Limoncito is only about an hour away." Carmilla stated. "We could easily go in the morning and come back that night. We can ask the front desk folks about the best way to get there." We headed back to the hotel for some rest.

Carmilla asked the desk clerk, "What is the best way to get to the Limoncito beach?"

The young girl looked us over and said, "If all four of you are going, you could hire a car. The drive is about an hour and we have maps. You could also take a helicopter ride, about fifteen minutes. The car is the cheapest. The helicopter will cost about two hundred US dollars each way. Would you like for me to make a reservation for you Senorita?"

Carmilla looked back at Leon and me. "I think that the helo would be fun, what do you guys think?"

Sarita looked at me, "But it is very expensive," she cautioned.

"Nate and I can split the cost. I think that it would be fun too." Said Leon.

Carmilla looked at us, "I never flew before today. First an airplane and now a helicopter, my nerves are going to be… I don't know!"

"Flying is safer than driving, at least statistically." I offered. "Helicopters are extra fun, they fly low and you can see so much more.

"Ok, if you guys are sure, I will do it," replied Carmilla.

"Did you guys bring your swim suits," asked Carmilla?

"Yes" I replied, "Alvaro just put a change of clothes in the suitcases for us from stuff that we left in Bogota".

Carmilla and Sarita looked apprehensive. "Don't worry the pilot doesn't want to crash either." I said.

Carmilla smiled, "I hadn't thought of it that way. The helicopter looks clean too."

We flew over lightly populated areas with lush green vegetation. The city of Jaco appeared to our left and the helicopter landed us right on the beach. The pilot shut down the engine, then said. "I do not have any other flights at this time. I will fly you back later today unless I get a call. Does that fit your plans?"

"That is very thoughtful. Yes, that will work for us." I agreed.

Leon and I tried to ignore the beautiful women that graced the beach. They were young and curvy in their skimpy two piece swimwear. The sun was warm and it did not rain until just after noon.

The pilot came over. "The rain front is going to be with us well into the evening. Would you like to go back to San Jose now?" Carmilla and Sarita had a quick conversation.

Sarita then said, "Ok, but you and Leon have to take us shopping when we get back to San Jose." Leon nodded and then we all boarded for the ride back.

Carmilla asked the waitress where the best shopping could be found in San Jose. She suggested, "The main shopping area is bounded by avenidas 1 and 2, from about Calle 14 in the west to Calle 13 in the east. For several blocks west of the Plaza de la Cultura, Avenida Central is a pedestrian-only street mall where you'll find many stores with inexpensive clothes shops. Depending on the mood of the police that day, you might find a lot of street vendors as well. Take care though the quality from the street vendors can vary considerably from what is found in the stores. Any taxi can take you there."

Carmilla and Sarita settled for some t-shirts touting the beautiful scenery of Costa Rica and the beaches. We then headed to the hotel and airport.

I got off in Bogota and sent Leon and the girls ahead to Sincelejo. After their plane headed away from the airport, I called Alvaro.

"How did things go in San Jose," he asked?

"No problems that I could see. Everything went smoothly. We had a good time, but next time we need to try the Caribbean side." I replied. "I sent the others back to Sincelejo. Are you at the Embassy? I would like to know some additional info."

"Sure thing, come on over." Alvaro offered. "There are a couple of new things that might interest you."

I met Alvaro in the conference room. "Our sources say that the cartel players are wondering what happened to their sub. It should have arrived in Galveston yesterday morning. They haven't hit the panic button yet, but it will not be long. There is talk of six tons of smack and forty million in US dollars on that sub."

"Could have been; the amount of cocaine sounds about right for the volume of the sub. The cash was what I could see. I almost didn't get any of it. Remember, I had already activated the time pencil when I saw those two bundles of cash. I did not want to delay and search for more. I guess that no one saw or heard the drug sub go down."

"We have not heard anything from that area," replied Alvaro. "The cartel will likely not panic until tomorrow."

"You did not mention the finder's fee for Eduardo. At least, I assumed that was what that extra hundred grand was about. He was really helpful and got everything done in one stop."

"I thought that a bright guy like you would figure it out." Alvaro quipped. "Did both of you give him a hundred K?"

"Sure did; he looked very satisfied." I observed.

"After you take down the second drug sub, we are going to move your team north of Cartagena. Actually, I want to move the team up north before you take the sub down. About a week before they complete the sub, return the horses to Domingo Alvarez and tell him that you are moving up north. You cannot justify spending much more time in Sincelejo and Rincon. I already have safe houses and boat docks setup. I will tell you where when the time comes. We can pack the Zodiacs and weapons in the vehicles and move everything at once."

"Oh Hell, I knew it was too good to last." I moaned. Alvaro chuckled.

"There are plenty of girls in Cartagena and Santa Marta to keep you guys busy."

"Sarita is special, I will miss her; but I suppose that it is not a good idea to bring them so close to danger without them knowing it." I responded.

"Yeah," Alvaro agreed, "We do want to keep collateral damage to a minimum."

"I got a report from Adan. He says that work on the second sub is going very slowly. They left for Costa Rica this afternoon from Cartagena. They will come back on Sunday. I made about the same arrangements with Eduardo for them. They are staying at the Presidente in San Jose. They chose not to take anyone with them."

Slightly Off

Art McGillem

I chuckled, "I know that they will have a great time. Leon and I could hardly keep our eyes off those Costa Rican women. Wow, what figures and pretty faces. We had two Colombian beauties with us and it was still a strain not to slip in a peek now and then."

"Leon and I will run up to Rincon in the morning and stay at the boat dock until Adan and Juan return. We will keep an eye on things and take care of the horses. Anything else that we should know?"

"Can't think of anything off hand," replied Alvaro. "Oh," he continued: "What do you plan to do with your million?"

"If I survive this, I can donate it to a worthwhile charity." I shook hands with Alvaro. "Thank you for all of the help," I said and headed out the door.

I got back to Sincelejo in the early evening. Sarita and Carmilla had just about finished making dinner when I came through the door. "Something smells good here," I said.

Sarita smiled and said, "We made extra. I thought that you would make it back in time for dinner."

"I made it back for dinner, but we have to leave in the morning. The Embassy wants us to finish looking around Rincon and move north. We will still have this as our base, but we will not be here as often, I am sad to say."

"That is so not good," opined Carmilla. We all ate quietly.

When we were in bed, Sarita snuggled close and said, "Nate, please do not forget me. I have not cared about a man in a long time. I know that I want to be with you for a long time." I pulled her closer and kissed her upturned lips. They were so soft and yielding that I knew Sarita had fallen in love.

Slightly Off

Art McGillem

We got to the boat house in the late morning. Leon went to feed and water the horses. I went inside to see if Adan or Juan had left a note. I opened the arms cache and Adan had left a note saying that the work on the second sub had almost stopped. They said that they rode the horses rather than take the Zodiac each night to do the recon.

"Adan took good care of the horses. They had plenty of water and still had some hay to munch on." Leon reported. "Adan leave us a note?"

"Yes he did. Sub building seems to have slowed down. I guess they used the horses to check on the sub progress. That was probably easier than hauling the Zodiac around." I speculated. "We should check on the sub tonight. I am going to skip lunch and take a nap. See you later."

I woke at seven to the smell of fresh coffee and beans. Leon had a skillet full of beans, peppers and onions working on the stove. We left about ten in the evening. The moon and stars provided just enough light for a safe ride. We tied and hobbled the horses about a half mile from the sub and walked the rest of the way.

There was a lot of activity around the sub. We could hear the men talking speculatively about what could have happened to the other sub and crew. I could see the shaft and propeller under the sub, so obviously work was suddenly progressing. Leon and I pulled back and waited for the crew to leave. We could easily hear their conversation from our hidden position.

At about four in the morning, the crew packed up and their boats headed back toward the farm. Leon and I quietly approached and watched the sub for about thirty minutes. I signaled Leon to wait and slowly approached the sub. I climbed up the ladder and was just about to put my foot down into the hatch when I thought that I saw something move. I waited a few seconds and it moved again. That is when I noticed the heavy twine leading down into the hatchway.

I turned on my penlight with the red filter and could see the fer-de-lance perched on the ledge between the sail and sub hull. If I had put my foot on the ladder, I would be dead now. I had heard about this trick from the Vietnam era vets. The VC would take a piece of wire and push it through a deadly snakes body and then tie the snake in a place where someone unaware would be bitten if they entered. The wire and limited movement gave the snake a bad attitude, making it even more dangerous than usual. I gingerly pulled on the string, gently lifting the snake from the sail and let it hang over the side. I signaled Leon to stay put and carefully entered the sub.

The fuel tank was in and everything was connected to the engine. The steering had also been connected. The electronics had yet to be installed, so the sub was not going anywhere yet. I took pictures of the layout. Then I installed the GPS Transponder in the same cavity that was in the other sub. I put the Fer-de-lance back on the shelf and took his picture also. Leon and I headed back to the horses. I told Leon what I had found and explained about the snake used as a guard. We mounted up and headed toward the boat house.

"Leon I think that we should begin a watch on the road to the farm."

"You may be right, but there are only two of us right now," replied Leon. "They did not have any electronics in yet, so I think they will want to test everything before sailing off into the deep. Then perhaps another night to load the smack."

"Two heads are often better than one." I said. "I am going to put Alvaro on alert and then we take the horses back to Mr. Alvarez. If you will saddle the horses, I will call Alvaro; then come help you."

"Ok, working on it," replied Leon.

Alvaro picked up on the first ring. "Nate here, if they put the electronics in the sub tonight, they may load the cocaine tomorrow. We could use your help for the second Zodiac. How do you want to play it?"

Alvaro thought for a minute, "Sounds like they are ready to move. I will come to Sincelejo this evening and stay at the other safe house. I can be in Rincon quickly if you need help."

"Works for me," I replied. "Leon and I are going to return the horses today. We will use the Zodiac to check things out tonight and give you a call in the morning." I hung-up and went to help Leon.

We had a late dinner and moved the Zodiac down to the water. Then we moved the motor and hooked it up to the Zodiac and controls. Then we loaded the weapons and slowly moved down the coast toward the stream cut between the Caribbean and the lagoon behind the river where the sub was being built. We hid the Zodiac in the mangroves and slipped along the edge of the lagoon until we came to the sub. We stayed all night, but nobody came to the sub.

In the morning, I called Alvaro to relay the news. Alvaro asked, "Did you already return the horses?"

"Yes, but Mr. Alvarez was not anxious to get them back. That gelding that Adan was training immediately threw Mr. Alvarez when he mounted. You must have paid him well. All Alvarez said was, "That horse never did like me," as he walked off. "Mr. Alvarez did ask why we were returning the horses. I just said that we were moving up north along the coast like we discussed. He did not ask any specific questions."

"I am already in Sincelejo, but I do not want to come where you are until I am needed. Based on the incident with the snake, they may be on high alert for any strangers in the area. I am driving a beat up greenish Land Rover this time, so do not panic if you see it coming your way. I borrowed it from a friend. There is news from the States. The Galveston drug network is running short of cocaine. I think that they may try to move that sub soon."

I interjected, "We will let you know if anything happens on our end. We cannot move that armored Zodiac without help, so expect our call soon. We will go tonight to monitor the process and call you in the morning."

Alvaro just said, "Ok." Then the line went dead.

Leon and I pulled into the lagoon just after midnight and hid the Zodiac. We closed in on the location of the sub and could hear voices. We monitored as the workers loaded the electronics that would help them guide the sub to its destination. At about four in the morning work ceased and the workers went off in their boats. Leon went forward to check the sub. He returned about an hour later.

"What took you so long?" I asked.

Leon answered, "Pictures and that damn snake. He didn't complain when I took him out of his roost, but it was a struggle getting him back in. That is one strong snake. Anyway, they installed a Sat phone in this baby. Good thing that you installed the GPS Transponder the last time that we were here. They mounted the Sat phone bracket just below the patch. If we had waited to install it, we would have had to find another place. The sub is ready to launch and there are extra fuel drums in the storage area near the engine."

We had just moved away from the sub toward the lagoon. A boat was coming up the lagoon toward us. It was still quite dark, but the sky was getting lighter. We could hear the two men in the boat talking. They would be guarding the sub while the cocaine arrived today. We could not hope to stay hidden where the Zodiac was. We had to get out of there quickly. We had just cleared the stream and were quietly moving back toward the Boat Dock when we heard another boat heading toward us. I cut power to the engine and we began drifting with the current parallel to the shoreline. The other boat passes within a two hundred meters of us, but we were not seen.

I called Alvaro about noon. "Alvaro old buddy, you need to be here before dark. I think that they are moving the cocaine in today or tonight. They sent some folks to watch the sub this morning and they were talking about the cocaine arriving today. We will agree on a plan after you get here."

Alvaro agreed, "See you guys about dusk. That way I will not have to use the headlights." Then he was gone.

Leon and I checked the weapons that we planned to use that night and placed them in the respective Zodiacs. Alvaro would be in the second Zodiac alone until the prisoners were transferred, then Leon would back him up.

Leon suggested that we not enter the lagoon. "Remember that white sandy beach just before we could see the lagoon. The mangroves at the western end come right down into the water. We could easily hide the Zodiacs in there and hoof it to the sub. Alvaro could stay with the Zodiacs if he wanted; less noise and less danger if he stays behind. I wonder when he was on his last sneaky-pete op."

I chuckled, "Probably has been a while, he has that desk-bound look.

"You and I will be in the armored Zodiac. You go ahead with the grenade launcher. Use the HE round right away on the thick part of the sub just below the sail. Maybe the round will explode this time. We will have Alvaro take the other Zodiac and follow us. After the sub is secure, I want you in the Zodiac with Alvaro and the prisoners. Then you can take them to the sub; how does all of that sound."

"Works for me," Leon confirmed.

"I think that we should put our sub on alert now. I picked-up the Sat phone and called the Ventura watch officer and explained that we will be operating in about the same area as last time and expected traffic tonight. Can you be in the area by about ten this evening?"

The Watch Officer replied, "We are already in the area. We had a call earlier today stating that our services would likely be needed tonight; any other traffic?"

I replied, "Negative, out here."

"Well we are set to play tonight. I think since the drug sub has their Sat phone mounted right next to the GPS transponder, I will wait to activate it until they sail. That way if there is interference from the transponder maybe they will sail on. We need to get some sleep so I will see you at dinner time."

Drug Submarine 2 Captured

Chapter 17

Alvaro arrived just before dusk. "What's for dinner," he asked?

"You are in luck, there are two left in this case; Chili with Beans or Pork Rib. Take your pick and I will warm it up."

Alvaro thought for a minute. "The pork rib is good, but I do not care for the clam chowder, so I will go with the Chili and Beans. Thank you. What is the plan for tonight?"

I pulled the map over to where we could all see. "We will take both Zodiacs, move down the coast to just past this beach and pull them up into the mangroves. Leon and I will then go and check on the sub. You can stay with the Zodiacs as our rear security. Just break squelch twice if you see trouble brewing. We will wait until either four in the morning or until the sub sails. Shortly after the sub sails, I will activate the GPS Transponder. We will take the sub about three miles from shore."

"Have you notified the Ventura of your plans?" Alvaro asked.

"Yes, they are already standing offshore waiting for our signal," I assured Alvaro. "I think that it is dark enough to move the Zodiacs down to the shore. Alvaro, I hope that you brought your muscles! That armored Zodiac is really heavy." "I may have a fix for that," Leon volunteered.

"What would that be?" I asked.

"When we were storing those bundles at the back of the Safe House boat storage; I found an axel with two wheels mounted. We can probably lash it to the rear of the Zodiac to take the weight of the motor and pull it to the water. I would have tried it already, but I could not lift the rear of the Zodiac by myself." We all went to see if that would work.

Alvaro and I lifted the rear of the Zodiac and Leon placed the axel under the transom. We used rope to lash the axel in place and easily pulled the armored Zodiac to the water. At about ten o'clock, we loaded up and motored down the coast.

I passed-up the first opportunity to hide our Zodiac and motioned for Alvaro to take it. Leon and I pulled our Zodiac well into the mangroves and secured the painter rope. I spoke into the tactical mike and told Alvaro that we were going to check on the sub. Alvaro gave one click to indicate message received.

We moved to where the sub should have been, but it was gone! We hurried back to the Zodiac and activated the GPS transponder. The signal on the tracker showed it to be about three miles at sea.

I spoke into the Tactical mike, "Alvaro, the drug sub is gone! The tracker shows that it is already out at sea. Follow us, but stay back until the sub has stopped and is secure. Your Zodiac does not have any armor."

I called the Ventura and the Watch Officer answered. "The drug sub has already sailed. It is already about four miles due west of our location. I gave our current coordinates. We can easily track them, but it will likely take us nearly thirty minutes to catch up with them. I will call you again before the interdiction point."

The Watch Officer replied, "Roger that, Out here."

In twenty minutes we had closed to within five hundred meters of the sub and slowed to a speed where we were just catching them and the motor sound likely could not be heard. We could see the sail above the water. I called the Ventura.

"We are about to interdict the drug sub," I said.

"Yes," said the Watch Officer; "We have been watching you both for the last twenty minutes through the periscope. Call us when you want us to do the pick-up. Ventura Out."

Leon moved to the front of the Zodiac with the grenade launcher. I maneuvered the Zodiac ever closer to the Sail. Leon was about to fire when a head and shoulders popped out of the sail and went back down. Leon fired the grenade. A perfect hit and a second later there was an explosion inside the sub. We quickly ran up against the sail and Leon tied us to the ladder running up the sail. He took out his .45 and started up the ladder when an AK74 was shoved out and sprayed the air around the sub. Leon fired a zig-zag pattern into the sail and the weapon did not reappear. "Manos arriba y salir ahora (hands up and come out now)," Leon shouted.

Slowly a pair of hands appeared above the sail hatch and the frightened men came out one at a time and stood dejectedly on the deck. Alvaro pulled his Zodiac up against the sub and told the prisoners to get in the back. Leon disappeared down the sail and pretty soon bales of money began coming out of the sub. I pulled them into our Zodiac. There were eight bales this time.

"I am going back down to set the explosive charge. I could not see any other bales of cash. I am going to bring their Sat phone with me when I come out," said Leon.

"Good idea and ride with Alvaro. We do not want any of these guys getting ideas when our sub surfaces," I said.

There was excited talk among the prisoners as the Ventura surfaced. The Marines on the Ventura took charge of the prisoners and put them in restraints. I waited weapon ready until the Marines had all of the prisoners secured. Leon and Alvaro pulled the Zodiac away from the Ventura as the deck slid below the surface.

We were about a half mile away from the drug sub when the explosive charge detonated. Like before, there was a muffled 'krummp' sound then the loud bang and short lived fireball. None of this could be seen from the shore, I was fairly sure. It was still early though and many people would still be up and about. I hoped that our luck would continue to hold up. We continued on toward home base.

We arrived back at the boat dock. Alvaro looked at us smiling. "I think that we should do another fifty-fifty. There must be a hundred sixty million there, if the same amounts are in each bail as last time."

I said, "I can't even imagine how much money that really is! If we divide the $80 mil six ways, that is a little over $13 mil each."

"Do not worry, Eduardo will help us take care of the money problem. Do not short him on his ten percent though." Alvaro assured us. Maybe Ryan and I can finally afford to get out of this business, he thought.

"When the rest of your team arrives tomorrow, pack everything up and move to this address in Sabanalarga. The house is on a corner lot and fronts onto Calle 37. I will take the $80 mil plus the cut of the rest for Ryan and I. We should probably count our bundles to see if each is $20 mil." We spent the rest of the night counting the four bundles that we were keeping and dividing it into smaller bundles. Each bundle had contained the $20 million as expected. Each of us would have close to $13 million from this haul or about $12 million after Eduardo got his cut.

Slightly Off

Art McGillem

"A week from Wednesday, there is another Embassy flight leaving from Cartagena. I will have seats for you. Do not plan to take any guests on this flight. I am going back to Sincelejo and will sleep there. Let me know when you get to SH 1 in Sabanalarga. I have a large ranch on the waterway with a three bay boat house to keep the Zodiacs. We will unload the Zodiacs at the ranch. When you pack the van; put the weapons on the floor, the armor on top, then the Zodiac and motor. You will not find anyone ambitious enough to unload everything to see what is on the bottom. I will see you at the Boat Dock in Santa Catalina Bolivar and fill you in on anything that Ryan comes up with."

Alvaro departed and Leon and I went in to get some much needed sleep.

When we woke up later in the afternoon, we buried the money with the other and covered the fresh dirt with the straw and hay that we had pulled back.

Leon said, "What say we head back to Sincelejo and see the girls?"

"Not a good idea," I said. "We have put them in enough danger already. Remember, people were already asking questions of them about us. If we go back after another drug sub has disappeared, no telling what could happen. We should just pack up and move as planned. I didn't realize that you liked Carmilla that much."

"She is ok," Leon said. "I wasn't too sure about her at first. I thought that she was too easy and maybe she is, a little; but she has a good heart and is a lot of fun. Not to mention how great she looks wearing just a smile."

"Yes, I remember how great she looked in that bathing suit. What a great figure!" I said.

"What are you complaining about? Sarita has a really great figure, beautiful face and a great disposition. Carmilla just has a little more of a full figure," Leon said with a gleam in his eyes. "I guess it depends if you prefer Shakira to Sofia Vergara figures," Leon continued.

"They both look great." I agreed.

Just after noon, Adan and Juan pulled in. "Whew, what a trip. We had a great time." Adan said as Juan nodded agreement. "Everything went ok with Eduardo. We are fully documented. What have you guys been up to?"

"Not much," Leon snickered. "We just took down the second sub destroyed a ton of smack and confiscated a boat load of cash."

"How did you manage that?" Adan asked.

"We asked Alvaro to help. We destroyed another billion dollar shipment of cocaine and collected a hundred sixty million in cash. I knew that there was a lot of money in drugs, but I cannot believe what I am seeing," I said.

"What are we doing with the cash this time," Juan asked.

I answered, "We are giving Uncle Sam eighty million and we are dividing the other eighty million six ways. We are all officially or rather unofficially richer than Croesus. We are scheduled to go to San Jose in about nine days on an Embassy flight. I am going to ask Alvaro to give us a week off. We can move much of our funds electronically to new accounts in Costa Rica. That will remove them from control by Eduardo and perhaps Alvaro and Ryan."

"By the end of next week we should each have twenty-five million dollars in the bank," I calculated. How close are you guys to retirement?"

"About a year," Adan and Juan responded together. Ok, I think that if everything goes well in Costa Rica we should try to complete this project or at least stick it out until retirement. Leon and I can resign our commissions at any time. We just have to play it cool until then." Everyone got quiet for a few minutes.

"You guys retiring will be the key. When you put in your retirement papers we will say that we want out also. The Team will be breaking up and if we are all still alive, we can just say that we think that it has also become too dangerous."

Adan said, "Actually I can put my retirement papers in nine months. If I have leave saved up, I may be able to leave about the same time." Juan said, "Same for me, but it is ten months."

"Sounds like a plan to me." I speculated. "We will tell whomever is in charge at the time when Adan requests retirement that we want to end our participation in this project. We can say, but hopefully it will not be true, that we are worried that our luck is running out. After all, a year in indian country is a long time.

Check for Strangers

Chapter 18

"TJ come here please." Carlos called his son. TJ walked from the veranda into the house and found his father looking angry and nervous.

"What has happened Sir?" TJ asked.

"Camilo did not heed your warning, maybe. The sub that left his farm has disappeared. It did not arrive in Galveston when expected and has been missing for three days. I fear that it is lost. Go and see Camilo. Find out what he knows. Then check for any strangers in the area."

"Escobar is going to blame us if the sub has disappeared. You know what he can be like when he gets mad," TJ cautioned.

"We did not do anything wrong, so he should not blame us." Carlos hoped that Escobar would blame others. Escobar had made lots of people disappear when he decided that they had cheated him or that they made a mistake that limited their usefulness.

"Go see Camilo again and make sure that he has good security on that second sub. We cannot afford to lose two in a row."

Diego drove and TJ was thinking about security at the farm. The dogs had come out to greet them barking and growling well before they got near the farm house. As they approached the farm house today, the dogs came out in the same way. He thought that security was pretty good at the farm.

Camilo was busy loading supplies into a boat as Diego wheeled the Land Rover into the yard. The dogs were jumping up to look into the SUV and did not look particularly friendly. Camilo paused in loading the boat and walked over quieting the dogs as he came.

"Hola Mr. TJ," Camilo greeted them. "What brings you to my poor farm?"

"The sub that sailed a few days ago has not reached the destination. We were wondering if you have heard anything from members of the crew or anything about the sub having an accident."

"No Senor TJ, I have heard nothing. They did not call us to report on their schedule, but I just thought that probably they had radio trouble. I did not call you, because there was nothing that we could do to contact them if they did not answer the radio or SAT phone. So they never arrived where they were going," mused Camilo aloud as he scratched one of the dogs behind the ear.

TJ swung a right into the point of Camilo's jaw and he went down and out. When Camilo woke up, he was sitting in a chair on the veranda with Diego at his shoulder and TJ looking balefully into his eyes. "If any sub misses even one scheduled call, I want to hear about it immediately." TJ's voice was low and deadly. "If you fail us again I will have your family killed before your very eyes. Have there been any strangers in the area lately?"

"Yes Senor TJ, there are two hydro engineers surveying the coastline and rivers to find sites for hydroelectric generating stations. They have a place on the coast just south of Rincon. I know this because my friend Domingo Alvarez rented them some horses to ride."

"I know Domingo also," mused TJ. "I think that I will visit him and see what he knows."

Diego and TJ got back into the Land Rover and drove to the Alvarez ranch. Domingo saw the Land Rover coming up the road and came out onto the veranda to greet them.

"¡Hola Senor TJ." Domingo greeted them. "What brings you to my humble ranch today? The coca crop is not ready to harvest yet, so it must be something else. You looking for a good horse, maybe?"

TJ smiled at his old friend. "No Domingo, we are wondering about the two strangers that rented horses from you."

"Actually there are four of them. They are hydro engineers employed by the US Embassy in Bogota to survey our rivers and streams. They want to help Colombia generate more electricity at a lower cost. They seemed to be nice fellows. One of them even tamed Ciclon. He will even let me ride him now."

"Were they doing anything suspicious that you noticed?" TJ asked.

"No, but they have moved up North now. I picked up the horses yesterday and received my payment. They left just after I did." replied Domingo.

TJ persisted, "Do you know where they went?"

"One of them asked my man what Sabanalarga was like, so perhaps they went there. They are probably going to study Laguna Guajaro and the rivers that flow into it. I do not really know. They talked quite a bit about their surveys and the rivers and streams depths and flow rates. Why do you ask?"

TJ picked right up, "They are strangers and we just wondered about them. From what you say, they do not seem like much to be concerned about. Cheaper electricity will be good for all of us." TJ motioned to Diego that it was time to be on their way and bid good day to Domingo.

Diego looked at TJ and said, "Now there are four of them. I wonder if they are really hydro engineers." This was more a statement than a question and TJ agreed saying, "I want to discuss it with my Father before we go to Sabanalarga. Head back to the house."

Safe House at Sabanalarga

Chapter 19

The Van and the Suburban were loaded. It was time to leave Rincon for Sabanalarga. The distance was about two hundred kilometers and should take us about four hours. We left early the next morning. The ride to Sabanalarga was uneventful and the roads were well paved and maintained. The police checkpoints just looked at our identification and passed us through without even asking us to open the cargo areas. We were all noticing the same thing. There were a lot more rivers, streams and lakes near the highway as we proceeded north. The coastal area around Sabanalarga held a lot of potential places for drug submarines to be built and launched. We would have good hunting in this area.

We arrived at Safe House 1 Sabanalarga during early afternoon. A high fence surrounded the compound. The gate was large enough for both vehicles to enter without difficulty. We turned the vehicles around so that the cargo doors faced the house and backed them close to the house. Hopefully curious folks would lose interest.

The house was well stocked with food and other essentials. We actually had a working television in this place.

Adan was checking the kitchen. "We are back on the MRE's until we get to the market or find some chicas to care for us."

Juan laughed. "I guess that will have to wait until we unload the vehicles. Not much room for anything else in them right now."

"I will call Alvaro and let him know that we have arrived," I said.

Alvaro picked up right away and was glad that the ride was uneventful. He then gave me the coordinates for the Boat House in Santa Catalina Bolivar. "I will fly up there first thing in the morning and meet you at the farm," he said.

"I have the location for the Boat House. We can go in the morning and get setup. Alvaro will meet us there," I said.

"Hold dinner," Juan said. "I think that I saw a restaurant just down the road as we turned-in. I am going to walk down and check it out."

"Hold on," said Adan. "I will go with you."

About two hours later they returned with food and local beers. The restaurant also had a cantina and the guys were feeling no pain as they laid the food before us.

We drove west along Highway 90 until it intersected with I-90, turned right and headed north. The total distance was about 60 kilometers, but took an hour and forty-five minutes. As we neared Santa Catalina Bolivar, Lake Totumo appeared on the right and we could see the blue of the Caribbean on the left. At least the roads surfaces were paved and in good condition, but looked like they could easily flood in a heavy rain.

Alvaro was already at the ranch when we got there. "How was the drive?" he questioned.

"The drive was easy and the roads well paved, but took more time than I would have thought to go only sixty kilometers," I responded. The ranch looks like a good place. No one is close enough to easily spy on us without being seen."

"Keep the gate locked whenever you leave," Alvaro instructed. "There are plenty of thieves in this area. We do not want to look like easy pickings. Do not hesitate to shoot at trespassers, but it is better if you do not hit them." Alvaro said with a wink.

"Ok, we will accept that as a word to the wise," I agreed.

"We might as well unload the Zodiacs and get them inflated before it gets really hot." I said. We got the Zodiacs inflated, motors mounted and moored in the boat house. Alvaro had two large fuel drums already installed in the boat house and both were full. We topped-off the tanks in the Zodiacs and were now ready to begin our search.

We had finished lunch and were sitting around the table. Alvaro cleared his throat and said, "I want you guys to just motor around in the Zodiac for the next few days. Let folks get used to seeing you. You did a good job keeping a low profile in Sincelejo and Rincon. They will probably get worried about that sub next week when it does not show up at its destination. We haven't heard anything yet about it except that they moved up the scheduled departure and delivery time for that sub. They also said that they had to send more cash this time to cover what was missing from the last sub. That means that you guys missed about twenty million dollars somewhere."

"We actually knew to look for bundles of cash this time," I said. "Finding cash was an unexpected event the first time. If I had not been so intent on blowing that sub, perhaps I would have found the rest of that cash. The time pencils are pretty accurate, but I am always paranoid to get out of the area as soon as I light one up."

"Now that you guys are wealthy, what do you plan on doing," Alvaro asked?

"Adan and Juan will put in for their twenty year retirement in about nine months. Leon and I will resign our commissions when they do that. That is assuming that we are still alive by then or have not been reassigned." I said. Leon and the others nodded agreement.

"Good, I was worried that you would want to take the cash and run," commented Alvaro. "Staying around until something normal changes the picture is a good cover. Ryan is due for rotation in about eight months. He has another year before he is eligible to retire. I can retire now, but my tour is not up for another four months. I guess that we will all do the normal thing."

Adan pitched in, "I am going to live the quiet life in San Antonio, Texas. Get myself a nice apartment a girl and kick-back, nothing pretentious to arouse suspicion."

"I am going to get a cottage out on Hatteras Island and run a bed and breakfast. I noticed a lot of single women spending time on the Outer Banks when I was stationed at Fort Bragg. I always thought that I would like to do that," said Juan.

"I always wanted to live in Montana," Leon confessed. "I like the changing climate, fishing, hunting and skiing. Missoula may be the place for me."

"I have something else in mind. When we decide to wrap-up this op, I will tell you about it. You will be welcome to join me if you think that it is worthwhile. I will probably end up in Virginia someplace at least temporarily. Maybe you or Ryan can show me the intel that you get on Senator Tweedle and his contacts having to do with your recent inquiry."

Alvaro gave me a skeptical look. "Senators are big game. Ryan probably has his dogs on the trail already. That book may be closed before long anyway."

"I would still like to know how the opera plays-out," I said.

Alvaro replied, "I'll mention it to Ryan and let you know."

"Back to earth now," I suggested. "Just to clarify, you want us to cruise during daylight hours in an innocuous manner just checking depths and flow rates?"

"Yeah, I want to make sure that you guys are not suspects that end up on the Cartel hit list. We need to make sure that any suspicions about you cool before we interdict another sub. I suggest that you stay away from permanent women because this will probably be your base of operations for the next year. We may move from the ranch, but the base in Sabanalarga will remain. I think that along this section of the coast, you will find plenty of chica's to keep you entertained. Anywhere along the shoreline of Laguna Totumo could be a sub building site. You can look for rivers flowing into the Totumo that may contain sites suitable for hydro power. No night surveillance until Ryan and I give the ok."

"Ok, you are the boss," I said. Alvaro waved goodbye and headed out to his rented truck.

"What say we go swimming? We have a lot of beach right in front of us." I suggested. We grabbed our suits and towels. The area in front of our beach was busy with boats of all sizes. Many of the boats were pleasure craft with girls sunning themselves. A nice twenty foot speedster flashed by, went a little further and then made a u-turn. We could hear the girls giggling and laughing as the boat approached. One called out, "Hey compañeros tiene alguna cerveza (Hey guys you have any beer)?"

"No, pero se puede conseguir un poco de rapidez (No but we can get some quickly)," Leon said brightly.

The taller slender brunette said, "Oh, you are Americano, No?"

"Yes, but our beer is Colombian," Juan responded. We were all thinking of the case of Budweiser Select that we had just put in the refrigerator.

"Bring some beer and come ride with us." The brunette said. Leon and Juan went to get the beer.

"My name is Laura," said the brunette. "Here is Carolina." Carolina was a petite brunette with big eyes and great legs. "Here is Natalia and Lorena," she continued.

"Natalia and Lorena look like twins," I said. They were both tall with average faces but with very fetching figures.

"Yes, they are identical twins," confirmed Laura. Leon and Juan returned with the beer.

"What have we missed," asked Leon? Laura went through the names again. Leon pushed the boat off and climbed aboard.

"MMMmm" said Laura, "This is not Colombian beer." "What brings you guys to Santa Catalina Bolivar?"

"Had we known, I would have had to say the beautiful Colombian women; alas, it is our work. We are hydrologic engineers surveying the waterways of Colombia to find new sites for hydroelectric power generating plants," I said.

"That does not sound very exciting," said Natalia.

"Actually it is kind of fun. We work for the American Embassy and they pretty much leave us alone as long as we send in regular reports. We spend most of the day riding in our Zodiac. If we are lucky, perhaps we have some ladies for company. The work is not hard and it is nice to be outside most of the time."

"What do you do when the weather is bad," asked Lorena?

Adan replied, "We find some good company and stay cozy."

"Do you ladies live here in Santa Catalina Bolivar?" Adan continued.

Laura answered, "The twins do. Carolina and I come from Sabanalarga, east of here."

"Oh, that is interesting," I said. "We also have a house in Sabanalarga. We just moved in yesterday. Leon and I will spend quite a bit of time there preparing the reports. Adan and Juan will probably be here most of the time."

We rode around, swam and drank beer, A natural pairing seemed to take place; Leon with Carolina, me with Laura, Adan with Natalia and Juan with Lorena. The arrangement could not have worked out better if we had planned it.

Laura laughed, "Carolina, you and I will have something interesting to do for a while." She looked at Leon and I. "There is nothing much to do in Sabanalarga. They have soccer and bullfights. There are a couple of good restaurants and you can usually find some music." Laura looked deeply into my eyes for a second; then continued. "I hope that we will have many memorable moments to share."

"Yes, I hope that is so." I replied.

"How do you guys stay in such good shape riding around in a boat all day," Lorena asked.

"I think that it has to do with two things," said Leon. "The number of times that we have to haul the anchor up each day and the amount of time that we take to swim keep us in shape. We also take a run each morning. All of the medical people say that exercise is the key to a healthy and long life."

"Nate how far do you run each morning," Laura asked?

"I run twenty minutes out, then twenty minutes back. That should be about four miles."

Laura looked at me speculatively, "Does that leave you any energy for late night activities?"

"I believe that it gives me extra energy for all activities." I smiled when I said that looking into her dark brown orbs. I got a smile in return.

Juan said, "Nate is our fastest runner. He does five and a half minute miles forever. He calls a one mile run a sprint and will be just over four minutes at the finish. You have a real jock on your hands Laura."

"Have you guys worked together long," asked Laura? "You seem to know each other very well."

"I guess that it has been about four months now," I said. "Two months in the States before we came here and then we were in Sincelejo for about two months. We did not find any useful new sites there, sad to say."

"There seem to be a lot of rivers between Cartagena and here though, maybe we will get lucky," Leon speculated. "We will also be looking North and East of here."

"Are you and Leon going back to Sabanalarga tonight," Laura asked?

"We had talked about it, but had not decided. Do you have something in mind?"

"Carolina and I could meet you and Leon at the Tono Parrilla Restaurante on Calle 14 for dinner if you are interested."

I looked at Leon and got a nod. "Sure, that would be great."

"Ok, my Dad will already be worried about us being out so long. We have to go back home. We will see you about eight." Laura said as the bow touched the beach in front of the ranch.

"The twins want to get off with you guys, keep them safe," Laura cautioned. We pushed the boat off and watched Laura and Carolina motor away.

Adan and Juan took charge of the twins while Leon and I got our stuff together and got in the van.

Tono Parrilla proved to be an open air restaurant with a good menu and very good food. We were early and told the server that we were expecting friends, Laura and Carolina. He assured us that he would personally insure that they found us when they arrived.

We sat at a table and ordered some fruit punch. They really put the punch in the punch. When Laura saw what we were drinking she asked, "How many of those have you had?" as she and Carolina sat down.

"We just started sipping on this one," Leon said. "They sure make them strong here."

"The alcohol that they put in that punch is about two hundred proof," said Carolina.

We ordered and switched to beer. Laura suggested we try the BBC Chapinero Porter; which turned-out to be very good. We ate dinner and were on our second beer when I asked Laura,

"Do you work here in Sabanalarga?"

"Yes, I am an accountant in the Atlantico Department Tax Office. Carolina and I work together, but in different sections. Why do you ask?"

"Just trying to get to know you better and make conversation."

Slightly Off

Art McGillem

"Ok, I am 30 years old, grew up in Sabanalarga, attended college in Bogota, and have a Masters Degree in Accounting and Administration. I was married but my husband was killed two years ago by the FARC. I do not have any children. My Mother and Father live in Santa Catalina Bolivar. Is there anything else that you would like to know?"

"Yes, do you always have that sparkle in your eyes?" I asked.

Laura laughed, "In truth the sparkle must have just returned, it has been missing for a long time." Carolina was nodding slowly and smiling; with her gaze fixed on Laura. Midnight was approaching when we finished eating and listening to the music.

Laura asked, "Are you guys going to show us your place?"

"Absolutely, follow us. Our house is on the corner of Calle 37 and Highway 90, just in case traffic separates us. You can't hardly miss our ugly van, but the compound has a high fence around it so the van would not be visible from the road." We got in the van and the girls followed us.

Laura looked around, "Quite Spartan even for a bachelor pad."

"Yes, we haven't had time to make it livable yet. The sofa and beds are comfortable though."

Laura took my hand and said, "Lead the way." I marveled at my good luck. Sarita and Laura were just wonderful in the bedroom. There was an edge to Laura, though. She was sort of keeping her distance emotionally. She proved to be a passionate and inventive lover.

In the morning, the girls walked across the street to the restaurant and returned with breakfast about forty-five minutes later.

Before they returned Leon came out. "Carolina is really different from Carmilla. Carolina's figure is not as voluptuous as Carmilla, but she really holds my attention. I hope that we get to stay here for a long time." Just then, the girls returned and began putting breakfast on the table.

The girls went to work after breakfast. Leon and I took the van and learned the layout of the roads in Sabanalarga. We exchanged phone calls with the girls during the remainder of the week and met for dinner on Wednesday. Laura called on Friday to say that she and Carolina were going to her Father's place in Santa Carolina Bolivar. She said that she would call us on Saturday and that we could go out on the boat for a picnic if we were interested.

I called Adan to see what plans they had. The farm house did have five bedrooms, but I did not want to interfere with their plans. Adan answered; "Sure, come on. The twins will be here on Saturday, but they said that probably Laura and Carolina would be here also."

On Friday, we had dinner and a couple of beers at the Cantina across the street; then we drove to Santa Catalina Bolivar. We arrived to find that the twins were already entertaining Adan and Juan. After saying hello, Leon and I walked down to the boat dock. The air was calm and the mosquitos were buzzing around like helicopters. We decided to go back and hit the sack.

The girls had stocked our larder and were busily preparing breakfast when Leon and I awoke to the sound of women chattering and the clatter of dishes. A pot of fresh Colombian coffee was waiting.

We had just finished breakfast when Laura and Carolina arrived. They had tied their boat up at the boat dock and walked up to the ranch house. They were already in their swim suits and looking very fetching. The twins quickly disappeared into their bedrooms.

Laura said, "Are you guys ready for a picnic?"

"Where are we going?" I asked.

"We will take the boat and go across the channel to that pointe of land just across from this ranch. There is a nice beach on the Caribbean side and we can put up a cabana and have a fun day. We have everything on the boat already. You may want to bring some beer. We can leave whenever you are ready."

Leon and I got up and headed for the bedrooms to change. Laura followed me in and closed the door. She pulled me close. "I have missed you Nate," she whispered and wet her lips. I bent slightly to kiss her as her arms went around my neck and her tongue came into my mouth." After a little, she relaxed away from me. "Oh that was wonderful she breathed." Then she turned and walked to the door. "See you at the boat after you change."

Obviously, it was going to be a great weekend. We got to the beach a little later and Laura and Caroline put the cabanas over the side. "You men set these up." I had seen these along the beach when we were in Tolu. The cabana was basically a very light duty tent. Aluminum poles stuck into the sand with a canvas top and side flaps that could be rolled up for cooling or lowered for privacy. We sat around talking and drinking beer. Laura started it, she tapped me on the shoulder and crooked her finger, stood and walked toward our cabana. I dutifully followed her.

"We should lower the flaps," she said. As I helped lower the flaps, I noticed that everyone else was doing the same thing. Laura pulled me down on top of her. "I have been waiting for this moment all week," she breathed as she undid her top. She wasn't kidding, her nipples were already erect. I started kissing her and after a little, she began pushing my head ever lower. Eventually her body shuddered and a small moan escaped her lips. "Come up here, it is time for me to tease you a little, but do not finish quickly." She wet her lips and took me in.

We had lunch and then headed north along the beach. We had walked about a mile and came to a secluded cove. Laura whispered into my ear, "I want to do it again. She was very skilled and exciting.

She looked at me happily. "Is this good for you? You are how do you say pene grande (large penis). I am so excited." she asked and smiled coyly.

"I think that we make a great couple," I replied happily.

"Yes," Laura replied, "The pill is a great invention. It allows women the freedom to explore their sexuality with little worry about pregnancy. I want you to understand that our relationship will be just fun and sex. My Father would never let me marry an American."

"Why is that?" I asked.

"He believes that everyone from your country is arrogant and untrustworthy," Laura said. "He had a business deal with a man from Texas a few years ago and the man cheated him. Father has never forgotten that. Maybe that explains why he does what he does now." Laura had continued thoughtfully.

"What do you mean by that?" I asked. "He has some very bad business associates that exploit weaknesses in America," she explained.

"You mean drug smugglers?" I asked.

"They probably are, I am not certain; but that is what it seems."

"That is a dangerous business. I would not want to get involved in that."

"I would not want that for myself either," Laura responded. "That is why I found a job in Sabanalarga and live there. I just thought that you should know about my family."

Laura put her swimsuit back on and began rolling up the side curtains. She lay back down on the towel for a minute and got up to get some more beer for us.

Later, we made a small fire and cooked our evening meal.

Laura finally said, "Carolina and I have to go back. Our parents will be wondering if we are ok if we stay out much longer." We put everything on the boat and headed back to the ranch. Laura and Carolina took the boat and disappeared into the night.

I guess that Leon and I looked dejected. Lorena laughed gaily; then said, "You two need to cheer-up. Laura and Carolina would be so happy to see your sad faces. They will probably be back here in about an hour."

Sunday evening, Laura suggested that she and I ride together back to Sabanalarga and that Leon could take Carolina back. We were driving along Highway 90 when I had a thought. "Off to the right there is a large lake, isn't that Laguna Guajaro," I asked?

"Yes," responded Laura. "Guajaro is a very large lake, fed by many rivers."

Well, we have just found a way to appear innocuous, Nate thought to himself. Tomorrow I will call Alvaro with the plan.

The next morning I called Alvaro. "Are we on schedule for Wednesday?" he asked.

"Yes, just tell us what time to be in Cartagena."
Alvaro continued, "The Embassy flight leaves at ten in the
morning."

"Ok, we will go down on Tuesday and stay in a
hotel. We would like to stay in Costa Rica for about a
week. We want to check out the Caribbean side of the
country. I then have a plan to cover our tracks when we
return to Colombia."

"What would that plan be?" Alvaro asked.

"The big lake Guajaro, we will spend some time
checking the rivers that breach the shoreline. A few months
of that should divert suspicion from us. If your other
sources develop a lead, we can check it out. We will need a
boat trailer and a tent. We can get both in Sabanalarga, if
you approve the expense."

Alvaro asked, "Will all four of you be exploring the
lake?"

"No, Adan and Juan will stay at the Ranch and
occasionally cruise the coastlines in the area during the day.
They might even get as far as Laguna Totumo. No night
activities, same for us, I replied."

"What is the tent for?" Alvaro questioned.

"I saw some islands in the lake. We can setup camp
on them and run surveys. There should be towns along the
shoreline where we can get supplies. Observers should
quickly lose interest in our activities," I replied.

Alvaro thought for a minute, "Ok, save the receipts
for any supplies that you buy. I will clear the plan with
Ryan; but I do not expect any problems. You can take ten
days in Costa Rica, but at your own expense. Also the
flight back is at your expense. Is that all good with you?"

"Sure thing, thanks for the ten days. We will be
going by ourselves as you suggested. We have all been to

Panama, but I have never been to the Caribbean coast of Costa Rica. I enjoy having women around. It is also nice when they are not around all of the time."

Alvaro chuckled, "I heard that! One thing; you will probably meet the FARC on the lake. They are a law unto themselves. If they approach you, do not resist. Keep your cool and they will probably leave you in peace. You have a good cover for being on the lake and in the rivers. Do not show much interest in anything away from the rivers or shoreline of the lake. Do not take any heavy weapons. The forty-fives should be enough and that does include the rifles. They will expect you to be able to protect yourselves from bandits. Your tickets will be waiting for you at the airport Reception Desk. You will need to show your passports. Have a good trip. Call me if you have any problems."

I looked over at Leon. "Everything got approved. We get ten days in Costa Rica, but return flight and hotels are at our expense. Now we need to go find a boat trailer, tent and stuff."

We spent the rest of Monday collecting supplies and the boat trailer. Monday afternoon we headed to Santa Catalina Bolivar to ride with Adan and Juan to Cartagena in the morning.

We rode in the Suburban and arrived at the Sofitel Santa Clara about noon and got four rooms. We lunched in the hotel restaurant. We put all of the luggage containing money in my room because I was not going out on the town that night. The guys took off for a night on the town. I shoved a chair under the door handle and took a shower. I felt so relaxed that I immediately went to sleep.

Slightly Off

Art McGillem

I awoke at six in the morning as usual. The wakeup call came from the Concierge at six-thirty. I was dressed, so I headed down for the complimentary breakfast.

We collected our boarding passes and arrived in San Jose just before noon and went to the Presidente hotel to check-in. Then we went to the bank. Eduardo was very complimentary as we were leaving. He had collected two million dollars from each of us. He said that he had given us a discount because we were such good customers.

We landed on Grand Cayman Island and checked-in at the Grand Cayman Beach Suites on Seven Mile Beach. The Reception Clerk initially told us that they only had rooms on the side of the hotel facing away from the Ocean, but when they saw our Platinum Visa cards; suddenly Ocean front rooms were found.

We then went to the Harbor Financial Services, opened and then transferred all but two million from the Costa Rican bank into the new HFS accounts. We each received black and gold American Express cards that directly accessed our accounts along with ten digit pin numbers. We each had about twenty-two million dollars at our disposal. HFS also assured us a favorable exchange rate for any foreign currency transactions.

We went back to the hotel for a late lunch and to watch the activities on the beach.

I found their exercise facility and worked-out for an hour each morning. We took the Atlantis Submarine ride one evening to see the undersea world at night. The submarine held forty-eight people in air conditioned splendor as we cruised along the reefs. The scene was quite beautiful, but I felt that snorkeling along this reef would be more fun. We went snorkeling the next day.

Slightly Off

Art McGillem

After seven days, we were feeling fat and lazy; so we booked our seats on Avianca to return to Cartagena the next day.

Adan and Juan said that they had someone that they wanted to meet that night. So we all got rooms at the Santa Clara. We used the credit cards from the Costa Rica bank. The girls came to the hotel and brought two new friends for Leon and I. We had a good dinner at the hotel and then went clubbing. Leon and I switched companions' shortly after dinner and we all had a great time.

Mary hugged my arm to her breast, leaned forward and whispered that we should go back to the hotel. We found a taxi and when we got to the hotel. She said. "Please show me your room."

We went up and after I closed the door she put her arms around my neck and gave me a long wet kiss. She pulled her head back and said, "I have never made love with an American before, what will it be like?"

I reached out and turned off the lights. The light coming from the Caribbean dimly lit the room and I said; "We are about to find out." Soon we were both naked standing in the moonlight. She put one hand on the back of my neck and pushed her tongue into my mouth. The other hand held my fully erect member. Then she whispered, "You are so big Nate, just like I had hoped." She was so wet that I did not need any lubrication. I felt how tight she was. Then she said, "Go slowly, this is my first time and I am glad that it is with you." There was a husky quality to her voice that let me know that she meant what she was saying. We did not get much sleep that night. She told me in the morning, "I am twenty-six and it was time for me to lose that complication. I hope that you do not mind. You were wonderful to me, everything that I had hoped for. Could we do that once more before I leave?"

I smiled, "Sure, but we should take a shower first. I will wash your back for you," I volunteered.

"Wow, that was exciting," she said. "I feel so unfair. I finished three times and you only once. If you come to Cartagena again, here is my direct number." She handed me a small business card with a hand written number on the back. "I hope that we will meet again" she said and walked out the door.

I went down to breakfast to find the rest of the team already seated at a table. "How was the new girl?" Juan inquired.

"Very nice," is all that I said.

Adan laughed, "I bet she was. The other girls met her at the elevator and were kidding her about it being her first time."

The other guys were grinning, so I countered; "She was well prepared for the final exam; she was also very excited and knew exactly what she wanted." We finished eating and headed back to the Ranch.

Laguna Guajaro, Colombia

Chapter 20

We collapsed the Zodiac and put it in the van. We also removed the armor cover from the other Zodiac and stored it in the back of the boat house. Leon drove us back to Sabanalarga.

In the morning I called Laura to say goodbye for a while. She pleaded, "Stay one more night, Carolina and I will come over after work and we can have dinner together before you leave." How could we say no to such a gracious offer?

We spent the time putting all of our camping equipment in the Zodiac and then placed a cover over all of it. After the girls arrived, I went out to close and lock the gate. "No escape until morning," I warned them.

Carolina looked up and said, "Does anyone want to escape." It was not a question.

It seemed that maybe I was the only one that Laura was seeing, because she was really excited and panting after the first kiss. In the morning, she moaned; "You should have slowed me down. I am going to be sore for the next week."

I laughed, "I know what you mean. It is a good kind of sore though. You will be on my mind for the rest of the week for sure."

"Only for one week?" She seemed to pout. A sudden flash seemed to jump from her eyes; "You had better remember me for more than one week or I will scratch your eyes out!" she joked.

After the girls went to work, we locked the gate and went West on Highway 90 until we found 90 Varasanta.

We followed it until we reached the lake at the small town of La Pena.

We found a safe place to leave the Suburban and trailer. The old fellow had a yard surrounded by a high fence and a big aggressive dog. He had several old cars and some machinery stored there.

We could see a small island about a half mile off shore. I asked Sebastian is someone owned the island. He said, "Yes Senior, why do you ask?"

"I was thinking of camping over there while we check the flow rates of the rivers in this area. We work for the Colombian government and are doing a survey to find good sites to generate hydroelectric power. Many rivers flow into this lake and some of them may provide good sites."

Sebastian listened, then said; "The owner does not live around here. He lets people grow crops on his land and many have parties over there. He only asks that we keep the place clean. We see him maybe twice a year. He comes on his yacht for a few days and then is gone."

"Thank you, we will camp over there while we are in this area. We will probably be back on Friday afternoon to get the van and return to Sabanalarga for the weekend. How late are you here?" Sebastian smiled, "We live here in the upstairs. If the store is closed, come up the stairs and call to us.

"We think that it will take us a couple of months to survey the rivers to this lake. We would like to leave our van here each week. What would you charge us to park here in your lot?" We agreed on a weekly rate and gave Sebastian the keys in case he needed to move the van and trailer.

We planned to spend the next three months surveying the lake, rivers and streams. We collected a lot of data and made many reports; that we kept at the house in Sabanalarga. We also kept a running journal in the Zodiac.

The FARC slipped up on us during the second week on the island. We had just returned from a trip to the south when a pair of large boats pulled up near our camp. Five heavily armed me got out of each boat and approached us. Their weapons were not directly pointed at us, but the threat was obvious. Leon and I just stood there as they approached. They could see our pistols and the rifles leaning against the tent. The leader was a really skinny Colombian with a very large mustache.

"Good afternoon Americans, what are you doing on my island?"

"Oh, is it your island, we do not know the owner." I said. "Sebastian from La Pena said that the owner would not mind if we camped here as long as we kept the area clean. If you want us to leave, we will."

"Why are you on this lake," Skinny asked? I responded, "The Colombian and US governments want to survey the rivers and streams around the lake with the goal of developing cheap hydroelectric power for the area residents. We are hydrologic engineers. Our job is to check flow rates and depths of the rivers; based on that data we can locate good sites to build the power generating stations."

"Is that all that you are here to do," Skinny asked agitatedly?

"I'm not sure what you mean." I said defensively.

"The rivers and streams around here are well known. Why does someone have survey them?" Skinny pressed.

"To decide where to place a dam, it is necessary to know the depth of the water and how fast it is flowing. The water has to flow forcefully enough to move the turbine fins. Those things have to be measured, they cannot be guessed at."

Skinny looked at me still suspicious. "Where do you go on the weekends? We have seen you leave every Friday and return on Monday."

I smiled, "We have some friends in Sabanalarga and visit them."

Skinny got the idea. "These friends are women, no?"

"Yes, they have made our stay in Colombia much more interesting. The fishing and camping here on the lake are good, but a man needs more than that to keep his soul alive."

Skinny finally relented, "Ok, you can camp here. I see that you are well prepared and your campsite is neat and clean." His men seemed to instantly relax. He waved his hand and his men got back on their boats and cruised away.

"Whew," Leon exclaimed. "I thought that we might be goners there for a minute."

Senate Committee Second Visit to Bogota

Chapter 21

Alvaro sat in the Conference Room waiting for Ryan to show-up. Ryan appeared about twenty minutes later. He held up his hand, "I know that your time is as valuable as my time. Those Senators are back in town and were pestering me with questions. I finally begged-off that I was already late for a meeting. I did not tell them that it was with you or they would have demanded to come along. You can thank me later."

"A couple of things have come up since the sinking of the second sub. I deposited our funds with Eduardo. He was moaning that our guys had transferred most of their funds to the HFS in the Cayman Islands."

"We did the same thing." Alvaro interjected.

Ryan continued, "They also deposited a much larger amount than they shared with us from the second sub."

Alvaro thought for a minute. "How much more was it?" Ryan replied, "Totaled about twenty million."

"Yeah, we suspected that might have happened". Alvaro continued. "Nate and Leon are no dummies. When I suggested a split of the first twenty million, they went right along with it without many questions. I know that they played straight with us once the game plan and trust were developed. What do you want to do about our share of the first twenty million?"

Ryan looked at Alvaro saying; "Well they are taking most of the risk. I say that we just chalk it up to new business relationships and forget about it. We already have more money than we are ever likely to spend."

"I'm cool with that." Alvaro replied.

Ryan then said, "Eduardo deposited our cut of the Teams handling fees in our accounts. Now, what are the guys' plans since they are all wealthy?"

"Nate laid it out for me." Alvaro explained the retirement plans and resigning of the commissions timing.

Ryan smiled for the first time. "That time-table will work for us. I can get you extended; then we will both find a reason to resign. Everything will look normal. If our true roles ever get exposed, we might not live to retire; which brings us back to Senator Tweedle."

"Tweedle has again demanded the names of the Delta operatives involved in the drug submarine hunt. He already knows about the second sub failing to arrive in Galveston, Texas. I wonder how he gets information so quickly. I told him that we do not have the authority to release that information. I informed him that he would have to request that information from JSOC on Fort Bragg. He was getting madder by the minute. He said that he was going to force the Ambassador to release the names and stomped out of the office. That guy is terminally stupid. If the names get leaked, he is the prime target for any inquiry. He must figure that he has some real protection."

Alvaro looked at Ryan with sympathy in his eyes. "Nate and the Team are on stand-down, or rather a cover operation. One team, Nate and Leon, are surveying the Laguna Guajaro area for the next few months. They are well inland, so little suspicion should fall to them. So far their cover is holding water. The other team, Adan and Juan, are cruising along the coastal areas in places where they should not find anything to do with drug submarines. Both teams are working a five day week and regular hours. Nate and Leon have setup a campsite on an island. FARC checked them out about a month ago and they seem to be ok."

Ryan smiled and said, "Now I know what the boat trailer and camping gear expenses were all about. You have some good men there."

Ryan continued, "I sent another Zodiac to the Ranch. We may have another op to run. Can you get some horses to Adan and Juan?"

"Not a problem. When would they be needed?" Alvaro asked. Ryan responded, "No real hurry, in a week or so. We have indications of another drug sub construction site just north of San Vicente. The location is about ten miles north of the Ranch. Horseback seems the best approach."

Ryan continued, "If we leaked Tweedles' specific interest to the Team. What do you think that they would do?"

Alvaro shook his head. "These are not the same type of guys on the local drug interdiction strike teams. I am sure that if Delta had a Presidential Order to hit a Senator, they would do it; short of that, no way."

"I figured that you would say that, but I wanted to ask anyway. Maybe I can get to the Ambassador before Tweedle."

Ryan handed Alvaro a piece of paper with the coordinates of the suspected submarine construction site and then walked out the door.

Alvaro went down to the Communications Center and asked the Watch Officer for a secure phone. Once in the booth, Alvaro called Mitch. Mitchell Doty was a long-time friend and currently manned the Cartels Colombia Desk at The Farm in Langley, Virginia.

Mitch answered, "Agent Doty here." Alvaro responded, "Hi Mitch, Duke here. How are we doing on the Senator Tweedle thing?"

"Duke, watch your back on this one. You should see the spider web we have on this guy. He even has compromising communications traffic with the VP. We have it all on tape and everyone is getting really paranoid as to where this will go."

"Who is everyone?" Alvaro asked.

Mitch laughed, "Only three people, but we all know that about half of the involved people could have us killed with almost no questions. How did you ever tumble to this guy?"

Alvaro explained, "The dumb ass keeps asking stupid questions in a loud and demanding voice. Questions like give me the names of all members of the Delta Team that is killing these drug submarines; or where is there next target. Then statements like: I am going to force the Ambassador to give me the names. Not subtle at all, like he could give a damn. Who is in the spider web; you can leave out the specific names?"

Mitch cleared his throat, "The V.P, two senior members of the Select Committee on Intelligence, six senior Senatorial Aids, one Supreme Court Justice, a senior Justice Department cabinet level attorney; do you want more?"

"Oh Shit, I see what you mean. Do you have any weak links among the four that know about the web?"

"I do not think so, at least for now."

"Mitch I need a favor. If you sense any weakness at all, put a copy of everything that is known into my dead drop. I am scheduled to come back to D.C. in about three weeks. I will retrieve the take then. Please include the voice tapes and voice prints. When I see what we have, I will try to get you guys off the hook. Do you have anything else?"

"God help us all," is what Mitch mumbled as he signed off.

Alvaro called Ryan on a secure line and gave him an update and warning: "Stay away from Tweedle. This guy can get us killed. Leave his answer resting at JSOC's door and do not challenge him."

Check the Americans

Chapter 22

Carlos called for TJ. "Son, tell me again about those four American engineers. I suspect that they are involved with the missing submarines. How could this be?"

"I have been thinking along those lines as well. Two seemed to be spending most of their time in Sincelejo while the other two were on the coast near Rincon. The pair in Sincelejo appeared normal. They even had steady women friends. The odd thing is that their vehicle was seen driving toward Rincon on several occasions. Domingo Alvarez said that his ranch hand saw all four together at the Rincon place on several occasions when he delivered grain for the horses."

"All four moved north a day or two before the second sub sailed. Two are in Sabanalarga and two stay at a ranch near Santa Catalina Bolivar. I have had people watching them. The two in Sabanalarga have found new women as have the two at Santa Catalina Bolivar. They do not seem to be doing anything more than hydrology research. FARC Captain Sergio Perez has been keeping an eye on the two in Sabanalarga for us. He says watching them is boring. They search the shoreline of Laguna Guajaro and go up any rivers or streams checking depth and flow rates. They do this about eight hours each day except for the weekends. They meet their women in either Sabanalarga or Santa Catalina Bolivar for fun and games. They appear to be doing just what is expected." TJ finished his report.

Carlos was not satisfied. "These four seem to be the only strangers in the vicinity of where we lost two submarines. Those submarines also carried large sums of money for laundering in the United States. None of the crew or any of the cocaine have appeared anywhere that we know of. We need to check on these four very closely."

TJ replied, "We asked the women from Sincelejo about these men. The women said that the men never asked about politics or the drug trafficking in Colombia. They just talked about the waterways and hydroelectric power generation. The women did say that both men had been in the military but separated and found civilian jobs as engineers. I have not spoken to the women in Sabanalarga or Santa Catalina Bolivar, but I can go there if you wish. Laura Munoz is the daughter of Andres Munoz whom you know. She is close with one of the Americans."

Carlos smiled an evil smile. "Go and speak with Andres. Ask him to speak to his daughter about her American friend. That should be interesting; he hates Americans. Just say that we want to know all that his daughter knows about these Americans. If they all meet at the ranch, we may have found the Delta Team. Caution Andres not to mention our interest to his daughter. He will know how to handle this situation. I am concerned because we have another sub under construction that is about ready to sail. I have put extra security in place already. Go now."

TJ paused to ask a question. "How many guards and fighters are at that site and where is it?"

"They have two highly trained men acting as guards. The rest are not really fighters, but they do have weapons. There are just seven counting the guards. Here is a map showing the location of the sub; take it with you. Also, take Diego and a couple of his men, just in case. If there is any indication that these Americans are other than they appear, make sure that something bad happens to them."

Slightly Off

Art McGillem

TJ and Diego arrived in Santa Catalina Bolivar and spoke with Andres Munoz. Andres became incensed when he heard that Laura was spending time with Americans and immediately called her to return home after work that day.

Andres grabbed Laura by the arm when she walked into the house. "Why have you been seeing an American engineer? You know that I hate Americans," he demanded.

"Nate is very nice," said Laura tearfully. The grip on her arm was painful and she had reason to fear her father's anger.

"He and the others are working to find sites to build hydroelectric generating facilities. They are helping Colombia to be a better place to live."

Her father asked her directly, "Are these men from the military?"

"No, Father, they were in the military but are now civilian contractors working for the US Embassy in Bogota. I believe them when they say this. Even their conversations are about water resources. I have not heard them say anything about the military unless one of us girls asks them."

Andres let go of Laura's arm in disgust. "You cannot trust Americans. I have told you this many times. Do not see them again. Do you understand?"

"Yes Father, I do understand. I do like and trust Nate. He has never given me a reason to feel bad towards him. I will stop seeing Nate if that will make you happy."

Laura knew that she had just lied to her Father, for she had been planning to see Nate and the others in just a few minutes. She still planned to see Nate that night. Laura left the house and went to her car.

Andres punched a number into his cell phone and TJ answered. Andres reported that his daughter believed that the Americans were engineers as had been reported by others. She said that she would not see the one named Nate, but she was not being truthful. He would have someone watch her and the Americans. TJ agreed that watching the Americans was a good idea.

"Diego, you and I need to take a ride. We are going to check security at the site where our submarine is being built. About thirty minutes later they arrived at the lagoon near where the sub was under construction. Diego was in the lead and had just turned up the riverbed when he was met by a man carrying an AK74.

"Senor, this is private property, you are not allowed to enter here." The guard said casually. His hand was on his weapon, but not in a threatening way.

"Do you know who I am?" TJ asked the guard. "No Senor, I do not know you." The guard replied.

"Do you know Senor Carlos Morena?" TJ asked the guard. "It is a common name," the guard replied. TJ took out his phone and dialed.

"Father, do you know these guards personally?" TJ asked. "Put the guard on," Carlos replied.

The guard listened for a moment, becoming less confident in his posture. He handed the phone back to TJ and said, "I am at your service sir. What would you like to see?"

"I want to see the submarine." TJ responded. The guard turned around and within a short distance the sub could just be seen on the other side of the river.

"We have to go a little farther along to cross the river. The water is quite deep here, but will soon become shallow enough to wade across." The guard explained.

TJ and Diego examined the submarine and could see that about all that was needed was the cargo. "When is it due to sail?" Diego asked the guard.

"I think a day or two," the guard responded. "I was told that the cargo will arrive tomorrow. There is a high tide that night, so I think that it will sail then."

TJ and Diego went back to their Land Rover. "We need to bring the men here this afternoon to reinforce this crew. Right now, we need to see what is going on at that ranch."

Senator Tweedle Calls Home

Chapter 23

"This is Senator Tweedle, put me through to the V.P.," he commanded. "Hey Doug, this is Jason Tweedle. Have you got a couple of minutes?"

"I can always make a few minutes for you Jason. What is on your mind?"

"You are on your secure line, right?"

"Yes, that is right." said the VP.

Tweedle continued, "I am having a bit of trouble down here in Bogota. Ryan the CIA guy will not give me the names of the Delta team members. I need you to pressure him or the Ambassador to give them up."

"What in the world do you need those for?" The Vice President demanded.

"I know that you do not keep up with the day to day activities of The Rubric, Doug. That Delta Team killed the last two subs out of Colombia. The loss of those subs cost us better than a million dollars each plus they were carrying our commission on the previous subs. The Rubric counts on those funds to operate. We cannot afford to lose another sub this year. We have quite a large payroll as you well know."

Vice President McConnell was thoughtful for a minute. "I will speak with the Ambassador and try to get those names for you."

Tweedle was not to be put off, "See that you do, we do not often ask your help. Make no mistake, if we lose another submarine, you will be in serious trouble."

"Do you dare to threaten me, Tweedle?" The VP roared. "I will have your guts for garters when you get back here."

"Now, now Doug, nothing bad will happen if you do as I ask," Tweedle cajoled.

The VP slammed down the receiver, ending the conversation. He was worried about the power of The Rubric. The Rubric had the influence to raise or ruin anyone in the World. If asked again, I will make the call; but it really is a very dangerous exposure for me, he thought. Maybe the Team just got lucky on the last two subs.

In fact the Homeland Security briefing this morning had mentioned that the cocaine supply in the Southern states had dwindled, raising prices and increasing criminal activities. The VP mused to himself. He called in one of his trusted Aides.

"Horace, get a hold of JSOC and see what they are willing to tell us about the submarine interdiction efforts in Colombia. I understand that they have a Delta Team operating down there that has had some success. Maybe we should do a photo op or something about winning the Drug War." Horace departed quickly on his mission.

Staff Sergeant Leslie answered the phone at JSOC. "Sergeant Leslie, JSOC, Sir."

The voice on the other end said simply, "This is Mr. Horace Feather calling from the White House. I need to speak to someone in charge of a Delta Team that is operating down there in Colombia. I was given the name of Lieutenant Colonel McMasterson. Would that be correct?"

"Sir, I can connect you with LTC McMasterson, he is the Executive Officer to Special Forces Operational Detachment- Delta. Please hold."

SSG Leslie rang LTC McMasterson, "Sir a Mister Horace Feather is on line two. He says that he is calling from the White House. He wants some information on a Delta Team working in Colombia. What should I do?"

LTC McMasterson thought for a second. "I will take the call. Find out who he is. Call the Chief of Staff at the White House and ask."

SSG Leslie called and verified that Horace Feather is an Aide to Vice President McConnell. Then walked into LTC McMastersons office and placed a piece of paper with the information in front of LTC McMasterson.

She heard LTC McMasterson tell Mr. Feather, "Mr. Feather, this is not a secure line, so I cannot discuss what you are asking about. I will call the secure line in your office in twenty minutes. You can ask your questions then."

LTC McMasterson thought, what the hell is the VP asking about Delta Teams for? He got on the phone to Ryan Dottmann at the Embassy in Colombia.

"Ryan what the hell is the Vice President of the United States doing calling me about Delta Team activity in Colombia?" McMasterson's voice was low and dangerous.

Ryan thought for a minute, "Bob, I can't be sure, but we have a bad situation developing. You probably know Senator Jason Tweedle."

"Yeah, I do, real pain in the ass," interjected McMasterson.

Ryan continued. "He was down here twice recently demanding the names of the Delta Team members that are involved in the drug submarine interdiction effort. He and some other Senators from the Senate Intel Committee came down here after the first submarine disappeared. After the second sub disappeared, he came down here again and threatened to force the Ambassador to divulge the Delta Team names."

"We became suspicious during his first visit and checked his phone calls and even have photos of him at the scene of a fire bombing of a bait Safe House. I had leaked that address only to him to see what he would do. The Cartel hit it early that morning and burned it to the ground. They did not even enter the building to check anything. The building was isolated, but under video and operator surveillance."

"Tweedle took the bait hook line and sinker. His face is clearly visible in the video. We already have him connected to a highly placed staffer that immediately called Carlos Morena down here in Cartagena. You are familiar with Morena, right?"

"Yeah, Cartel controller if I remember correctly," replied McMasterson.

"Exactly, after the staffer called Morena; the bait safe house was destroyed that night. NSA is working on the voice traffic. It was Tweedle who contacted the VP. We have all of his voice traffic recorded. What a bucket of worms!" Ryan paused thoughtfully.

"Where is all of this headed right now?" McMasterson asked.

"The Ambassador has not asked me for the Team member names yet and might not. He is an honorable guy and would know that giving those names could mean."

Ryan was thinking out loud. "I have the Delta Team in cover mode, looking totally innocent. We also have a line on a third drug submarine. The Team is going to very quietly check the status of the sub probably this next week. I had no idea that Cartel connections went this high up in the administration. Each of those subs represents about a billion dollars in drug sales and millions in profits." Both men were quiet for a moment.

LTC McMasterson spoke first, "I am going to talk this over with the General. He is straight, but as a career officer he is also a political animal. When he hears that the VP is involved, he may decide to shut us down. I've got this guy Horace Feather an aide to the VP asking me questions. I have to call him back in about ten minutes. I am going to stall him, but not cut him off. I will call you after I speak with the General."

Ryan started thinking out loud again, "I am not going to give up the real names of the team members. If I am forced, I will give the names that they use here and send them to Costa Rica until you can think of where to hide them. I want to take down that drug sub before I have to disband the Team. I will call you when I know how far along the submarine build has progressed. If the Ambassador asks for the names, I will say that I need to let you know before I give them to him. That might give us a few more days. This development is a big disappointment. We have been really successful with this operation. I would like to keep it active. Maybe Tweedle could run into a bad situation down here."

McMasterson quickly interjected, "We should not do that. We would be immediately suspected given the way that this has developed. A later time might work to eliminate future problems. Keep working on your op. I will keep you posted." McMasterson ended the call thoughtfully. He already had the secure number for Mr. Feather and dialed.

"Horace Feather here," came back the answering voice. "Lieutenant Colonel McMasterson here, what do you want to know about the Delta Teams in Colombia? We have several teams with DEA and some with other duties in Colombia."

"The VP is thinking of giving some recognition to the Delta Team doing the drug submarine captures down there. They have apparently been successful on at least two occasions. Homeland Security briefed that cocaine supplies in the south were getting low. A good report would provide our citizens with an update on the government effort to reduce drug dependence in the country."

"Mr. Feather as you should know, the submarine interdiction effort is a clandestine operation. The whole purpose is to insure that the submarine, drugs and crew simply disappear without a trace. We would not want to have the involvement of our government known at this time. We are just beginning to have success. Knowledge of our efforts would immediately alert the Cartels and they would begin looking for our people. As of now, the Cartel only knows that the submarines and crews have disappeared. They do not know why and that is just what we proposed. We want the Cartels to stop using submarines. Each sub that we interdict means that six or seven tons of cocaine do not reach the US market. We do not want any publicity for this program at this time."

"Colonel McMasterson political life dictates that politicians must constantly be seen as getting the public's work done. We do that by publicly declaring our successes. I believe that VP McConnell will want to publicly declare the successes of this operation and personally congratulate the members of the Team in front of the media."

"Mr. Feather, we do not publicize the names and faces of Delta members under any circumstances. If the Vice President insists, I may be able to provide the names of the Team members. I will need a request that I can take to General Teabury, Chief of JSOC. I do apologize, but the very lives of our personnel depend upon our discretion."

"I will report to the Vice President that you resist accepting public accolades for the Delta Team. If he wishes to persist, I will contact you again." The line went dead.

LTC McMasterson clicked-off and pressed the direct dial to Commander JSOC. He heard the Aide answer. "Hello Captain, this is LTC McMasterson, I need to speak with General Teabury when he is available."

"He may have time now, let me check, Sir."

Major General Teabury came on the line, "What is it Bob?"

"We just opened a can of worms down in Colombia, Will. The Vice President is asking to publically acknowledge the success of the drug sub interdiction program. He had Horace Feather give me a call. Unfortunately, it gets worse. I just wanted to give you a heads-up. Someone may call you directly."

"That doesn't sound like a particularly difficult can to close back up. We will just say that we do not want any publicity for this operation. End of conversation." Replied Gen Teabury.

"It may not be that easy. It all started with questions by Senator Jason Tweedle to Ryan and Alvaro down in Colombia. He demanded to know the Delta Team members names and location. Alvaro gave him a false location and it was completely destroyed that night. They have video of Tweedle at the site; recorded calls to a senior staffer in D.C. who called Carlos Morena in Cartagena. Tweedle is also recorded discussing the drug submarine with the VP in a manner that suggests direct involvement with the drug profits."

"Holy shit!" exclaimed the JSOC Commander. "What did you tell them?"

"I said that I needed to see the request from the VP in writing and that I would bring it to you for a decision."

"That was a good move, gives us some time to figure things out. What is the Team doing now?"

"Anyone checking on them would just see them doing hydrologic surveys. The men are keeping regular work hours; nine to five with weekends off. We have reports of a third sub under construction and plan to check the progress very quietly next week. The report came from a DEA source known to be reliable."

"Damn Bob, just when we get something good going some politician wants to screw it up. Keep doing what you are doing and let me know if they take the next step." The General dropped the connection.

McMasterson stepped to the door and called out, "Sergeant Mack please step in here."

Master Sergeant Mack was arguably the best intelligence analysts in Special Forces Operational Detachment – Delta. I have a new project for you. Call Ryan Dottmann down at the Embassy in Colombia and get all of the information that he has related to the submarine interdiction operation. Use the secure line and do not talk to anyone but me about anything involved in this project. The team is not in any trouble from me. I want to know everything there is to know about Senator Jason Tweedle and anyone that he is involved with. When you read the reports, you will understand about the secrecy. All of this is to be classified Top Secret."

"Yes sir," Sergeant Mack replied. He went to the secure phone and called Ryan and made the request. "Sergeant Mack, be sure to keep all of this quiet. I will send you everything that I have and any updates that I get. What we have here is more dangerous than foo gas. A single leak could mean a death sentence for all of us. I mean that literally not figuratively."

Ryan clicked-off. He put a copy of everything including the voice prints, recorded conversations and videos into a box for the diplomatic pouch that evening; stamped the box Top Secret and addressed it to LTC McMasterson at Fort Bragg. A State Department courier would deliver the documents to JSOC after they arrived in D.C..

Drug Submarine 3

Chapter 24

Alvaro brought two horses, tack and feed to the Ranch. The barn had stalls for four horses. Adan and Juan helped put the horses into their stalls.

Alvaro had called ahead and Leon and I were supposed to meet him at the ranch. We dropped the Zodiac and trailer at the Safe House in Sabanalarga. When we arrived at the ranch, the horses were already taken care of and everyone was down at the Boat Dock.

"What is up Alvaro," I asked?

"I came here to give you guys a heads-up. Senator Tweedle has gotten the Vice President on our case. Stay loose, but if I say pull out, that will mean now in capital letters. Right now, they are stalling the VP in D.C., but that could change at any moment. They want your names. If we give them that you are soon dead. General Teabury, Commander JSOC does not want to give our operation up, even to the VP.

"One of the DEA informants says that they are building a sub near a small river north of here. We want to take that sub before you may have to leave Colombia.

If you have to leave Colombia quickly, I have another set of ID's in the works for each of you. If this op crashes, use your current in-country ID's to get to San Jose, Costa Rica. Rent a couple of cars to drive to Nicaragua using the new ID's. I think that it would be best if you travel in pairs. Your bank accounts are in your alternate ID's, do not use those while traveling. We do not want to compromise those names under any circumstances. Fly into the US with the ID that you use to rent the cars. Destroy those ID's and report to Fort Bragg as yourselves. LTC

McMasterson knows about all of these plans. We are planning that none of this will be necessary, but we need to be prepared for the worst case. Have you guys got any questions?"

"What are we doing about Senator Tweedle," I asked.

"Senator Tweedle has become a person of interest to a very select group. He will be sorry that he ever encountered Delta. I will tell you more, if you need to know. For now we need information on that submarine."

Alvaro continued, "The site where the submarine is being built is close to a beach area. Someone put up fences and a gate to charge for admission to the beach. That restricts access and may have been done to keep people away from wandering into the sub construction site. I was thinking that you could ride the horses up there on the weekend and see how close you can get before you see a reason to shy away. Tuesday and Wednesday will have just a sliver of moon. Anyway, you guys make your own plans and let me know what you find. I am heading back to Cartagena, then on to Bogota."

Today Alvaro was riding a motorcycle and we heard it fire-up and roar off.

"We had better keep our weapons closer at hand." Juan complained.

"I think that we still need to play it cool, keep the rifles handy; but not in plain sight. We have been working the cover in an obvious way for the last couple of months without any suspicious questions, even from the girls," I said. "The twins are probably coming to see you this weekend, so if we use Alvaro's plan Leon and I should do the horseback recon. I did not tell Laura that I would be here. Leon did you say anything to Carolina?"

"No I thought about calling her, but just have not gotten around to it." Leon said.

"That settles it, Leon and I will make the recon in the morning. We will probably be gone all day since it is about a twenty mile round trip."

While we were talking, the twins had arrived and waived excitedly, seeing all of us together. Natalia had her cell phone out and was talking excitedly as they walked toward us.

When they reached us, Natalia announced; "That was Laura she and Carolina will be heading this way in a few minutes. I can stop them if you want me to." I looked at Leon and we both shook our heads no and the twins smiled.

"Leon and I had planned to take a horseback ride up north tomorrow, but I guess that it can wait." I said.

"Maybe you should ask Laura, she loves horseback riding," volunteered Lorena. "When did you guys get horses?"

Quickly I said, "Oh, they just arrived today. We haven't ridden them yet. I hope that they are friendly." We walked into the barn and gave the horses some oats and brushed them down while the girls watched.

"They seem tame enough," I said. "Remember Ciclon?" That horse looked kind of tame until Mr. Alvarez put a foot into the stirrup," Juan cautioned.

Lorena asked, "Do you guys have anything in the refrigerator except beer?" Adan and Juan had a guilty look and said "No" almost in unison.

I reached into my pocket and gave Lorena two hundred thousand pesos. "Will that be enough to get us through the weekend?" I asked as I handed it to her.

"Oh yes, we will do very well with this". Lorena grabbed Natalia's hand and they wandered off toward their car.

Lorena and Natalia returned just as Laura and Carolina pulled into the parking area. They walked toward the ranch house talking excitedly. They all had their arms full and were waiting for one of us to open the door.

"Dinner will be ready in thirty minutes." Laura said. "Nate you are bad. You have not called me in almost a week." Laura was showing her best pouty face, but her eyes were smiling.

"We were in a dead zone for cell phone reception until this morning. I was going to call you when I got here, but then we had to take care of the horses and then the twins arrived?"

"Ok I will forgive you this time."

We went in and grabbed some beers from the refrigerator and went out onto the veranda to await dinner. Leon leaned over and asked, "What is the plan now?"

I had already been thinking about it, so I said, "I am going to ask Laura if she would like to go riding tomorrow. I will suggest bringing along a swimsuit. I can use that beach as a destination. If she says no we will think of something else."

We were walking along the beach when I asked Laura to go riding in the morning. "Oh, that will be such great fun!" She said excitedly. "I used to ride often, but about five years ago my father moved the family to Santa Catalina Bolivar. We did not have enough room for the horses in the new place, so they were sold."

"Bring along a swimsuit. There is a beach up that way that is supposed to be nice," I said.

"Yes," Laura replied. "I have been there, but you have to pay to get in. The cost is not high though and the sand is clean." We walked up toward the ranch house and bed.

To my surprise, the next morning Laura saddled her own horse and checked her tack with a professional eye. She turned to me and with a shy smile said, "You were too gentle with your horse. The cinch is one hole too loose. You will be much happier if you tighten the cinch."

She watched me tighten the cinch and added saddlebags to her rig. "I brought some sandwiches and bottled water for later. There are not many places to find food out that way."

We rode along the shoulder of Highway 90A and stopped occasionally to rest the horses. A few houses dotted the roadside. We came to a road junction and I started to turn toward the Caribbean coast. Laura reined-in and said, "That road leads to Hacienda Villa del Mar, they do not encourage visitors. We should go on. The beach there is not good either."

We rode on and began seeing roads branching off toward the coast. Laura said that most of these roads led to homes along the shoreline. We came to a narrow track and she said, "This road leads down to a nice secluded beach. Maybe we can be alone there and have lunch."

We rode down the track and soon could see the surf. The closer we came, the more a small sandy beach was revealed. A good sized stream flowed into the Caribbean there also. We hobbled the horses and let them wander along the beach. Laura began taking off her clothes and smiled enticingly when she noticed that I was watching her every move.

"See something that you like?" she asked.

"Yes very much," I responded as I moved toward her.

She held up her hand saying, "We should swim first." I kissed her and held her for a minute as she pressed against me. We parted and I began taking off my clothes. I also had worn my swimsuit. We swam around and I gradually worked my way over to the stream. The water at the confluence was deep and colder than I had expected. I climbed out onto the bank and began to walk upstream when Laura called me to come for lunch.

We finished our sandwiches and I said, "What is for desert?" Laura pulled me over on top of her and simply said, "Me." I took the hint and we were soon lying sated and naked on the beach. I heard it first. Someone was walking toward the beach and singing. Laura and I scrambled into our swimsuits and were just finishing when a man appeared from the stream defile. He saw the horses first and then us. He started to unsling his rifle, but noticed that we were not carrying weapons. He said, "No debería estar aquí (You should not be here)."

Laura asked, "Se trata de una playa privada (Is this a private beach)?" "Se Senora, (Yes madam)" he responded.

I answered for us, "A continuación, vamos a dejar (Then we will leave)."

He replied aggressively, "Yes you should do that immediately and do not return." He now had his hand on the rifle. Laura and I dressed, caught the horses and continued north along Highway 90A toward the Water Park.

The Water Park did not have an attendant and the gate was open. We rode the horses down to the beach. I could see a fence that stretched along the south side and extended to the beach and into the water. At low tide the fence would still extend into the Caribbean.

We placed our blanket on the beach. Our nearest neighbors were about fifty feet away. Only a few couples could be seen scattered along the beach strand. The couple next to us was in a playful mood and the woman removed the top of her bikini and teased her boyfriend.

Laura saw me looking and said, "Do you want me to remove my top also?"

"No, I am the jealous type. I do not want to share you with anyone." That got me a quick kiss and a shy smile.

Later, I suggested it was time to head back to the Ranch and Laura agreed. As we left the Marina, I noticed a river across Highway 90A and asked Laura about it. She said that the river got quite large a little farther north and flowed directly into the Caribbean. We rode on and stopped at a local gas station for some fresh squeezed fruit drinks. We sat in the shade provided by the sign and drank thirstily.

We got back to the Ranch just in time for dinner. We took a slow walk on the beach and then headed for the bedroom. Despite our afternoon activities, Laura whispered in my ear, "Please give me your tongue for a long time. I have been waiting so long for you. This afternoon was just not enough even though it was wonderful." She moaned lustily as I removed her bra and teased her nipples to full erection. She was really wet, but I did as she asked and after her third orgasm she pushed me gently away. The rest was pure ecstasy. Laura giggled, "Shh, others may hear you."

Sunday we spent the day on the barrier peninsula swimming, fishing and laying around. The girls prepared dinner using the fish that we had caught. Then suddenly we were on our own again.

Spies in the Woods

Chapter 25

TJ and Diego parked the Land Rover in the trees near the entrance to the ranch and began watching. Toward dark two cars arrived. Two women were in each car. Diego chuckled, "Those men will be busy tonight and the next two days, no need to watch them."

TJ thought for a minute. "Ok you are probably correct. They will all be busy until the women return to work on Monday. Laura did lie to Andres; we just saw her arrive here. I do not see any concern on her face though," TJ said as he put down the binoculars. "We will return on Monday to see what they do.

After the happy group returned to the Ranch house, Diego started the Land Rover and slowly moved onto the road toward Santa Catalina Bolivar. TJ decided not to speak to Andres about his wayward daughter. She is a beauty TJ thought. There might be some advantage in keeping what I know to myself.

"Diego, pick me up early in the morning at five o'clock. I want to see if the cars are still here. We will find rooms here tonight."

The next morning, the cars were still there. Good information to know thought TJ as he snapped pictures of the cars parked near the ranch house.

A Plan in the Making

Chapter 26

Monday morning, I got the team together at the kitchen table. "I think that I was close to the sub building site Saturday. An armed guard appeared out of nowhere while we were lying on the beach. He told us to leave and not come back. Obviously, there is something to hide there."

Monday also found, TJ and Diego hidden in the trees across the road from the ranch. The cars belonging to the women were already gone. TJ and Diego stayed until about five o'clock in the next morning without seeing anything out of the ordinary. TJ finally said, "We need to get some sleep. We can come back tonight."

Although they could not hear, plans continued to be made inside the ranch house.

"Juan and I could go in tonight." Adan said.

"I think that it is too soon, they may be more alert than usual," I countered. "On Tuesday, we can all go in the van. We will drop Adan and Juan about a mile short of the access road and they can recon along the stream. We will drive on up Highway 90A and check where the river widens at the Caribbean outflow. We will take some fishing gear as a cover. We will return to the pickup point in four hours."

Adan and Juan eased along the ridge on the south side of the stream. There were enough trees and shrubbery to cover their movements, but the underbrush made quiet movement almost impossible. Finally the rumble of the surf began to cover the noise of their movements. They were about four hundred yards from where the stream joined the Caribbean when they saw activity on the other side of the stream. Adan called a halt and they began moving slowly back along the stream. After about five hundred meters, Adan waded slowly into the stream and disappeared from sight. He came up about a hundred meters closer to the activity and scrambled out on the other side. He motioned Juan to stay and cover.

Adan moved away from the stream and slowly approached the area of activity. There it was, he could dimly see the hull of the submarine. The men were working by red filtered battery powered lights. The hull of the sub was about seventy percent complete. Four men were laying fiberglass sheets on the skeleton and smearing the resin into the fiberglass.

Adan froze instantly. He sensed rather than saw that someone was approaching his position. The guard had silently moved within about four feet of Adan and was standing still listening. The guard took six more steps and then stood looking and listening. The guard repeated these movements until he disappeared beyond the location of the sub. Adan breathed a sigh of relief. That was too close for comfort he thought to himself. He checked the time, four o'clock. The workers began packing their stuff and then got into a truck and drove off. The guard had not returned and so must still be in the area.

Adan slowly moved in the direction that the guard had taken. Soon he found the guard sitting on a rock overlooking the Caribbean, apparently waiting for sunrise. Adan crept back for a quick look at the sub. It was about the same size as the other two. One more night and the hull would be closed-in. Adan eased away from the sub toward the road. He signaled Juan to follow him and they moved toward the pickup rendezvous.

Slightly Off

Art McGillem

The rendezvous point was in a thick group of trees next to the road. Juan was waiting when Adan arrived. "What happened to you in that stream? One second you were stepping across and the next, you disappeared?"

"Well you know how you cannot judge the depth of a puddle from the top? It works the same way for streams and rivers." Adan quipped with a grin. "They must have dug that stream out. When I crossed it above, near the road, it was little more than knee deep. I bet it was ten feet deep where I tried to cross. The current carried me about a hundred yards before my feet found bottom again. I see headlights; that may be our ride."

Adan and opened the side door of the van and they climbed in. "This is the place." Adan stated as Juan closed the door. "The sub hull is about eighty-five percent complete. The engine and gas tank are in place. They have a sentry. The one that I saw is very experienced. He was within four feet of me before I noticed him. I watched him high-stepping slowly along until he went out of sight. We will need to take care approaching and leaving this location."

I thought for a minute. "We will return Wednesday night. If the sub is complete, we can place the GPS Transponder in the usual place. Did you find a good observation spot?"

Juan looked at Adan; then said. "Observation from across the stream was good. It looked like the view from the hill behind the sub would be blocked by vegetation and the slope." Adan confirmed Juan's estimate.

"If the crew quits work at four o'clock each morning, we will have a little less than an hour to get in and out before it is light enough to be observed. I hope that guard stays down by the shore." I said. "Leon and I will go in tonight on the next recon. We will plant the GPS Transponder if possible."

We arrived at the drop-off point just after midnight and made a stealthy approach to the submarine site. Leon found a tree with a wide branch that gave good support and began watching the sub construction crew. I backtracked and crossed the stream at a shallow point. I found a gap in the shrubbery that gave a good view and settled down to wait. Suddenly my peripheral vision picked-up movement to my right. There was the armed guard easing along about six feet from where I was hidden. He had approached so silently that only his movement alerted me. He had an old AK47 slung over his shoulder. He stopped to talk with one of the workers and then continued on toward the beach. The crew ceased work and left the area.

I slowly moved to the sub and climbed in. The space that we had been using to hide the transponder did not appear to exist in this sub. I found a bad joint where the sail mated with the sub's hull, placed the transponder there and covered it with fiberglass cloth and resin. I was just finishing when I heard a noise outside. I ceased all movement and stood quietly. I noticed that the steering and prop-shaft had been installed and that the hull was completed. I heard a foot strike the ladder rung on the body of the sub and got my .45 pistol in my hand. Next time I would bring a silencer; I swore to myself. The guard changed his mind for some reason as I could hear him hurry away. I got out of the sub and hid nearby. The guard returned a few minutes later and entered the sub. He apparently went directly to sleep and he made loud snoring noises.

I headed back to the rendezvous point. Leon was waiting. "Whew, that was close. I threw a chunk of dead wood into the bushes and the guard went to check on it. I saw you come out of the sail and get clear. The guard disappeared into the sub and did not come out. Did you plant the GPS Transponder?"

"Yes, but this sub design did not have the gap like the others. This sub may be a newer design. I found a place to hide and conceal the GPS though. They need fuel, electronics and powder and they will be ready to sail." Adan and Juan slowed but did not stop while we climbed into the suburban.

"I think that it is too dangerous to cross to the sub side of the stream. We will do well to monitor from the south side. I will call Alvaro later. The sub could be ready to sail in a day or two."

I called Alvaro later that morning and filled him in on the plan. We needed to insure that the USS Ventura was back on station as the drug submarine was likely to sail within a few days. Alvaro said that the drug shortage on the east coast, US of A, was becoming critical. He thought that the Cartel would be sending the sub as soon as possible. He became concerned when I explained about the professional demeanor of the guards at the construction site. The guard at night was not the same one that I had encountered when Laura and I were swimming in the cove.

We agreed that the drop-off technique was best to avoid any prolonged visibility in the area of the sub construction site. Alvaro said that he would come to Santa Catalina to help and that he would arrive that evening.

After we got some sack-time, we put the armor covering on the second Zodiac. Now we were prepared to interdict the sub on short notice. Alvaro arrived just as it was getting dark.

"You guys got anything to eat around here?" Alvaro asked.

Juan tossed a Beef Ravioli MRE on the counter and said, "Help yourself, there is a pot of hot water already on the stove."

"Ugh, just what I was hoping for." Alvaro forced a smile and began opening his meal.

"We plan to leave here about ten o'clock tonight. You might want to catch a few winks after you eat." I said. "Before we leave tonight, we will move the weapons down to the Zodiac's. Adan and Juan will remain here ready to meet us if the sub sails tonight. Alvaro, you can switch with Juan if you want to stay here or you can accompany Leon and view the sub. I will continue up the coast and do some fishing until pick-up time. Just let us know what you want to do."

Alvaro responded, "I will go with Leon to see the activity around the sub. I want to see what is up with the guards. What is the plan if the sub sails tonight?"

"If the sub sails tonight, Adan and Juan will meet us at Latitude 10.48.15.62N, Longitude 75.12.59.11W. That location should be vacant at that time of night, but is easily accessed by road. We will leave the vehicle there and recover it on the way back."

Adan looked concerned. "If we leave a vehicle exposed like that, we should report it stolen and leave it somewhere after we wipe it down. It would seriously weaken our cover if it gets seen and reported and we still have it." "I agree." Alvaro said. "I will see that you get a new vehicle if we have to burn one. You will then have to slip back into your cover activities and stay away from the coast in that area for the near future."

"Not a problem, if Laura wants to ride up to that beach again, we will just go to the water park. Too bad that the secluded beach is going to be off limits from now on."

Adan and Juan looked at each other, "Did something memorable happen on that beach?" Juan asked.

"Yes, that guard with the AK told us in no uncertain terms to stay away. It is a nice little secluded beach." I responded guardedly. Leon winked at Adan and Juan.

TJ and Diego were parked in the trees and had seen Alvaro arrive. They did not know who he was. At about ten o'clock in the evening they watched as three men got into the Van. It was too dark to see the faces, but the fishing poles were easy to spot.

Diego said, "Looks like they plan to do some night fishing." "Yeah, I guess so. We will follow them and see where they go."

Diego let them get a good lead and then pulled out onto the highway. After they left the city, Diego turned off the headlights and continued to follow. He and TJ did not see the brief stop to drop-off Alvaro and Leon. They followed the van and watched as Nate began fishing. "I wonder what the other two are doing." TJ questioned absently.

"They must be sleeping in the Van," suggested Diego. They sat back to watch and finally both were snoring loudly. When their snoring noise finally woke them up Nate and the van were gone. Diego started the Land Rover and headed back toward the sub. When they got to the sub, it had already sailed. They then headed toward the ranch.

Alvaro and Leon approached the spot from which the sub could be watched unobserved by others. "We need to crawl the rest of way." Leon whispered. Alvaro nodded and followed on his belly. He parted the tall grasses and could see bales being loaded into the submarine. Leon made the sign for quiet and Alvaro stopped moving. They were under a low growing shrub, well concealed. The guard had appeared on this side of the stream and was about twenty feet away. The guard stood perfectly still for several minutes and then began turning his head in all directions, listening quietly. He then took several high steps and repeated the watching and listening routine.

When the guard was out of sight, Leon slowly exhaled; then whispered. "I was really worried that he heard us crawl under the bush. He appeared just as you parted those grasses in front of you. I think that was why he listened for so long. I wonder when high tide is today."

"Why think about high tide?" Alvaro asked.

"The stream flows into the Caribbean, but it is shallow at the sand bar during low tide. So they will only be able to sail out at high tide." Leon explained.

"Look over there." Alvaro whispered and pointed. The workers had stopped loading the submarine and were moving it along logs toward the stream. The sub launched with a splash. Ropes attached fore and aft quickly pulled the sub against the bank. The ropes were then tied to trees. Loading of the cocaine resumed and the sub sunk lower into the water. As usual, work ceased at four o'clock, but several of the workers picked up weapons and remained as guards.

I picked-up Alvaro and Leon and headed back to the Ranch. Alvaro said worriedly, "They may move that sub during daylight."

"Not likely," I predicted. "High tide is not until about nine o'clock this evening. They would have trouble getting that sub over the sandbar until about seven o'clock.

We can activate the GPS Transponder occasionally and see if they move."

Alvaro looked at me questioningly, "Why not just leave the transponder activated?"

"We have thought about that before. I just worried that it might cause some effect that we were not aware of with some of their electronics. If we use it intermittently, they are less likely to pinpoint a cause if anything occurs."
"Good thinking," Alvaro complimented.

"We should start two hour watches. At the beginning of each shift we will activate the GPS until we get a firm coordinate, log it and shut-down."

The drug submarine began moving at seven o'clock in the evening. We moved the weapons down into the Zodiac's and waited. We wanted to see what direction the drug sub would take. The USS Ventura was standing by about four miles off the coast near the drug sub launch point. The drug sub crossed the sandbar into the Caribbean.

Sub 3 did something different. The sub followed the coastline heading toward us. A large powerboat came from the shore and began following Sub 3. The powerboat kept pace with Sub 3, about a quarter mile behind. This posed quite a dilemma for us. We could kill the powerboat, but it would alert the sub and if we attacked the sub, the powerboat would then attack us. The sub was also keeping within sight of land.

They made their mistake off the coast of Tolu and headed out into the Caribbean. I called the commander of the Ventura. "Commander Ryker, this is Nate. Sub 3 has headed out to sea. They have a powerboat following them about a quarter mile behind. We cannot take them both. Can you help with the powerboat?"

Commander Ryker responded, "The powerboat is the easier target for us. We have him on radar. How soon will you take Sub 3?"

"We want to get about another mile out into the Sea before we hit. I will call you about ten minutes before the strike point. How do you plan to take the powerboat down?"

"The Marines have been itching for some action. They want to use a Stinger missile with just our sail above the surface. The powerboat will never know what hit them. The water will probably carry the sound of the explosion to the sub though."

"We will have already hit them with the first shot by then," I countered.

"Roger that." Ryker responded, "Good hunting. Out here."

"Time check;" we all looked at out watches and I said. "Leon, nail that sub with HE in nine minutes, forty seconds. Alvaro, please guide the boat. I will back Leon with the HK416."

Alvaro moved into position and pointed the Zodiac toward the sail of the drug sub. We were about thirty feet from the sub when the powerboat exploded. "Dang, 20 seconds early," I muttered. Just then a head popped above the hatch and looked toward the sound of the explosion. Then it swiveled in our direction. There was a shocked expression on the man's face and he closed the hatch and disappeared from sight. Leon fired the M320 into the sail base and I cross-stitched the sail with the HK416 rounds. Leon had the chamber of the M320 open quickly and sent them another round through the hull. Neither round detonated.

The hatch in the sail opened and an arm with AK74 came out. I stitched the sail again before the AK could send rounds our way.

Leon commanded, "Armas de gota, Hands up salen (Drop weapons, hands up come out)." I watched closely as four men assembled on the deck. One was the guard that I had seen previously and he still had a pistol in his holster. Leon had noticed it also. "Take that pistol out of the holster and drop it into the water." Leon commanded. He tried again in Spanish, "tomar pistola y colocar en agua."

The man looked at us with contempt and said, "vete a la mierda (Fuck you)". He drew the weapon and was bringing it up when I fired.

The other three began chattering excitedly. "haz lo que te digo y no te lastimas (Do as I say and you will not be hurt)," I shouted. When I did not shoot, they got quiet. Juan guided the other Zodiac up against the hull and I jumped aboard to insure that none of the prisoners were armed before putting them on the boat with Adan and Juan. Juan headed toward the Ventura with the prisoners.

I started to climb the sail when Alvaro said, "Let me do it this time." I stepped back and said, "It's all yours, but be careful." I exchanged places with Alvaro and waited in the Zodiac. Alvaro tossed down three bundles of cash. He was about to toss the fourth bundle when I saw the red flash. "Something flashed in that bundle. Do not open it, see if you can see what it is. Is that the last bundle of cash?"

"Yes" Alvaro replied. I was busy examining the bundles already in the Zodiac, but could see nothing suspicious. "Leave it on the sub and set the explosive charge. We need to get out of here." Alvaro disappeared into the sub and reappeared a short time later. He climbed into the Zodiac and I got us out of there. We had only gone about two hundred yards when the sub exploded. We felt the concussion and were sprayed with sea water, but suffered no damage.

"I wonder if that was the result of a timer or was command detonated?" I said to no one in particular. Alvaro said, "The sat phone was on and I could hear people on the other end asking what was happening. I suppose that the last thing that they heard was the explosion."

We were heading back to the Ranch when Alvaro's explosives detonated. We could just barely hear the thump. "I guess that it was command detonated." Alvaro said. "I did not see any way to activate or deactivate the package with all of that plastic around it."

We returned to the Ranch. Alvaro said, "If those bundles of cash are the usual amounts we should give the Embassy the forty million and divide the twenty million six ways." Alvaro looked at us evenly. Leon was the first to react. "Sure why not. I can't imagine running out of cash, if I live long enough to spend any of it." We all nodded agreement.

Leon and I headed back to Sabanalarga with our cash. It was early morning when we reclaimed our Zodiac and motored along the eastern shore of Lake Guajaro. When we got far enough south, we crossed to the city of Repelon to get gas and supplies. We setup camp on an uninhabited island in the middle of the lake across from Repelon.

We heard boats coming to the island just as we started our campfire to prepare breakfast. We had a pot of coffee brewed by the time that Skinny and his crew arrived. They piled off of the boats with weapons out. "Hello and

Good Morning," I said. "Would you like some coffee? It has just finished boiling."

"Where have you been?" Skinny demanded. "You have been gone for five days."

I laughed, "We did not think that anyone would miss us. We needed some cooling and companionship; if you know what I mean. We just came back from the Embassy in Bogota, but we were in Cartagena before that. Cartagena is a beautiful city and that hotel we stayed at was really beautiful. The seven mile beach area has a lot to offer."

I found our spare cup and filled it for Skinny.

Skinny took the cup and held it thoughtfully. "What do you know about drug traffic in Colombia?"

"Not much," I said. "Probably it is good for the Colombian economy, but not very good for the people who become addicted to the stuff. People use it by choice, so it is their hard luck. Why?"

Skinny looked at me quizzically, "Do you know where you are?"

"If we are trespassing on another of your islands, we will leave. Is that the problem?" I asked.

"You are standing in the middle of a coca plantation." Skinny retorted. Leon and I looked around neither of us had seen a coca plant before. It was plainly written on our faces.

"Which ones?" We asked almost in unison.

Skinny laughed. "I wanted to see what you said to that. I was not being truthful. The bushes are not coca plants."

"You had me going there for a minute. The Embassy would not take kindly to us camping in the middle of a coca farm." I said.

"Camp here as long as you want. Continue to keep the place clean as you have done in the past and we will get along fine." Skinny and his crew boarded their crafts and motored away.

"Whew," Leon exclaimed after Skinny was out of sight. "I thought that we were dead meat for sure."

"Yeah me too." I agreed.

After two weeks of cruising along the shoreline of Lake Guajaro, it was time to take some R&R (Rest and Relaxation). We headed back to Sabanalarga and some feminine company. I called Laura on Thursday and asked if she wanted to go out to dinner on Friday. She said that she would come to the house after she finished work.

Leon called Carolina. Laura had already called her and they would come after work. We were in good spirits when we put the Zodiac on the trailer and left it with Sebastian. The FARC had a checkpoint setup on the road leading to Sabanalarga.

Skinny walked up to the van and asked, "Where are you guys going?"

I answered, "After two weeks on the river we want to go to Sabanalarga for dinner and female companionship."

Skinny looked at Leon and then at me. "Senior, you should leave Senorita Laura Munoz alone. Her father does not like North Americano's. He would not approve."

"I am sad to hear that." I said. "I like Senorita Laura. She is good company. I will ask her if this is going to be a problem."

Skinny just said, "You have already been told. You are doing good work for my country or I would not have warned you." Then Skinny waived us on.

"Skinny is sure beginning to keep us on a short leash." Leon observed.

"I wonder how serious that warning is?" I thought out loud. "I will mention it to Laura after dinner tonight."

"I will ask Carolina about Laura's family. Maybe there will be a clue there." Leon said.

Laura and Carolina arrived with dinner in baskets. After we ate and sipped some wine. She took my hand and led me to the bedroom. "Two weeks is a long time to make me wait."

Laura said as she began undressing me. "I like the way that you do me." She sighed as I slipped fully into her. She rocked back and forth for a few minutes and quivered and gasped deeply. "Oh I needed that." She whispered into my ear as she collapsed onto my chest. "I will finish you in a minute," she promised into my ear and gave me a long wet kiss.

When she had enough, she went to wash and brought back a cloth to remove the traces of our love making. When she finished, I asked her about Skinny with FARC. She said, "I think that I know who you mean from your description. He definitely is part of the drug smuggling gang that controls this area. I am not sure what his warning is about though. Maybe he just does not like North Americans seeing Colombian women. That said, my father does not like North Americans. He feels that he was cheated by one a long time ago and has never forgotten. If Father says anything, I will let you know. He does have some dangerous friends. They would do someone harm if he asked. I am sure that you have nothing to worry about." She had been gently massaging me and I began to feel that it was time to start round two.

We had just finished breakfast on Sunday when Laura's cell phone trilled. She went to answer it. When she returned, she told us that her father had asked her to come to the house and that she would leave shortly. I told her that we were going back to the lake on Monday morning.

Carolina stayed with Leon until Laura picked her up on Monday morning. Laura and I managed a quickie before she and Carolina left for work. She did not say anything about her father.

We spent the next three weeks touring Lake Guajaro. We did not find any promising dam sites or rivers leading to the Caribbean or Pacific.

Alvaro called to suggest that we spend a few days out of the country. He said that an Embassy flight to Grand Cayman Island was leaving on Wednesday if we wanted to go. He suggested that we take companions.

I called Laura to ask if she had time to leave for the Cayman Islands on Wednesday and return some time later. She called back a little later and said that Carolina wanted to come along if it was ok. We spent the next ten days in the Grand Cayman Beach Suites Hotel.

On the tenth day, Alvaro called to say that we needed to return to Bogota the next day if possible. We put the girls on a flight to Santa Marta and we flew direct to Bogota.

At about the same time, TJ was meeting with his Father in Cartagena. Carlos was livid. "You and Diego saw nothing? Nothing at all!"

TJ was nervous but said, "We only saw them go fishing and then they flew to the Cayman Islands with the women. Captain Perez with FARC said that when they came back, they just cruised farther south in Laguna

Guajaro. The women returned home yesterday, but the men went to the Embassy in Bogota."

Carlos thought for a minute. "When the men return to the ranch and house in Sabanalarga kill them. If the women are there kill them also; except for Laura Munoz. Her father is important to the organization. The last submarine also did not reach Galveston. I would rather kill them than take a chance of losing another submarine. Now leave me."

Return To Fort Bragg

Chapter 27

Alvaro greeted us as we entered the Embassy. Adan and Juan were already in the conference room when we arrived. Ryan walked in shortly after we did.

Ryan began, "You guys have really done a great job here. We apparently stepped on some toes in Washington along the way. The Delta Team has been recalled to Fort Bragg. I think that Senator Tweedle got to someone higher up and forced our hand. The Vice President wanted to make public awards to the team members. Can you imagine how stupid?" Ryan had a disgusted look.

"Your cover up North was getting a little thin anyway. We were going to have to move you down south soon. According to your reports FARC was already closely monitoring your activities. You all did one hell of a job and none of our guys got hurt. We stopped about three billion dollars' worth of cocaine from getting into the United States."

"You guys will get to leave tomorrow. Sorry about the short notice, but the orders arrived this morning and there is nothing that we can do about them. Your personal gear is already being packed and will be shipped to Delta at Bragg. Alvaro and I are being sent back to Langley for debriefing at the end of the month. We are both going to put in for retirement. Maybe Delta will let you hang around Fort Bragg until you can put in for retirement. If you guys want to move into CIA let me know and I will make the recommendation. Hell, I will make the recommendation anyway. Who knows, you may change your minds about retiring or getting out."

"We have already talked over retirement and we are all getting out of active duty." I said. "I have something that I would like to propose to you. I have come to trust everyone here and I have something that I would like to propose to you."

"Alvaro briefed me about the involvement of Tweedle and the VP. He also mentioned something called the Rubric. Apparently, Tweedle and the VP are members of this organization. I cannot help but wonder if The Rubric works to the benefit of a few highly placed individuals at the expense of everyone else. I want to investigate this Rubric on my own terms and if it is bad, root it out. I think that I have enough money saved up to facilitate a thorough investigation. The problem is that I will likely need a good intelligence source to help me find the information that I will need."

"Adan and Juan have already said that they are taking retirement and do not want to work on this project. Leon has not answered yet. If either of you plan to stay in CIA, perhaps you will help?" I looked expectantly at Ryan and Alvaro.

Alvaro spoke first. "I am tired and burned-out. Thank you for your offer, but I am going someplace quiet and put my feet up. I have had more than enough adventure to last me a lifetime."

Then it was Ryan's turn. "I am with Alvaro. I am getting out, way out. However, I do have a rope for you. A long-time friend of mine has just been appointed Deputy Director of Operations at CIA Langley. He should be there for three or four years. Let me know a little more about what your plan is and I will ask him to help you. I am sure that he is trustworthy."

Ryan handed a package to Alvaro and then Alvaro passed it to me. "The package contains all of the information on Senator Tweedle and his contacts as of yesterday. When I get back to Langley, I will talk with my friend. I am sure that he will be interested to help you. If he is, I will insure that the intel feeds get sent to him on this matter. I will then contact you Major Thomas." Ryan said.

"It has been a pleasure knowing you guys. I wish you the best." Ryan said. We shook hands all around. Alvaro handed us our passports and tickets for the outbound flight.

Duke looked thoughtful for a minute then said. "I know that you have the right idea about this situation with Senator Tweedle, but getting to him and the others will be very dangerous. My suggestion is to enjoy the rest of your life. Buy an island and live fruitfully.

"I am going to be very careful. I think that I need to follow this lead and am glad that I have the means to pursue justice. If I find that the drug skim is going to a good purpose, I will back-off. I may be going it alone. I already know where everyone stands except Lyman and respect your decisions. We all have done enough for our country."

"Ok if the DO agrees to help, I am in." Lyman agreed. Scott and Adam had walked on ahead.

"I am going to miss Scott and Adam. They are good at surveillance and that is mostly what we will be doing for some time." I said.

"Once we get setup, we can see if they are bored enough to come work with us." Lyman suggested.

Three days later the four of us met again at Camp McKall, North Carolina. LTC McMasterson greeted us.

"Excellent work down South he commended. Too bad about how things developed on the political side. MSG Dwell tells me that you and CPT Gleason are resigning your commissions. I sure hate to lose two operators like you. You can stay on as civilian contractors if you want. I can make all of the arrangements."

"MAJ Thomas, I got a secure call from a Deputy Director at Langley. He says that he wants to talk with you. Are you planning on switching teams?"

"Sir, I do not know about switching teams. What I want to do does not seem within the purview of the CIA. The organization that I am concerned about may be mostly within the States."

"You referring to The Rubric?" Asled McMasterson.

"Yes Sir I am." I said.

"Captain Gleason, are you in on this also?" Asked McMasterson.

"I think so sir. I think that good Intel will be the problem. Without that, I cannot see much chance of success. Someone has to have the NSA link for the current intel."

"What about you two?" Asked McMasterson; looking alternately at Arceneaux and Ridley.

"No sir." Said Arceneaux and Ridley simply shook his head no.

LTC McMasterson nodded, then said. "You two can go. We will keep you here as Cadre until your retirement ceremony. I am glad to have you as part of the team." Adam and Scott got up and went out.

"Nate, I want you to call the DO and tell him that you have changed your mind and that you are going back to a quiet civilian life." LTC McMasterson could see the black clouds forming in my mind and quickly added; "I have something more interesting to offer you."

Prologue ~ The Rubric

"Delta or maybe I should say JSOC has a small civilian component; very secret, very special. I want you two to become part of that. The General and I agree that we need to know more about this Rubric. Actually you will be Secret Service Agents. I think that GS 14 should be enough rank. You will have all of the intelligence support that our government has to offer. You will only answer to me or the General. You will not actually have a budget, but be reasonable in your expenses. Does this appeal to you?"

LTC McMasterson smiled to the chorus of, "Yes Sir's".

I looked at LTC McMasterson and said, "Sir, I have some personal matters to attend to. I would like to take a month off while my resignation is being processed."

"Does this have anything to do with Laura Munoz?"

"No Sir, but it does have to do with Sarita Emmanual. She has no family alive in Colombia. I am thinking of asking her to join me here in the States. We can come up with a cover if she agrees to join me."

"Let me know what she says before you commit to an arrangement." Admonished LTC McMasterson. "Lyman do you have similar plans?"

"No Sir. I have no problem working with Nate even if Sarita is in the picture. I do not see any security risk there. I did not meet a woman that I want a permanent relationship with while I was down south. I did meet some exciting women though."

"Sir, my first thought is to find an apartment in Maryland. Then I will meet Sarita in Costa Rica and discuss our future relationship. I will return to consult with you when I know what my plan will be." Nate explained.

"Ok, Mister Thomas. Take the rest of the month to make your decisions about Ms. Emmanual. Call me if you need anything. Lyman call me at the end of the month. That is all gentlemen.

Puerto Viejo ~ The Rubric

Chapter 1

I took out my cell phone and called Sarita. When she answered I said, "Hi Sarita, this is Nate. I am sorry that it has been so long since I have called, but I did not have a choice."

Sarita decided not to be angry. "You have been gone for so long that I did not believe that I would ever hear from you again. What has happened? I was very worried about you."

"It is a long story and I would like to tell it to you in person. Can you come to Costa Rica? I will have a ticket waiting for you at the airport in Cartagena."

"Why do you want me to come to Costa Rica?" Sarita asked.

"I want to talk to you about our future." I responded. "I have been thinking of you since I had to leave Sincelejo."

"Can Carmilla come also?" Sarita asked hesitantly.

"Yes, but Leon will not be here to greet her. I think that their relationship has ended. We do not work for the Embassy now."

"Ok, I will come to you then. Where should I go?"

"Your flight will land at Puerto Viejo on the Caribbean side. We will be staying at a hotel there. I have reserved a suite for two weeks. You should be able to make up your mind about us by then. You can tell Carmilla where you are going if you wish, but ask her not to mention it to others. It is better if she never mentions me again."

"When is my flight? There is one tomorrow if you can come that early. If not, just tell me when and I will arrange the ticket."

"I am so glad that you have called me. Yes, I will come tomorrow."

"Sadly, you will be landing in San Jose. We will have to drive to Puerto Viejo or maybe we will take the helicopter. I will meet you at the San Jose airport."

Sarita smiled to herself. She could hear the excitement in his voice. "Until tomorrow then." She said as she dropped the connection.

Nate met Sarita at the arrival gate. She only had a small carry-on bag. Two large suitcases were waiting at baggage claim.

Nate gave Sarita a big hug when she came through the gate. The hug was returned with surprising strength. They walked a short distance and mounted the helicopter to the hotel in Puerto Viejo. The helicopter flew with the doors open. Conversation was nearly impossible. They enjoyed the scenery as they flew.

A car was waiting for them at the helipad and whisked them to the hotel Le Cameleon. Nate led Sarita up to their suite. When he closed the door behind them and turned, Sarita was standing looking up at him. He bent to kiss her and hold her close. The explanation came next.

"Sarita, I am so sad about the way that I treated you in Sincelejo. I wish that I could have said goodbye and given you an explanation. I just left because that was the safest for you." Sarita reached up and put a finger over his lips.

"Is this explanation because you were not really hydrologic engineers?" She asked.

"Yes." I answered.

"I thought so. I was visited again by some bad men and they were asking about you. You had been gone for about a month by then. They believed me when I said that you had gone away without saying goodbye or any explanation. So they did not bother Carmilla or me anymore. What were you doing in Sincelejo?"

"I work for the US Government. I probably will never be able to tell you what I do on any given day. I know that I want to share my life with you. The part that I can share with you is when I am not working. All of my friends are in the same situation with their wives and friends. We just have to put-up with that inconvenience. I do not expect you to give me an answer right away. You will need time to think it over. I have two or three weeks before I have to go back."

"If you decide to come with me we will find an apartment in Maryland or Virginia. I hope that at some point we will decide to get married. I know that I am not offering you much right now, but I am sure that our situation will get better with time. I will take good care of you."

Sarita smiled up at me. "I cannot offer you much either. There is only me. I was hoping that you would come back for me. I will go with you wherever you say. We shall see if our love can grow. She kissed me slowly and held on tightly."

"I need to get a shower and freshen up before dinner."

I sat on the sofa and watched as she removed her clothes. She looked at me shyly and did not remove her bra and panties before going into the bathroom. Her lithe body looked very inviting. I was captivated by the way that she moved.

After we ate dinner, I suggested that we shop for her new clothing. We quickly found the clothing stores and she started to go into a low end shop. I stopped her. "We do not need to buy things in that kind of shop. The shop two doors down looks much better."

"That is an expensive shop. They do have nice things, but they also cost a lot of money."

I smiled. "Money is not one of our problems." I said and guided her into the exclusive shop.

Sarita bought four complete outfits including purses and shoes. The bill was unbelievable, but I did not flinch as I handed over my black American Express card.

After we were outside of the store Sarita said. "Where did you get that credit card? I have heard that you have to be very rich to have one of those. Also, you are now Natanael Gomez."

"I suppose that I could say that we are rich. I do not want to use that to push you toward a decision." I said. "Sadly, for now I have several names. You will only have one name to keep track of unless something unforeseen occurs."

"Didn't you hear me up in the suite? I said that I would follow you wherever life takes us. My decision to be with you was already made when you asked me to join you." She brushed her shoulder against me playfully. I would have taken her hand, but my arms were full of packages.

When we got back to the hotel, the questions started. "Tell me who I am dealing with, please."

"You should never hear of Nate Calero again. He ceased to exist when I left Colombia. My real name is Nathan Thomas. I was an US Army Major until last week when I resigned my commission. I am also the wealthy Natanael Gomez. If the cartel does not learn my real name, I will eventually move all of my money into accounts for Nathan Thomas and I am employed by the US Secret

Service a fact not to be discussed in public. You should be isolated from all of this once we arrive in the US. You will be the fiancé of Nate Thomas."

"You sure have a complicated life, Nate! Get a shower and come back here." Sarita ordered.

I had just soaped up good when Sarita joined me. We scrubbed each other all over and then dried each other and headed for the bed.

In the morning, I called LTC McMasterson's private line. "Hello Nate, what's cooking?"

"Sir, how much trouble is it to get an Entry Visa for Sarita? Do you have any good contacts?"

"You know that I do." McMasterson gave me an address in San Jose. Take her Colombian passport there. Do not take her there. Send her shopping or something. The Visa just takes a few minutes there. Emmanual is common enough, but not the Sarita. We will give her a US passport when she gets here and break the trail. I want to meet her socially after you get here. Give me a call when you are ready.

Sarita and I took the helicopter to San Jose the next morning. I fixed the Visa and she went shopping. We met back at the heliport and flew back to the hotel.

The next day we entered the United States at Ronald Reagan National Airport. I had our passports ready as we approached the Customs Officer and handed them to him. He just asked, "Anything to declare?" We said, "No." and he stamped our passports and waved us through.

Sarita was surprised and said, "That was easy. I had heard that it was hard."

I showed her my passport and where it said United States Secret Service as my employer.

"Darn" she said. "Now I am just the fiancé of a poor civil servant. I am so happy." Her smile showed that she was very happy.

I leased a new Chevy Impala from Hertz car rentals and we drove to The Boar's Head Inn in Charlottesville, VA. We registered for a two week stay in one of the suites.

"This is so beautiful." Sarita exclaimed excitedly as she surveyed the grounds of the Inn.

I had setup an account for Nathan Thomas in the Cayman Islands and filled it with most of the two million that I had left in Costa Rica. The credit and debit cards had direct access to the funds.

Sarita had a good conservative style to her attire, but one thing was missing. We got into the Impala and headed into Charlottesville. I found the mall and we went into the jewelry store. Sarita's eyes kept getting bigger as she looked around and little oh's escaped her shapely lips now and then. We found a nice one carat diamond that she liked for an engagement ring and I put it on her finger. She was disappointed when she had to give it back and they put it into a box. I put the box in my pocket for later.

We returned to the Inn for dinner and then went up to the suite.

I barely got the door closed when she was in my arms kissing me passionately. I could feel the heat from her breasts as she held me close. I gently pushed her back and removed the box from my pocket. I opened the box and held it out in front of me.

"Sarita, will you marry me?" I asked.

"Oh, yes I will Nate." I took the ring out of the box and placed it on her finger.

Sarita simply said, "I love you. Make love to me Nate."

Slightly Off

Art McGillem

In the morning I called McMasterson and since he was already at the Pentagon, he agreed to meet us at the Inn for dinner that night.

McMasterson had gotten a promotion and was now a full Colonel. I introduced him to Sarita in the lobby of the Inn. "Sarita, please call me Bob. I look forward to seeing you and Bob often. I assume that you two have not found permanent accommodations yet?"

"No Sir, we just arrived yesterday."

"Drop the Sir. We are Bob and Nate from now on."

"If you are interested, I know where there is a small ranch available for rent in Culpeper. There is a three bedroom house with three and a half baths, two barns and twenty acres. The rent is three thousand per month. I will give you the address if you are interested."

"Yes Bob, we sure would like to take a look at it."

"I thought that you might, so I brought the keys along. What is on the menu here?"

Near the end of dinner, Sarita went to the powder room. Bob handed me an envelope. "Inside you will find a new legend for Sarita. Passport, driver license, social security card, shot records and other stuff. It is obvious that she loves you dearly. I think that you have chosen well."

"How much have you told her already?"

"Very little actually; mostly, that because of my work I use aliases. That she would not be involved in what I do for the Secret Service and that I would not be able to talk about my work with her. She was actually waiting for me to come back to Sincelejo for her. So maybe she can take the partial isolation that comes to a wife of people in our line of work."

"You can make a suite here at the Inn your drop point. We have an arrangement with the owner. Delta will pay for the suite here. The suite that you will use has a private exit if needed. The suite is on the third floor, but the exit is on the first. You will have to pay for the rent at the farm."

"Um Bob, show much does a GS 14 make?"

"Bob laughed, "Oh, about eighty-seven thousand a year. The income should be enough to take care of the farm expense. You still have all of your pay sitting in the account that you setup before you went south."

"We will check-out the farm tomorrow morning and let you know."

Sarita returned and Bob and I stood. Then Bob said, "I am really glad to meet you Sarita. I am sorry to eat and rush off, but I have another meeting tonight. Welcome to your new home."

We drove to the ranch. The house is a rambling one story with about five thousand square feet of heated space. The wrap around porches immediately drew Sarita to the house. The inside was nicely appointed with top of the line appliances. The wood floors were twelve inch wide quarter sawn white oak. Sarita wandered from room to room while I checked-out the den. I walked up to the built-in gun cabinet and moved the second stop from the left and the cabinet opened to a large collection of firearms. I hurriedly closed the cabinet. Sarita came into the den.

"I approve." She said. "Do you like this place?"

"Yes, we should take it." I said. "We have a three car garage so there is room for you to have a car also. What kind would you like to have?"

"A Land Rover would be nice." She said. We went and bought one the next day and she drove it home and put it in the garage."

I called Bob and said that we would stay at the farm. He said, "I see that you found the arms room already."

"Yep, but do not do any audio or video surveillance in the bedrooms. I warn you."

Bob laughed. "Audio and video are full outside, in the inside hallways, den and great room only. Your suite at the Inn is 710. The key that you have will work in the door. Let me know when you are ready to start work."

I called Sarita. "Bring your passport and other IDs into the den."

Sarita came in with her purse and I held out my hand. She placed her passport and IDs in my hand and gave me a quizzical look.

I took out the manila envelope and gave her all of her new IDs. "Am I suddenly a US citizen?"

"Yes, all of the IDs are valid. These pages have your history. Take some time to learn it. You probably will be asked about your past by new friends. We are doing this for your safety. The cartel does not forgive or forget. You can see how our government will go to great lengths to protect us. I hope to retire after I finish this project, so be patient. I am going back to work next week."

(Check for "The Rubric" on Kindle eBooks and in print!)

If you are reading this book on a web enabled device please review this book at:

https://www.amazon.com/author/arthurmcgillem

Thank you for your support.

www.ingramcontent.com/pod-product-compliance
Lightning Source LLC
Chambersburg PA
CBHW072211170626
46813CB00003B/885